The 90s Club and
the Hidden Staircase

Eileen Haavik McIntire

Amanita Books
Imprint of Summit Crossroads Press
Columbia, Maryland

Copyright © 2012 by Eileen Haavik McIntire

Library of Congress Control No. 2012903466

Publisher's Cataloging-in-Publication
(Provided by Quality Books, Inc.)

McIntire, Eileen Haavik.
  The 90s club and the hidden staircase / Eileen Haavik
McIntire.
  p. cm.
  ISBN 978-0-9834049-3-4

  1. Older people--Fiction. 2. Retirement communities
--Fiction. 3. Crime--Fiction. 4. Detective and mystery
stories. I. Title. II. Title: Nineties club and the
hidden staircase.

PS3613.C5422012   813'.6

QBI12-600017

Editors: Judy Rice, Holly Berardi

Cover Designer: Six Penny Graphics

Published by Amanita Books, fiction imprint of Summit Crossroads
Press, Columbia, MD, USA.

Acknowledgments

As a child, I was a fanatical reader of Nancy Drew books. She was my heroine. Her interests were boundless, she was always learning something new, and most glorious of all, she had her own car! One day, as I sat on a pool deck watching a lone woman, ninety-one years old, swim laps, I wondered what Nancy Drew would be like at ninety. That became the impetus for this book, which features Nancy Dickenson, *not* Nancy Drew, but a retired detective, nonetheless, and her friends in the 90s Club at Whisperwood Retirement Village.

Whisperwood is like many retirement villages nowadays. They are not depressing "old folks' homes" for cast-off relatives but more like cruise ships, offering cheerful complexes with enjoyable, sociable dinners in attractive dining rooms every evening along with classes, hobby areas, dances, trips, gyms, tennis courts, pools, and ways to participate in about any activity imaginable.

Young people expect the elderly to dribble Pablum, but I've learned that for some people, age is no barrier to anything they want to do. I often read articles about people who are ninety, one hundred, or older who are still working, active, and alert. My former father-in-law at ninety-seven drove from Arkansas to Texas and back and did his own home maintenance. A family friend at ninety-two was tennis champion in his retirement community. As of this writing, famous actors Kirk Douglas, Ernest Borgnine, Eli Wallach, and Kevin McCarthy, are all in their nineties and still active. Even greeting card companies now have birthday cards for those turning one hundred.

The Whisperwood in this novel portrays the kind of lifestyle that residents of such communities enjoy but, of course, my Whisperwood takes a sinister turn. The evil that occurs is totally fictional and does not in any way resemble the actual events or people at any real retirement village.

Many people helped me research, write, and critique this novel. My husband Rog is first on the list, always supporting my efforts. Pat and Allan White and Janet Rochlin at Riderwood Retirement Village supplied countless anecdotes about life in this community. The Columbia Fiction Critique Group, the White Oak Writers, Holly Berardi, and Judy Rice provided invaluable criticism and suggestions for the plot and writing. Any errors are entirely my own.

- Eileen Haavik McIntire

Chapter 1

The old man shuffled down the silent hall toward the open steel door at the far end. The tap, tap, tap of his cane echoed from the tiled floor and concrete walls. He stumbled along hoping that the door ahead led to the warmth and comfort of home. When he arrived, he opened the door and steadied himself against the door frame to rest as he gazed not at the familiar furnishings of his living room but instead at a cold, stone stairway.

"Where is my home?" the old man wondered. "I want to go to bed. I'm tired." He peered in at the stairs. "Is this the way?" He pondered the question, looking alternately down the steps and then at the hall behind him. "I'll go down," he decided.

Gripping the rail with one hand and steadying himself with his cane, he descended the stairs one step at a time, each step down darker than the one above. His knees throbbed with pain. When he reached the bottom landing, he found himself standing at the side of a road lit only by the low-wattage bare bulb hanging in the stairwell behind him. He squinted both ways down the road. In each direction, it disappeared into the darkness of a tunnel.

"Maybe this is the bridge between the buildings," the old man thought. "But which way is home?" He turned to the right and hobbled down the rough, narrow road carved out of rock.

Now the tapping of his cane added a rhythmic percussion to the dripping, bubbling sounds emanating from the tunnel walls. The old man stepped carefully, steadying himself with his cane in one hand, the other feeling its way along the wall. The light behind him cast a long, misshapen shadow on the road ahead and then faded into the blackness of the walls on each side, reflecting here and there a faint sparkle.

The smell of dust and exhaust fumes choked him, and he gasped for breath, but he struggled onward into more darkness. Unseen puddles lay like booby traps in his path. He could not help splashing through them as he tottered forward. The wet penetrated his shoes, and he could feel his wet socks rubbing blisters into his feet.

"What is this place?" the old man thought, weeping from fatigue. *Whisperwood.* The word surfaced in his mind and floated away. "How do I get out of here?" he said out loud as if someone could hear him. "I want to go home."

The dripping and bubbling noises reverberated around him. He gripped his cane and wound an arm around his head to block out the sounds. He closed his eyes and opened them but could see nothing in the black void. He felt as if he had been struck blind.

"I've got to get out of here," he muttered. "I'm tired and I want my bed. Where is it?"

Tapping his cane, he staggered forward, reaching out until he touched the cold hardness of a rock wall. Then he felt his way along, but the absolute darkness suffocated and terrified him. He had no idea which way would get him out of there, but he pieced his way forward, step by step, thinking that he must be in a nightmare and would soon wake up.

Chapter 2

A silent ambulance made its way down the mountain, creeping past the van approaching the wrought-iron gates of Whisperwood Retirement Village.

The van driver glanced at Nancy Dickenson through the rear-view mirror. "No hurry for that one, I guess."

Nancy watched the ambulance pass with misgiving. It might carry her down the mountain one day. The gate attendant held up his hand, and the van stopped. Nancy fumbled through her purse with trembling fingers, pulled out her official new resident papers, and handed them to the driver to give to the attendant.

She heard a low growl. With woods encroaching on the road in this part of central West Virginia, her first thought was bears, but then she noticed a large, blackish-brown rottweiler in a pen next to the gatehouse. The powerful dog watched her with hard brown eyes, but Nancy knew how to handle dogs. Why did Whisperwood need a guard dog in such an isolated, pastoral setting?

The attendant finished scanning the documents and nodded to her as he opened the gate. "Welcome to Whisperwood," he said.

She smiled at him, but she couldn't help a shiver of apprehension. She hoped she would like living here.

The van pulled around the circular drive in front of the building, drove under the portico, and stopped at the entrance, scattering a flock of grackles. The building itself was six stories high, with a wing one city block long extending on each side of the central building. The driver hurried around and helped Nancy out. He hesitated at the cat carrier but took a deep breath as he picked it up, held it at arm's length, and took it into the lobby.

"Don't worry," Nancy called after him. "The cat's sedated."

The driver nodded as he set the carrier down and returned to the van for her suitcases.

Nancy paused at the threshold. The movers should have unloaded the furniture and boxes into her new apartment yesterday.

"That all, ma'am?" The driver looked expectantly at Nancy.

"Yes, that's all." She handed him a tip and took a deep breath.

"Take care now." The driver bounded into the van and gunned the engine. In a few moments, he disappeared down the drive and around a curve, leaving her stranded at the doors of Whisperwood. She fought down a mad urge to run after him and steeled herself to meet the future. Then she saw the white-haired old lady reflected in the glass doors to the lobby. Surely she didn't look that old. She didn't feel it.

She stood straighter and lifted her chin. The doors opened automatically in front of her, and a middle-aged, stocky man in a tailored gray suit and grim expression strutted out. A younger man sauntered gracefully behind with one hand in his pocket, the other holding a leash to a dog that matched the one at the gate.

The man's sapphire blue eyes lazily raked Nancy up and down as he winked at her and stepped aside to let her pass. Then he strolled out the door, pulling the dog behind him. His pressed blue shirt and creased khaki pants gave him a prep school look.

Nancy watched both men head for the parking lot before she stepped forward through the opening door. She took a deep breath, squared her shoulders, and walked into the lobby.

A plump young woman in a flowered dress stood by the reception desk, expressionless, speaking to a white-haired woman leaning on a cane. Both women seemed nervous and upset, and neither one looked at Nancy, who recognized the young woman as the resident coordinator. Nancy waited for the conversation to end. The coordinator's hands fluttered. "We were preparing the papers to transfer him to assisted living, but he wandered out and got lost. I'm told he died of heart failure and exposure."

She glanced down at her feet, and Nancy heard her mutter, "I suppose that's true. It was cold and windy last night."

Nancy's ears perked up. *No wonder they were upset. What a terrible thing to happen.*

The elderly woman said something Nancy couldn't hear and then turned away to tap her cane down the hall. At the same time, the young woman looked up and noticed Nancy. She saw the luggage, and the blank expression gave way to a smile. She walked toward Nancy with hand outstretched.

"I'm Amanda Fellows, resident coordinator here. You must be Ms. Dickenson. We've been expecting you."

Amanda's kind, open face reassured Nancy. "I'm pleased to see you again." Nancy shook Amanda's hand and nodded back toward the front doors and the two men out in the parking area. "Do they live here?" she asked.

Amanda laughed, fluttering her hands. "The shorter one is the president and CEO of Whisperwood, Nat Bryerson. The other one with the gorgeous blue eyes is his assistant Perry Greenshaw." Amanda leaned over to the receptionist. "Mattie, please run out and tell Mr. Bryerson that Ms. Dickenson is here." She turned back to Nancy. "He wanted to greet you when you arrived, but he's been distracted today. We had an unfortunate incident last night."

Nancy looked at her and asked the obvious question, interested in how Amanda would respond. "What happened?"

Amanda waved off the question. "Just a problem with one of our residents, but," she smiled, "nothing for you to worry about."

"I see." Amanda was going to cover it up, especially for a new resident. Nancy made a mental note to find out what really happened as she stared out the doors at Bryerson and his assistant talking in the parking area.

Amanda fingered her cameo necklace. "All of us try very hard to make Whisperwood a pleasant, safe place to live."

"Why do you keep a rottweiler at the gate? He doesn't seem very friendly."

"The dogs. Don't worry about them." Amanda's laugh seemed forced. "They're just here to help us find lost residents. Some of them don't," she paused, "track well, you know, and sometimes they get lost on the grounds. Without the dogs' help, we'd have a hard time finding them."

Nancy raised an eyebrow. *Rottweilers are guard dogs, not bloodhounds.*

Amanda glanced at her watch, then looked up at Nancy, and smiled. "Welcome to Whisperwood, Ms. Dickenson. We're pleased to have you join our family. We've heard so much about you, and I'm sure you have fascinating stories to share."

Nancy followed Amanda to her office. "Are those golf carts outside just for staff?" she asked.

Amanda nodded. "We always keep them handy."

Nancy liked options. "How fast do they go?"

"I'm afraid insurance regulations won't let you drive them. The staff use them to carry supplies around to the different buildings. The receptionist keeps the keys." Amanda laughed. "But the residents who use the power wheelchairs and scooters go fast enough that I had to post 'rules of the road' for them. Watch out for the speed demons in the halls."

She waved Nancy into her office and took her place behind a desk crowded between file cabinets. "You might feel a bit nervous and uncertain," Amanda's hands fluttered, "about moving here. All new to you, I expect."

"A bit." Probably everyone was nervous about moving into such a place.

She watched Amanda sift through a pile of folders, select one and pull out some papers.

She spread them in front of Nancy. "Sign these to show you received the keys, please, Ms. Dickenson, and I can give them to you."

Nancy read the document and said a silent prayer. Was she doing the right thing to move here? She thought of the odd death of an old man. She'd retired years ago and the new technology had passed her by, except for her computer, but she sniffed a mystery. At heart, she was still a detective. Perhaps Whisperwood needed her. She smiled at the thought and signed the papers while Amanda reached into a desk drawer and brought out three keys jangling on a small metal ring. She handed the ring to Nancy.

"Your building, apartment, and mailbox keys. You're down the hall from the dining room. That will be convenient for you."

Nancy swallowed her misgivings. "Yes, thank you. I'm not much of a cook—found that out a long time ago. I'm looking forward to the meals."

"We seat people in groups of four or six, so you'll get to know the other residents, and your friend Louise has been asking about you."

The reception clerk poked her head into the office. "Excuse me, but Mr. Bryerson is ready to welcome Ms. Dickenson now."

Mr. Bryerson wanted to welcome her? Did he welcome everyone who moved in here? Nancy waited for Amanda's response.

Amanda picked at the cameo. "He knew you were coming today, but the tragedy upset him as it has all of us." She sighed and stood. "He's excited about meeting you. He likes to have celebrities choose Whisperwood."

Nancy brushed the idea away. "I'm hardly a celebrity."

"But I've heard of you and read about your cases," Amanda protested. "I hope you'll give some talks about your work to our residents."

Nancy looked up with surprise. "I'll be happy to if you think they'll be interested." Some people, even the most harmless and innocent, felt uncomfortable around her.

"Of course they will." Amanda stood and walked to the door. "I'll take you over to his office. Don't worry about your suitcases or your little pussycat." Her eyes softened. "We'll get them to your apartment for you. I love cats myself." She took Nancy's arm and guided her two doors down the hall and into a small, paneled office.

The thin man with the sapphire blue eyes no longer held onto a dog. Now he lolled in a chair beside the desk where a woman stared at a computer. She glanced up over her glasses at Nancy. "Ms. Dickenson? Go right in."

Nancy walked through a heavy oak door onto plush beige wall-to-wall carpeting. The stocky man who had passed her at the entrance now sat at a massive mahogany desk in front of the window, silhouetting him against the sunshine outside. After all the turmoil of moving here, Nancy was too tired to be impressed or intimidated, but she was interested in meeting the man who had built Whisperwood.

She stepped forward as he set down his bottled water and stood, offering his hand.

"Ms. Dickenson. Welcome," he said with a smile.

Nancy shook his hand. It was sweaty and calloused and belied the well-tailored, expensive appearance of the suit he wore. She resisted the urge to wipe her hand on her slacks. He was trying to be friendly, for goodness sake, but the effort seemed forced, which made Nancy peer closer at the facade.

He gestured toward one of the man-sized, dark-brown leather armchairs. Nancy sat on the edge of the seat, prepared to be courteous. Bryerson did not take his eyes off her as he too sat, but his smile did not reach his eyes. Was he thinking about how much trouble she'd be? Did he pet the dogs? Did his family live here? Wife? Kids?

He cleared his throat. "We're pleased you've chosen Whisper-wood as your new home, Ms. Dickenson. I apologize for not greeting you earlier. My mind was still back here in the office." His voice was soft and cultured, each syllable enunciated clearly. He lifted the papers in a stack in front of him. "We've all been excited about meeting you."

"Thank you. I'm excited about being here," Nancy said. Her sharp eyes darted around the room. Such masculine decor. No photos of wife or kids.

She spotted a stack of cartons containing bottled water beside his desk. On top lay a bag of potato chips. They made Bryerson seem more human. No other warm touches at all. She looked at him and waited, hands folded in her lap to appear like a prim and proper little old lady. This was the most reassuring image for people wary of her past as a private detective.

Bryerson sat back and nodded. "Yes, we've planned everything here for your convenience and comfort. If something's not right, talk to Mattie out front or Amanda, of course. They'll take care of it for you." He leaned back in his chair and steepled his fingers. "We've put a lot of thought into building Whisperwood. We designed it to be a first-class place we ourselves would want to live in."

"That's good to know." His words were friendly. He was trying to appear congenial, but she felt as if he were sizing her up. Why? She was harmless. She was almost ninety years old, for Pete's sake. And she hadn't worked as an investigator for thirty years.

"I'm glad to have this time to chat with you," Bryerson said. "I always like to know why people choose our facility above all the other retirement villages in this country." He smiled. "Especially someone with your impressive background."

Nancy answered the smile. "Your marketing team does an excellent job, and my friend Louise Owens lives here." She looked down at her hands, remembering her loneliness. "I needed to meet new people, make new friends, and I like West Virginia."

"Beautiful state. Wild and wonderful." Bryerson rolled his eyes at the state slogan. He rose, signaling that the interview was over. "Welcome to Whisperwood, Ms. Dickenson."

***

Life at Whisperwood: In Memoriam

The Whisperwood Community regrets the passing of the following residents May 15-31.

JOHN O'CONLEY
ALLISON HORNER
CALISPELL YOHO
DEXTER WHITE

ABIGAIL ROWEN
MARY LOU CARTER
LAURENCE ROGERS
WHITNEY WALLACE
PATRICIA ALBERS
KEVIN BEECHER

-From *The Whisperwood Breeze*, newsletter
of Whisperwood Retirement Village

Chapter 3

Nancy entered her new apartment and relaxed. Most of the furniture was placed in a logical arrangement, and the boxes were stacked in a corner of the living room. Amanda followed her, pulling a cart with the cat's carrier resting on it.

"Everything seems to be here," Nancy said. She picked up the cage and placed it on the floor against the living room wall.

"You can unpack as you feel like it." Amanda pushed the cart out into the hall. "Don't do too much at a time." She followed the cart and added, "Let me know if you need anything." She closed the door behind her.

Nancy took a deep breath and looked around her new home, relieved that the move was over. She heard a yowl from Malone.

"Poor kitty," she murmured, opening the carrier door. "Come on out and see your new home."

Malone stretched, sniffed the carpet, and glared at Nancy as he tentatively stepped out of the carrier. Nancy set out water, food, bed, and litter box, then sat quietly for an hour, letting him prowl. He'd occasionally cast a reproachful look at her or rub himself against her legs. Gradually, he grew comfortable enough to curl up in his bed. Nancy watched him a few more minutes and then left to seek out her old friend Louise. She arrived at Louise's door just as a short, pudgy man ambled out.

"Welcome to the neighborhood," said Louise, grinning at Nancy. She tugged on the man's sleeve with long, thin fingers that matched her frame. Her hair was pulled back into a single gray braid that reached to her waist. "Meet George Burroughs. He's a pain in the neck, but I put up with him."

"I put up with her, you mean," George stopped and straightened his sleeve. "I'm the only one who'll listen to her crusades." He pointed to the lapel button on Louise's khaki shirt. *Save the Whales.*

"Don't mention plants or animals to her, or you'll be stuck all day." He bowed to Nancy. "Pleasure to meet you. Louise has told me a lot about you." He winked at her. "I don't believe half her stories." He grinned. "Course we could use some excitement around here." He nodded at Nancy and walked down the hall toward the elevator, tapping his cane with each step.

Louise and Nancy sat down for a long chat, catching up with the news of old friends and new ones. As they exhausted this topic, Nancy leaned forward to bring up the question of Amanda's muttered words. "What do you know about the old man found dead on the grounds? Amanda seemed to have doubts."

"That's another reason why I'm glad you're here," Louise said, sitting back and tapping her fingers on the chair arm. "I don't like the way they've hushed up the details. All we know is that John Hanson was found dead outside early this morning."

"Did you know him?" Nancy asked.

Louise shook her head. "Barely. Saw him in the halls now and then. His friends told me he was 'losing it,'" she tapped her head. "Amanda is telling everyone," she raised an eyebrow, "that he must have wandered outside for some reason, then had a heart attack and fallen and wasn't discovered for hours."

Nancy nodded. "That could happen." And no mystery at all.

Louise folded her arms and raised an eyebrow. "But his shoes and socks were sopping wet, and his hands were black with soot. Where did that happen? We haven't had rain for days and dew might dampen shoes and socks but wouldn't soak them."

***

Life at Whisperwood:
Welcome to New Residents

All new residents are invited to an informal tea party in the dining room at 2 p.m. on Wednesday, June 10. Don't miss this opportunity to meet the staff and representatives from the many organizations flourishing at Whisperwood. You will also be assigned a "buddy" who has lived here awhile that you can contact at any time with your questions.

-From *The Whisperwood Breeze,* newsletter, Whisperwood Retirement Village

Chapter 4

Louise took Nancy by the hand the next several days, showing her where the gym and the pool were, waiting while Nancy signed up for classes, and introducing her to tennis club members. George had helped, too, insisting that Nancy enroll in his beginning Spanish class, even though it was near the end of the semester. Nancy had even signed up for two bridge groups, but finally, she called a halt.

"I really appreciate your help, but my poor cat Malone is feeling neglected," she said. "I'd like to spend the afternoon reading in my apartment. That'll reassure Malone, too."

Louise flicked her braid. "I guess I was a bit over-eager. Just want you to enjoy this place as much as I do."

"I do. I'm going to be very busy here, and I like that." They had stopped in the central lobby outside the pub. Nancy smiled at the cheery friendliness around her. "I can hardly believe how nervous I was about leaving Morgantown. I should have moved here years ago."

"Yeah. I know. We all feel that way," said Louise. "No fun being independent if you're lonely and worry a lot."

Nancy looked at Louise in surprise. "You worry?"

"Fooled you, huh?" Louise raised an eyebrow in irony. "Used to get panic attacks all the time, thinking my body would be found mummified months after I died...living independently in my own home."

Nancy nodded, remembering her own fears. "I didn't eat well either." She laughed. "No problem here."

The full-course meals served each evening were hard to resist. Every day she felt grateful that someone else was cooking her meals again. A fond memory of her beloved housekeeper and cook flitted across her mind.

Louise took Nancy's arm and walked her over to the lobby bulletin board. "They post announcements here. Worth keeping an eye on." She tapped a note labeled, "In Memoriam."

"Obituaries too." Louise read the latest announcement. "Uh oh."

Nancy looked at Louise, then read the announcement. "Dexter White. Did you know him?"

Louise pursed her lips. "Yes. And he was one of the younger ones here. No health problems that he talked about. I'll have to find out what happened."

Later, Nancy, Louise, and George walked across the grounds toward a picnic table, Nancy stopped to pick a stray dandelion. "I have a birthday coming up."

"Your ninetieth, right?" said Louise.

Nancy nodded.

Louise winked at George. "That makes three of us." She laughed.

"Sounds like a new club," added George. "The 90s Club."

"I think Whisperwood needs some watchdogs," said Louise. "That's what we can do. I've got a few projects in mind."

George groaned.

Nancy smiled. "I'd like to get involved in something worthwhile."

"The 90s Club it is, then," said Louise.

They stopped and shook hands.

"We don't have to hold meetings, do we?" asked George. "Keep minutes? Plan things? Recruit new members? Schedule meetings?"

"I vote that this particular club be ours alone," said Louise, "much as that goes against my inclusive, democratic instincts."

"No work, all fun that way," said George.

"Okay," Nancy agreed. "Our own unofficial club."

They laughed but somehow forming the club cemented their friendship and made Nancy feel the comfort of a close community within the larger circle of Whisperwood.

The only thorn was the cat. In the early morning he would jump on her chest, yowl at her, and swat her face till she got up and fed him. Bill's cat, really. He'd had some idea about using the cat in his magic act. The memory always made Nancy wince. She and Bill used to wonder what breed he was, since they'd found him as a kitten under their cabin in the woods. Their best guess was maybe part bobcat. He certainly looked like one. A short-haired, fawn-colored cat, larger than a normal housecat but skinny with long legs and tail. Despite his difficult temperament, Nancy found herself touched by his odd and unexpected vulnerabilities. One day she surprised herself by realizing she loved the poor animal.

One morning with Malone curled up and snoring at her side, she lingered in bed, pondering the fact that the day was her birthday, and she was now ninety. She had never thought she'd get that old. She'd lived beyond her first husband and her second. There were no children, and now her only family was this tawny cat. She petted Malone with a wry smile on her face.

The petting woke Malone. He stretched with his claws full out, then withdrew them, and batted Nancy before leaping out of bed. He rubbed against the door and meowed, then he stalked regally toward the kitchen. Nancy fed the cat quickly before he could nip her ankles.

After breakfast, she opened the door and found Amanda placing a rose on the hall shelf outside her unit. Every apartment had such a shelf for displaying personal mementos, flowers, welcoming signs, or whatever the resident chose to represent him or herself. Our "lawn ornaments," Nancy had thought when she walked down the hall on her first day.

"You caught me." Amanda smiled, fluttering her hands. "We always give a rose to residents on their birthdays with us, so happy birthday! How are you feeling today?"

"Very well, thank you. And thanks for the rose." She sniffed its fragrance. "I do love living here." Her eyes sparkled. "I've made friends, and I'm involved in so many activities, I don't have time to feel sorry for myself. Now I'm off to the gym and this afternoon, tennis." She turned toward the kitchen to find a vase. At the same time, Malone stalked into the foyer, saw the door open, and ran out into the hall.

"I do like kitty cats," Amanda said, reaching down to pet it. Malone eyed her beckoning fingers as if they were fish filets. He swatted at them with claws extended.

"Oh dear!" Amanda withdrew her hand and looked at the blood dripping from her fingers.

"I'm dreadfully sorry," Nancy exclaimed. "Just a minute." She ran into the kitchen with Malone close behind. Any activity in the kitchen drew Malone. Nancy opened the refrigerator and took out a package of hamburger. She gave him a bit of the meat to keep him busy and in the kitchen while she found bandages and ran back out into the hall, shutting the door behind her.

"I'm sorry. He's not a friendly cat," said Nancy. "Not at all." She pulled out a bandage. "Let's go down to the water fountain, wash your hand, and put on a bandage."

"He's a very big cat, isn't he?" Amanda said tremulously. "I usually like cats."

"He was my late husband's pet," said Nancy.

"Oh, I see." Amanda smiled tentatively at Nancy as they walked down the hall. "I do like to see our residents happy with their pets here."

Nancy did not respond. Happiness was not a word she'd use in thinking of Malone.

***

Life at Whisperwood:
Club Fair This Saturday!

Don't miss the Club Fair on Saturday, June 13, 10 a.m. to 3 p.m. in the auditorium. Refreshments will be served.

Find out what's happening at Whisperwood and meet people with interests similar to yours. Representatives from all the clubs, groups, and religious organizations at Whisperwood will have exhibits and sign up sheets. Chess? Bridge? Model trains? Travel? Tennis?

Whatever your interest, we have it all at Whisperwood!

-From *The Whisperwood Breeze*, newsletter of Whisperwood Retirement Village

Chapter 5

Nancy met Louise in the gym that morning. As they worked through their exercise routines, Louise said, "I found out about Dexter White."

Nancy sat in the cruncher. "What happened to him?"

He slipped in his kitchen and hit his head. By the time anyone checked on him, he'd died."

"How terrible," said Nancy. "Must have been quite a fall."

"Yeah." The look on Louise's face was grim. "Amanda wouldn't tell me how he died. I had to find out from his neighbor who happened to be on hand when Dexter was found."

They finished their routines and walked out together into the hall.

"There's something else," Louise whispered.

"About Dexter?"

Louise nodded. "I met his son outside Dexter's apartment—he was just down the hall from me." She shook her head. "The son said several of Dexter's valuable antiques are missing."

Nancy stopped. "Has he talked to Amanda?"

"He said Amanda thinks Dexter probably sold them or gave them away. She can't believe anyone here would steal from a resident's apartment."

What did Dexter's son say?"

Louise shrugged. "He agreed with her."

That evening after dinner, Nancy sat at her table in Spanish class, stifling a yawn. She sat up and tried to look alive for Señora Lopez who trilled her r's and flailed her arms like a Mexican traffic cop.

Even though Nancy joined the class late in the semester, she was able to keep up because of the repetitive lessons, but it was held after dinner. Tonight the dining room's offering was Nancy's favorite, baked chicken and mashed potatoes followed by the sundae bar. She really had to watch the fat and sugar, and she'd eaten too much. She yawned again. Hard to stay awake. It was a shame, too. She'd always wanted to improve her Spanish.

"Pay attention, Nancy," she scolded herself. She had taken classes all her life and wasn't going to stop now, especially when depression shadowed her, ready to spring if she let her guard down. She was glad she had moved to Whisperwood, but despite its charms, she had never seen such a variety of ills in her life.

She glanced at the walkers stacked against the wall. They came with the territory, along with wheelchairs and canes. She blessed her lucky stars that she was able to keep up her walking and swimming and tennis. Or probably, she grinned to herself, walking and swimming and tennis gave her the stamina to keep up.

Nancy forced her eyes open to watch Señora Lopez write a new word on the board. Then she spotted the vividly painted moon face and sausage arms of Glinda Spencer gliding in her scooter down the hall toward their class. Nancy glanced at her watch. Seven-fifty. Glinda was almost an hour late as usual for the two-hour class.

Nancy scribbled in her notebook. "Here she comes. We should leave right now," she wrote. She nudged George who sat beside her. He read the note and grimaced. His round pink face turned red. He sat up and straightened his red bow tie. They glanced at each other, but even though they both wanted to leave, they stayed in their seats out of pity for Señora Lopez. She taught high school students during the day, but Nancy could see that she was no match for Glinda Spencer.

Glinda steered her power scooter across the front of the room and halted directly in front of Señora Lopez. "Sorry I'm late. Long line in the dining room," she said in her bell-like voice.

The teacher nodded, visibly gritting her teeth. "We're on page 156," she said.

Glinda remained in front of the class and under the nose of Señora Lopez. "Page 156." Glinda reached around to the basket hanging off her wheelchair, rummaged around in it, muttering, "Where is it? I can't find it. It's got to be here." More mutterings and fumbling produced the book. "I have it now. What page?" She peered up at the teacher expectantly.

Nancy sighed, staring down at her book and running a hand through her hair. The class continued drearily along as Glinda interrupted every sentence, asked irrelevant questions, and repeated anecdotes they'd already heard. At last the misery was over. A universal sigh rose among the students as they gathered their books and papers. A few malevolent glances were cast in Glinda's direction, but the subject was oblivious.

"I like this class," Nancy muttered to George, forgetting for the moment that he was hard of hearing, "but Glinda ruins it for everyone."

George nodded and grumbled, his voice too loud for the whisper he intended, "Thank God we only have a couple more sessions before summer break." He tugged on his red sweater. "Got to get going. See you later." He picked up his cane and stepped toward the door.

Nancy scurried down the hall, but she couldn't escape Glinda's power scooter. Glinda never bothered with Amanda's "rules of the road." She whirred up alongside Nancy. "Hey, slow down," Glinda said. "I want to talk to you."

"What's on your mind?" Nancy kept walking even though she was curious. Glinda was such an odd specimen.

"I want to show you something." Glinda slowed the scooter to match Nancy's pace. "You'll find it fascinating."

They stopped at the elevator, and Nancy pressed the up button. She turned to face Glinda. "And what is that?"

"Been going through my stuff. I've had an interesting life, you know." Glinda nodded, a smug smile on her face. "Come up to my place. I need your help." It was an order.

Nancy debated whether to comply, but her good nature and curiosity won. She rode up on the elevator with Glinda. On the fifth floor, she stepped aside to let Glinda swing out, then tagged along behind her down the hall to her apartment.

Glinda waved at Nancy to follow her in. "You can help me set it up. I can't lift it from my chair."

Nancy hesitated, overwhelmed at the strident pink walls and plethora of stuffed animals on the fuzzy white sofa. Several stuffed cats stood on a credenza across from the sofa but, Nancy realized with awed surprise, they had been stuffed by a taxidermist, not a toy factory.

Nancy averted her eyes from the staring glass ones of the cats and walked behind Glinda as she glided into her bedroom, also painted that same, Nancy sought for a word, *vivid* pink. The white fuzzy bedspread matched the sofa cover. She noticed a lovely Tiffany lamp on the desk in the corner next to an older model computer. Several floppy disks were stacked next to the mouse pad. No flash drives. She wouldn't have expected Glinda to have a computer, even if it was an old one, although a lot of residents, including herself, had PCs or Macs.

Glinda pointed to a heavy steamer trunk at the foot of her bed.

"I haven't seen one of those since I was a girl," said Nancy, seizing on the one pleasant object in the apartment. She remembered the long-ago cruise to South America and the friends she had traveled with. All of them gone now. She ran her fingers across the trunk lid, feeling its hard, shiny surface.

Glinda poked her. "They call it an antique, but it was new when it was given to me sixty years ago. Those are genuine brass hinges there. Not brass-plated like nowadays." She glanced at Nancy. "Open it up. It's not locked."

Nancy flipped up the latch and lifted the heavy lid. A wool blanket covered the contents of the trunk.

"Pull off that blanket," ordered Glinda.

Nancy was slim and active enough to kneel down and reach into the trunk. She pulled aside the blanket. Underneath, resting on another blanket lay an iron plaque, about twelve inches square and a half-inch thick. Embossed on the top were a cross and a strip of letters that appeared to be Russian or Cyrillic. A separate strip of metal inscribed "No. 11" was affixed to the plaque at the bottom. Glinda leaned forward in her wheelchair, gloating in admiration of her treasure. "There you are privileged to see a genuine boundary plaque, found in Alaska by someone I once knew. The letters say, 'Country in Possession of Russia.'"

"This must be very old." Nancy lifted it out of the trunk at an awkward angle. Thank goodness the plaque wasn't too heavy. She turned it over, but the other side was blank and pitted with corrosion.

"Russian traders planted plaques like that around Alaska to claim their territory. Early 1800s, that was." Glinda reached over and stroked it. She peered up at Nancy. "Only one other is known to exist and that one is Number Twelve."

"How did you get it?" Nancy turned the plate over and studied the design on top. The surface felt grainy like wrought iron.

"I'm from Alaska, you know," said Glinda, lifting her chin and sitting tall. "I was in show business there—they called me The Singing Canary."

Nancy winced. Singing canary?

Glinda grinned. "A man I once knew found it and gave it to me."

She smiled into a mirror hung on the wall at her wheelchair height. "To pay off a debt."

Alaska. Nancy would never have thought a hot house plant like Glinda could have spent any time in such rugged country. "Anchorage?" Nancy guessed.

"Anchorage is the only town worth mentioning in Alaska," Glinda said. "But I was glad to leave even though," she patted her odd golden hair, "I had boatloads of admirers there."

Nancy kept her face blank. "Shouldn't this be in an Alaskan museum?"

"Maybe so. Eventually. Right now it's mine."

Nancy sat down on the bed with the plaque in her lap. She felt awed at its history. "What are you going to do with it?"

"I'm displaying it on the shelf outside my door, that's what." Glinda frowned at the plaque. "That oughta wake up the people around here," she muttered, looking like a cat at a mouse hole.

Nancy ran her fingers over the cold, grainy iron. "This is too valuable to leave out in the hall—anyone could take it."

Glinda's cold eyes turned to Nancy. "People around here need to know that I've led an exciting life. I was a star. I'm to be reckoned with."

They already think you're something, all right. Glinda reminded Nancy of several egotistical politicians she'd met. She studied Glinda for a moment, hearing in her words all the pathos of a has-been and feeling sorry that the plaque should be used for such a small purpose.

Glinda stared back at her defiantly. "I dare them to steal it. I'll deal with them. Anyway, it's too bulky to just carry away, and lots of other people here put valuable things on their shelves." She thrust out her lower lip in a pout.

"I know." Nancy traced the odd Russian letters with her fingers.

Glinda leaned forward, her eyes glittering. "And none of their things have disappeared."

"Did you get this appraised and insured?" Nancy stood, still examining the plaque as she carried it past Glinda out of the bedroom.

"Why should I do that?" Glinda tossed her long golden curls, turning her wheelchair to follow Nancy.

"I know the person who gave it to me, and I know it's authentic. I know what it's worth. Go ahead, put it outside on the shelf."

Nancy hesitated, not wanting to comply, but she felt tired and didn't need an argument. She followed orders and turned to say good-bye.

Glinda's eyes narrowed. "Wait a minute. I want to talk to you."

Nancy shook her head. "It's late. I need to go."

Glinda frowned. "Okay, Miss Know-It-All Detective. You're mighty proud of that pearl necklace, aren't you? You're always wearing it. Why don't you get it appraised and insured?" She drew herself up and stared at Nancy like a fat, feathered ostrich would stare at a juicy worm.

Nancy's mouth dropped open. Her hand involuntarily fingered her necklace. So now Glinda was attacking her? "What I do with my pearls is beside the point. We're talking about your plaque."

"I'll tell you why you don't get it appraised. We all can see it's just a string of fakes made of glass balls and fish paste." Glinda sat back, a smug smile on her face, as if they now played a game. She waited for Nancy's next move.

Nancy's eyes sparked. "It most certainly is not. This was a gift from my father to my mother. After she died, he gave it to me." Nancy turned to leave. How dare Glinda mock this precious memory of her mother and father.

"Thank goodness it has sentimental value," Glinda rolled her scooter to the door as Nancy stepped into the hall, "because it sure doesn't have anything else."

Nancy ignored her.

"I know all about jewelry," Glinda added. "I made it my business to know. Men were always giving me pearls—real pearls—and diamonds and sapphires and rubies and all set in genuine 18 karat Alaska gold." She paused, squinting up at Nancy.

"And I know all about you. Don't think I don't. I know who you are. A private detective," she snorted, "indeed. Some of the people around here would stay as far away from you as they could get if they knew the kind of nosy stuff you used to do. And I don't care who gave you those pearls, they're still fake, fake, fake."

***

Life at Whisperwood: Class Registrations

Descriptions and registration forms for fall classes will be available at the reception desk beginning next week.

Although enrollment is open throughout the year, early registration can ensure that you are included in the classes of your choice. Art and craft classes do limit the number of participants because of the space and supplies required. The Model Train Club and other organizations also run classes. Contact the club liaison for information about those.

From *The Whisperwood Breeze*, newsletter of Whisperwood Retirement Village

Chapter 6

"Just wait'll you hear the latest," Louise muttered to Nancy as they joined George the next day for dinner. The threesome arrived early, so the evening's hostess allowed them to sit by themselves without adding a fourth person. Louise wore khaki slacks and shirt, but today the buttons pinned to her lapel said *Stamp Out Invasive Species* and *Support Your Local Humane Society*.

Louise and George, both leaning on canes, hobbled after Nancy through the dining room, navigating their way around tables covered with white linen. Mauve napkins were rolled with the silverware and lay at each place, while long, twisted candles with tiny, flickering electric bulbs on top served as centerpieces. Their table stood between the windows across the back wall and a wide pillar that provided a partial screen for an illusion of privacy.

"This is table fifty-six. Remember to ask for it when we have something private to discuss." George's baritone projected across the room as he hooked his cane on the chair arm, straightened his blue polka-dot tie, and draped his yellow sweater across the seat back.

"Pipe down, George," said Louise. "We can hear you, and so can everyone else in the room."

Nancy glanced around the pillar at the diners nearby to make sure they weren't listening but caught herself, knowing that she needn't worry. At Whisperwood, most of the residents were hard of hearing and had enough trouble keeping up with the conversation at their own tables.

Louise flicked her long, gray braid and said through gritted teeth, "I do have something private to discuss."

A server filled their water glasses and set a basket of rolls on the table. She gazed down at them with intelligent brown eyes and a shy smile while she noted their orders.

After she left, Louise exploded. "There's been another victim."

Nancy paused in the act of unfolding her napkin. "Another victim?"

"Sorry, Nancy." Louise softened her voice. "This is the second old man who's been found dead on the grounds. I'm not buying their story that he wandered off into the woods and died of exposure."

"How could that happen?" Nancy asked. "Everything is so secure here. And the security guards patrol this place."

"That's what we're wondering," George took a roll and passed the basket. "Twice is too damn often."

"I knew him," added Louise. "He was always nosing around. Last time I saw him, he said he was onto something here. Wouldn't say any more." She took a roll and tore a piece off. "Damn fool."

George eyed the butter. "Sounds like a crusade for you, Louise."

Louise nodded. "I'm looking into it."

"Let me know how I can help," Nancy said and then, because she had been fuming all day, brought up Glinda's obnoxious behavior. "Most of the people I've met here try to be pleasant, but I had a run-in last night with Glinda. . . "

"Don't tell me." George sat back with a chuckle. "Glinda Spencer. The delight of our Spanish class."

Louise looked up. "They should never have given her that power scooter. She's all over the place with it, fishtailing down the halls, poking into everyone's business. Almost hit me the other day, then accused me of being in her way."

George's pink face grew red. "She scares me." He frowned. "But I'll get even. I'm putting her and all her loathsomeness in my novel." He rapped his knuckles on the table for emphasis.

"Good idea." Louise lightly slapped George on the arm. She winked at Nancy. "I'm still waiting to see one word of what he's written." She sat back in her chair, stretching out her long legs under the table.

George lifted his chin. He ignored Louise's comment, turning his attention instead to unrolling the silverware from his napkin. "Glinda's always looking for trouble. One of these days someone's going to do her in."

Nancy glanced at George and again raised her voice so he could hear her. "I'm surprised, George. Glinda tells me that men fall all over her, giving her diamonds and pearls and . . ." she mimicked Glinda's bell-like tones, "genuine 18 karat Alaska gold."

"Not me, no sir." George shuddered. He held a fork up to the light. "Gotta make sure they clean the utensils."

"So how did Glinda get to you?" Louise asked.

Nancy leaned forward. "Glinda claims these pearls are fake." Nancy held the necklace out from her neck so the others could see it clearly. Its soft patina glowed in the light. "This necklace is the only thing I still have that belonged to my mother. She died when I was very young—I hardly knew her."

"I've always admired it," said Louise.

Nancy smiled at her. "My dad bought it for Mom. I know it's genuine. I don't care how much it's worth, and I don't want anyone mocking it." Nancy stared down at her plate.

"Sounds like Glinda sounding off," Louise said, patting Nancy's hand. "Don't worry about it."

Nancy shook her head, not trusting herself to speak.

George reached for his water glass. "I know what you could do about your necklace. Get it appraised. I'll bet there are retired jewelers living here."

"George is right," added Louise in her gravelly voice. "Read through Whisperwood's Bio Books. And while you're at it, check out Glinda too."

"I've leafed through them, but I didn't know Glinda then." Nancy sat back in her chair.

"Everybody has a page in those books," said Louise. "Even me, and I haven't done anything." She winked at Nancy.

Nancy smiled. "I have to challenge that, Louise. I'll bet your page is quite impressive." She knew about Louise's lifelong battles to protect animals and the environment. "I've even seen you quoted in the newspapers."

George glanced at Louise with interest. "You mean we have another celebrity here besides Nancy?"

"No, you don't." Louise banged her fork on the table. "A lot of people would rather shoot me."

"I'd like to rewrite my page," Nancy said. "They made it up. Doesn't sound like me—except for the bit about playing bridge. I do love that game. Three mornings a week. Keeps the brain sharp."

"You're all too modest for me. Wish I'd made up something colorful for my page. Big game hunter, maybe. Astronaut even." George motioned to the server several tables away and pointed to his cup. "Speaking of colorful, you wait until I get through with Glinda in my book."

Louise groaned as she tapped on her cup to echo George's signal. "Please, don't go on about your novel till you've finished it." She paused as the server returned with coffee pots. She filled their cups and moved on to the next table.

Nancy looked over at Louise. "Glinda said she was in show business in Alaska, and," Nancy grinned, "they called her the 'singing canary.'"

Louise snorted. "All the singers in Alaska are called singing canaries."

"I would never have guessed she was from Alaska," George said, twirling his water glass. "Peoria, maybe."

"I would have said Pittstown." Louise leaned back in her chair, hands in her pockets, gazing up at the ceiling.

"It's odd. Don't meet too many people from Alaska around here. Wonder who else is from Alaska." George looked around the dining room as if Alaskans were all fur-covered Eskimos. "Maybe they know her."

"Could be. Her sister lives here," Louise said. "Barbara Elmo and her husband Donald."

"No kidding." George whistled.

"I'll look for others while I search for a jeweler." Nancy said. She took a sip of water. Her detective instincts were taking over. "I should just ignore Glinda, but now I'm curious." She looked up as the server arrived with their salads. "What's your name?" Nancy asked.

"Taneesha, ma'am. I'm sorry I forgot my name tag today." She gestured at her white blouse—clean and pressed—as were her black slacks.

"That's all right. I always forget mine. You're in high school, aren't you? What grade?"

"Eleventh." She glanced over at the food station. "Excuse me. I'll be bringing your food out in a few minutes." Taneesha hurried on to the next table.

Nancy turned to the other two. "It's great they hire high school kids here," she said. "Gives them job experience, a little extra money . . ."

"Sure." Louise fidgeted in her seat as she surveyed the dining room. "And don't forget the scholarships we provide."

"The only bad thing is we have to eat dinner so damned early so the kids can leave by seven," George grumbled. "My wife and I never ate before nine. We'd have a couple of drinks, appetizers, then dinner. That's the way I'd like it."

"Yeah. They think we're old so we like to eat early." Louise poked her fork towards Nancy. "Are you going to pursue the appraisal?"

"I'll never rest until I know for sure." Nancy set her lips into a firm line.

"Thatagirl." Louise's blue eyes twinkled in the narrow, craggy face.

Taneesha arrived, carrying a tray loaded with covered plates. She uncovered them and placed them correctly in front of each diner. "Now is everything all right?"

"Just fine, Taneesha," George said, studying his plate. Nancy and Louise nodded at the server as she moved on.

Louise flicked her braid. "Forget about Glinda, Nancy. What

else does she have to brag about?"

Nancy speared a piece of tomato. "She does have one thing to brag about, and that's the reason she asked me to her apartment. She couldn't lift it."

"What is it now? Photos from her checkered past?" George mumbled as he lifted a piece of fish with his fork and peered under it.

"Have you ever heard of Russian boundary plates?" Nancy asked.

"Does this have anything to do with Alaska?" Louise shoveled up a forkful of peas.

"Or maybe dinner?" George pointed to his plate.

"It has something to do with Russian traders staking out Alaska as their possession," Nancy said. "Anyone know when it became a U.S. territory?"

"Sure," Louise said. "Bought from Russia in 1867." She tapped her lips thoughtfully. "I remember seeing an iron boundary plate in the Alaska State Museum in Juneau a long time ago. They said it was the only one ever found. You gotta wonder where the others are."

Nancy nodded. "Glinda has plate number eleven."

Louise stopped with her fork in the air.

George looked up from his fish. "Probably worth a lot, wouldn't you think?"

"Yeah," Louise said, "If it's genuine, there are only two in the world that we know of."

"I told Glinda not to put something so unique on her shelf," said Nancy.

Louise nodded. "You were right. No telling who might be roaming the halls."

"It doesn't look like much. Most people would think it was an old house number plate," Nancy said. "It's worn . . . and ugly, too."

Louise sipped her wine. "I'll have to go by Glinda's apartment and take a look at it." She stared down at the table for a moment. "Anyway, she's not all bad." Louise took another sip of wine. "I found out that she sends big checks to the local humane society. Surprised the hell out of me."

"Surprises me too. Have you been in her apartment?" Nancy asked.

Louise shook her head as she reached for a roll. "Let me guess. Red-fringed lampshades . . . ."

"Worse. Bright pink, like a palm reader's cottage." Nancy described the dead cats as she passed the butter and margarine.

Louise laughed. "Hard to keep something like that out of your nightmares."

"I get enough nightmares. That's why I keep busy," Nancy said. "Now I've got perusing the directories to sandwich in between bridge games, tennis, swimming, and the gym."

"And I'm working up a plan of projects for the 90s Club," Louise added.

"Looking forward to it. It's hard not to feel redundant and," Nancy searched for the word, "passé at our age. Bridge is just a game, after all."

"Okay," Louise sat up and poked a finger at her. "You're on. You can pet those dogs at the gate, for one thing. Their names are Ham and Eggs." She snorted. "Perry's idea. They're nice dogs, but nobody but me pays any attention to them."

"But they're guard dogs, aren't they?" Nancy asked. "Are they attack trained?"

"Of course not," Louise said. "I think Perry got them because they look mean. And they're powerful, but they're good dogs. Depends on how you treat them. I go out and pet them, talk to them, give them some attention. People don't have to be afraid of them."

She cleared her throat. "And I'm getting up a campaign to recycle stuff here. Can you believe they don't do that in this place? Incredible, but you can help me change that."

"I hate to put recyclables in the trash," Nancy said.

"Give them to me." Louise pushed her chair back and tossed down her napkin. "I make weekly runs to the recycling center. Our landfills are close to capacity, but Bryerson doesn't think that's of any concern to us. Most self-centered man I've ever met."

"He certainly is odd," Nancy agreed.

***

Life at Whisperwood: Too Precious to Lose

We all enjoy the mementos, photos and knickknacks on the display shelves, but please be sure
that the items you put on your shelf can be replaced. No original photos or valuable keepsakes
should be left out in the hall. Instead, display your
important and valuable items in your apartment and
invite your friends in to visit.

-From *The Whisperwood Breeze*, newsletter of
Whisperwood Retirement Village

Chapter 7

Every morning, Glinda perched like a brooding sentry on her power scooter in the lobby, watching the comings and goings with hawk-like eyes. Nancy often passed her to reach the lobby's coffee bar. Today, she lifted her cup to Glinda in a mock salute, but Glinda ignored her.

Nancy turned away. Being friendly to that woman was a waste of time. She walked over to the couch outside the office of Whisperwood's administrator, Harry Doyle, as he rushed out. He waved in passing and said, "I'll get the article to you later this morning."

Nancy watched him run down the hall, amused at his earnest attempts to look professional. Unlike most of the other staff who wore casual clothes on the job, he dressed like Mr. Chamber of Commerce. Today he wore a gray suit with a red-checkered tie.

She felt annoyed at the brush-off, but she knew he still hadn't written his article for Whisperwood's house newsletter, *The Whisperwood Breeze*, and it should have gone out yesterday.

Even though she was a new resident, Nancy volunteered to edit the newsletter when the previous editor died. The job put her in the inner circle and on top of what was going on. She stirred her coffee. She was curious about Bryerson, for one thing. Who was he? He must be brilliant. Look at what he had accomplished here. He was well-mannered and spoke quietly, but something about him seemed, Nancy sought the right word, secretive? He was friendly enough to the residents, but the friendliness never went beyond the usual courtesies. Pleasant, but revealing nothing. She didn't even know if he had a wife and family. If he did, where were they? So far, Nancy's cursory Internet searches had only turned up superficial articles on his success as a businessman.

In contrast, Harry's openness and enthusiasm made him likeable and approachable. Why had Bryerson selected Harry? Nancy had read Harry's framed business degree, displayed with pride in his office. Whisperwood must be his first job after receiving his MBA. She would have thought Bryerson would hire someone with more experience.

As she sipped her coffee, a middle-aged woman approached. "I'm looking for Mr. Doyle or Amanda. Have you seen them?"

"Harry just left for a meeting," Nancy said. "Can I help you?"

"I was just clearing out my sister's things," the woman said. "Elizabeth Cochran, you know? She used to edit the newsletter?"

"I'm so sorry. . ." Nancy began.

The woman waved that away. "I just wondered if she left anything down here."

"You can look at the desk," said Nancy, "but I've taken over as editor and didn't see anything personal there."

The woman hesitated. She tapped her finger on her lips. "I guess she gave away a lot of stuff. . ."

"We do have a thrift shop here," said Nancy. "Was there something missing in her things?"

"Yes. Several things. Valuable, I would have thought, but she was worried about leaving too much stuff that others would have to get rid of. I'm sure she probably gave them to the thrift shop."

The woman turned away. "I'll just go down there and check."

"Good luck," Nancy called after her, noticing that Glinda had observed this exchange with a look of malevolent curiosity.

Nancy finished her coffee. She was not sitting in the lobby this morning to pester Harry about the newsletter but to wait for Louise and her friend, Dr. Tom Gerrard. The two activists were closeted in Bryerson's office, confronting him about the invasive species growing on the grounds. The Japanese honeysuckle and multiflora roses that lined the drive, for instance, were an obvious sore point to Louise, Tom, and the other environmentalists at Whisperwood.

"Those alien plants take over," Louise had told Nancy, "and crowd out all the native species like the raspberries and blackberries that I used to enjoy picking when I first moved here. They're all gone now, smothered out." Louise stuck out her jaw as she wound up on one of her favorite topics.

"And those ailanthus trees by the tennis courts are truly evil." She'd thumped her cane. "They're fast-growing and, yeah, attractive, but in a couple more years, that's all you'll see. Forget about oaks, hickories, sassafras, poplars. Take heavy, repeated doses of a tough weed killer and a full-scale forest fire to get rid of those ailanthus— not that we'd advocate fires, but you see what I mean. Meanwhile we're losing a lot of the other trees."

Nancy looked up as Bryerson's door opened. Louise stalked out, lower lip protruding, one fist clenched, the other clomping her brass-topped cane hard on the floor as she stomped over to Nancy. Tom followed, leaning on his walker, but he turned around and slammed Bryerson's door behind him.

"That barbarian," Louise muttered to Nancy. "Whisperwood is not his baby. It's ours. We all live here, and we have rights too."

"What happened?" Nancy asked, rising to meet them.

"That . . . that . . . jackass refuses to let us eliminate the Japanese honeysuckle and multiflora rose." Louise spit out the words.

"We told him we're willing to replant with native species—and to pay for it," added Tom, clenching his lantern jaw and banging his walker on the floor.

"He won't consider any of your suggestions?" Nancy walked alongside Louise as they headed toward the front doors. "He seems so intelligent and well-read."

Louise glared at Nancy. "Intelligent and well-read, maybe, but he's still an asshole and everyone knows he's a cheap son of a bitch. Oh, he's willing to let us walk around the grounds—as if that were a huge concession. Don't we expect to walk around the grounds? Isn't that why we came here? 'To walk through the fields?'"

Nancy recognized the quote from the Whisperwood brochure. "Smell the flowers—and I don't mean the multiflora rose either.

The man is a total jerk. He kept trying to derail us by pointing to all the framed awards he's received for the design of this place." Louise growled in disgust.

"He had no interest in my opinion either," said Tom, sweeping a hand across his bald head, "and I'm a botanist. I could have given him any facts and figures he wanted."

"He should be interested in involving the residents— probably save him money to let us do some gardening," said Nancy. "He and Harry are always complaining about the expenses here."

Louise waved Nancy's comment aside. "Yep, you'd think he'd want us to be environmentally conscious, but he kept telling me not to worry my little head—that's what he said!—about the grounds or anything else." Her mouth twisted with scorn.

"We're supposed to enjoy ourselves," Tom added, "as if we're already dead and in some kind of insipid paradise—not that I believe in any such thing." His green eyes flashed. He wiped his hands on his jeans and tucked in his white polo shirt with the words, "Native Plant Society," in a circle of blue letters decorating the pocket. The shirt matched Louise's, but she wore her usual khaki slacks instead of jeans.

"It's not as if Bryerson's trying to hide a dumpster or sewer pipe," added Nancy. "We can see the whole campus from our windows. We even walk around the honeysuckle and roses. Those shrubs aren't covering up anything."

"Of course not. We'd know if he was making moonshine or burying bodies on the grounds." Louise thumped her cane. "He doesn't want to be bothered with us."

"Ignorance, I guess," added Tom. "He probably thinks it would cost him some money."

"Yeah." Louise stuck her chin out. "So then I asked him about the dogs." She started walking toward the lobby door to the verandah. "They're caged up in that tiny area most of the time." Louise folded her arms.

The door opened automatically, and they stepped out. Nancy looked down towards the gatehouse, but it was hidden by the curve in the road.

"Doesn't anyone walk them?" Nancy asked.

"Not that I've ever seen—except when they're using them to hunt down one of us lost on the grounds." Louise shivered. "It's cruel to make them stay in that cage all the time." Louise thumped her cane again. "He says they're work dogs, needed to find residents who get lost, like those two men who died of exposure here." Louise paused and stared at the trees in the distance. "There's something really funny about that." She frowned at Nancy. "Why would their hands be covered with soot?"

"Coal dust?" Nancy thought a moment. "Maybe they fell down a coal chute."

Louise snorted. "This place doesn't use coal. I checked on that before I moved in here. I would have voted for wind or solar power, but they use natural gas."

"Terrible that such an accident could happen."

"Yeah," said Tom. "Should have better safeguards here."

"Bryerson says everyone's on the alert to make sure that kind of accident—accident!" Louise snorted, "doesn't happen again. Then he threatened me." She laughed.

"Threatened you?" Nancy's mouth fell open. "With what?"

"He hinted that we wouldn't be welcome here if we insisted on making trouble." Louise kicked at a turf of grass. "Can you believe it?"

"I don't think he has the right to terminate your residency," Nancy said, "just because you made some suggestions."

"Of course not. I could sue the hell out of him."

Nancy surveyed the lawn and shrubs before them. She took a deep whiff and fingered a honeysuckle tendril, thinking that its flowers were as pretty as its scent. "I suppose this land was cheap—even for West Virginia, but Bryerson must be a powerful business-man to put together the resources to build this place."

"I heard he was in manufacturing." Tom squinted as he stared back at the monstrous white building, their home, at the top of the mountain. "Never bothered to look into it. Maybe I should."

"I'd like to know more about the history of this place," Nancy said. She felt a twinge of excitement as her curiosity took hold.

"What was here before? If it was a reclaimed mine site, how stable do you suppose the ground is under us? Are we all going to disappear in a tunnel cave-in?" She gazed out at the slight ups and downs of the lawn. Was that normal?

"Who knows?" Louise flashed her cane as if it were a sword.

"Not Bryerson, I bet."

Nancy nodded. "Let's walk around this place and take notes."

"We might see some other no-good plants he's got growing here." Louise stalked across the lawn.

"Or sink holes," said Nancy.

Louise snorted. "Tonight I'm gonna tell George about Bryerson's attitude so he can add this little fiasco to his novel."

***

**Life at Whisperwood:
Garden Plots Available**

Whisperwood still has garden plots available for residents with a green thumb. The plots are ten feet square and located behind the long-term-care building. Whisperwood Administrator Harry Doyle requests that residents confine all gardening and yard work to the garden plots to avoid injury and damage to the landscaping.

-From *The Whisperwood Breeze,* newsletter of Whisperwood Retirement Village

Chapter 8

The posted obituaries listed ten residents who had died in the last two weeks. Nancy read the names, feeling sad and a little sick at the length of the list. She pulled out a pen and notebook and noted the times of several memorial services. Depressing the way they mounted up here.

May Brooks walked up alongside. "I recognize most of these people." She tapped the list. "Long-time residents here."

They both stood close to the bulletin board out of the way of the speed demons who raced their power wheelchairs and scooters through the halls. Nancy could hear them coming. They reminded her of droids, none more than chest high, sitting on their mobile chairs and gliding down the halls like a hissing army of robots.

"I recognize some names too," replied Nancy, smiling down at the short, stout person beside her. "What a shame, but then nobody expects any of us to live here very long."

"I just hope I don't lose my mind and wander the halls getting into trouble." May tugged at Nancy's sleeve. "Did you hear what happened to me?"

Nancy shook her head.

"I woke up in the middle of the night and heard a noise in my apartment." May shuddered. "So I pulled the emergency cord and when the security guard came, he found a naked old man in my bathroom." She stopped to take a breath, grimacing up at Nancy.

"How scary for you," Nancy said. "How did that happen?"

"The old guy said he was going for a walk and had to go to the bathroom, so he decided to use mine." May folded her arms across her ample bosom. "That's the last time I'll leave my door unlocked."

Nancy nodded. "Most of the time, I feel so safe here I don't bother to lock my door either." She laughed. "Not that I ever need to lock it with Malone on guard."

May rolled her eyes. "Yeah. Malone. I don't have a watch-cat like Malone, and I was terrified when I heard that old man." She shivered. "I hope it never happens again."

She pointed to a name halfway down the list. "Mary Lou Carter. She promised to give me a Lenox vase I'd admired. I better go see if they've started moving her stuff out yet." She sauntered down the hall.

Nancy settled at one of the card tables in the lobby. She picked up the Bio Book, filled with page-length biographies of the residents, and began leafing through the pages, looking up once to see Glinda speeding by on another of her exploring expeditions. Nancy smiled in silent amusement. Her friends always said she was nosy, but Glinda beat her by far. Nancy liked to explore too and often saw Glinda in odd places around the complex—basement, attic storage areas, every hallway.

Nancy continued to peruse the directory for someone with a background in jewelry, detouring time and again as she read with interest the brief histories of the residents. Each person had a page randomly placed in the loose-leaf notebook. The listing for Barbara Elmo was bland enough. She had been a homemaker and her greatest accomplishment was a "long, happy marriage." No mention there of her sister Glinda.

The other person hailing from Alaska was Bernice Nelson, whom Nancy vaguely remembered as another member of the bridge-playing network. Eventually she found the name of a retired jeweler, Simon Smythe. Had she met him? Nancy searched her memory. She didn't think so.

Nancy repeatedly called the jeweler that afternoon, but neither a person nor a machine answered. She shook off the feeling of frustration and an hour later walked up to his apartment. She knocked on the door. Again no response. His neighbor opened her door and peeked out. Nancy greeted her, then gestured toward Simon's apartment. "Is he away?"

The woman stepped out into the hall, but her hands trembled, and she clung to the door. Nancy reared away from the whiffs of alcohol as the woman nodded at Nancy, surveying her from head to foot, then followed Nancy's gesture with her eyes and rolled them.

"You wanted to see him?" she asked, slurring her words. "He's away again. Never saw a person travel so much. Leaves with a box and a suitcase. Comes back with the suitcase. I have to wonder . . ."

Nancy hid her disappointment as she tucked these odd tidbits into her memory. "How long do you think he'll be away?"

"He's usually gone a couple of days at a time." The neighbor scratched her arms. "He'll be back soon." She retreated into her apartment and shut the door.

Nancy stood in the hall, absently staring at the closed door. Maybe she could visit Barbara Elmo, Glinda's sister, on some pretext to fish for her take on Glinda, but she didn't know Barbara. Nancy decided to wait for a casual opportunity to meet and chat. What drove a person like Glinda to attack, belittle, and bully others?

***

Life at Whisperwood: Know Your Neighbors

An updated phone directory listing apartment and phone numbers and e-mail addresses is now available at the reception desk. If you'd like to know more about your neighbors, look through the Bio Books in the lobby. The books include photos with brief biographies to help you get acquainted with all the interesting people living here at Whisperwood.

-From *The Whisperwood Breeze*, newsletter of Whisperwood Retirement Village

Chapter 9

The summer mornings were sunny, warm, and breezy, luring Nancy out onto the paths for long walks. She avoided passing her apartment windows so Malone wouldn't see her from his perch on the window sill. If he did, she'd have to endure his biting attacks when she returned as well as the complaints from her neighbors about his shrieks and howling because he couldn't go outdoors. She didn't mind wearing the heavy leather biting glove half as much as listening to Malone's and the neighbors' complaints.

This morning, Nancy had gone down to the gatehouse with treats for the two dogs, and now she was late for a meeting in Louise's apartment. As she walked into the building, she nodded at Perry who sat on a bench in the sun, but when she passed him, she could see that he was tearing a butterfly's wings off in tiny pieces.

She didn't quite believe her eyes. Why would he do such a cruel thing? She glanced at his face and their eyes met.

He laughed.

Nancy walked faster into the building. Did he hurt the dogs too when no one was looking? What was his job around here anyway? No one was quite sure, only that Bryerson seemed to find him indispensible. Probably something to do with security or maybe maintenance.

She climbed the stairs to Louise's apartment on the fourth floor and knocked. Louise ushered Nancy into her living room where George already sat, teetering on the edge of a rickety antique chair. Louise's living room featured several antique Chippendale oak chairs and two small, round, mahogany tables covered with lace tablecloths.

"Anyone like a cat?" Nancy asked. Malone had been particularly irritating that morning.

"Not that one." Louise laughed. "Earl Gray or English Breakfast?"

"English Breakfast." Nancy had never been able to connect robust, tough Louise with such a dainty array of furniture. She watched Louise place a teabag into a fragile, flowered tea cup, then pour hot water into it from a china teapot. Of course, all the furniture and the tea set were inherited along with the sterling silverware. On the wall behind the credenza was an array of plaques and certificates from various organizations honoring Louise for her support.

She looked up to see Louise watching her.

"I keep all this stuff," explained Louise waving at the china cabinet and furniture, "because my daughter wouldn't know what to do with it, and she'd put it all in a yard sale. I couldn't stand to see that happen." Then she grinned. "But I use it everyday so to hell with it."

Louise handed her the tea cup. Nancy took it and sat down on the other side of a table from George. She took a second look at George's shirt, a riot of Hawaiian flowers, but said, "So let's get down to business, shall we?"

Louise brought in a plate of cookies, set it on a table, then sat down, stirring sugar into her own tea cup.

Nancy began. "We all know that once in a while someone picks up the keepsakes we put out on our hall display shelves."

George nodded. "Usually on the way to the Alzheimer's Unit." He laughed. "Don't mean to laugh. Pretty sad, you know."

"I know." Nancy feared Alzheimer's like everyone else at Whisperwood.

George peered at Louise over his glasses. "I bet you could take any small item out of these apartments, and no one would report the theft."

"Stealing the display items is different." Nancy tossed her head. "We all saw them on the shelves, now they're not there anymore, and the owner doesn't have them. We have to consider theft."

George peered at her over his cup. "Nothing of any value was stolen, so no one wants to make a fuss."

"Tom's framed photo of the aircraft carrier Yorktown is missing now," Nancy said. "He's very upset, having served on that ship. So what if it has no value? It was important to Tom and nobody should have taken it, Alzheimer's or no Alzheimer's."

"Ingrid down the hall from me had a wooden troll souvenir stolen." Louise waved a cookie in the air. "Just a knickknack, but it reminded her of her last trip with her husband."

Nancy nodded. She had so many years of memories herself, which always surprised her. She could not reconcile herself with the elderly white-haired woman she saw in the mirror. She didn't feel old. She looked at Louise. "And now someone has stolen my musical fan doll."

Nancy gazed into the distance, remembering. "That doll was a gift from a family I helped. It used to be quite pretty with a tiny bouquet in one hand and fan in the other."

"Was it a collectible?" George flicked a crumb off his trousers. "It might be worth stealing."

Nancy shook her head. "No one would want it as a collectible. A friend's child lost the doll's arm and cracked the head. Anyone could see that it was too damaged to be worth anything. I was only being ironic by displaying it at all."

"How's that, Nancy?" George asked.

"You know, don't we all feel a bit worn like that fan doll sometimes?" Nancy kept the quiver out of her voice.

"Oh. Yeah." George paused with his cup in the air.

Louise picked up her cup. "I've heard of several other items being taken in the last week too."

"Whoever's stealing them is a nut case." George sat back and folded his arms. "Anyway, this is a good incident to put in my novel."

Louise groaned. "We have yet to see one word you've written."

"Never mind," said George. "What about Glinda's boundary plate? Has anyone stolen that yet?"

"It's still there on her shelf." Nancy bit into a cookie. "It's heavier and larger than most knickknacks on the shelves. Harder to carry and worthless, most people would think."

Louise shrugged. "I suppose a staff person might take something he fancied as he passed by."

"Sometimes people order deliveries from that restaurant down the road," added George, munching his cookie thoughtfully. "All kinds of people roam these halls."

"Even visitors could pick up an item and carry it out," Nancy added. "I warned Glinda about the thefts, but she brushed me off."

"Forget about it, Nancy," said Louise, flipping her braid.

Nancy eyed the braid, quelling an impulse to cut the damn thing off. How many times did Louise have to fiddle with it in one conversation anyway?

Louise talked on, oblivious to the danger her braid was in. "You can't help someone who won't listen. But we can try to find out what's going on around here." She stopped and frowned. "Anyway, I don't think it was a visitor or delivery person because most of the items were on the shelves in the evening and gone the next morning."

"We could roam the halls to see who's wandering around late at night. We might learn something." George lifted his cup.

"I'll drink to that," said Louise, sitting up in her chair. "Of course if we see anyone, they might think we're the thieves—and vice versa." She shrugged.

Nancy laughed. "You're right, but I'm in." Her eyes sparkled in anticipation.

Louise and Nancy clinked their cups.

***

Late that night, Nancy, Louise, and George began their watch, each taking separate halls and floors. Nancy enjoyed this kind of adventure, and she was grateful to do something that kept the night away and made sleep come easily when she finally did go to bed.

By three that morning, the adventure had lost its charm. Nancy was almost sleepwalking as she dragged herself down the empty, dim halls of Whisperwood. Only the security guards and members of the Insomniac Club, playing bridge in the lounge, were awake. None of them noticed Nancy as she passed. Good. She wanted to be invisible.

She walked around a corner, feeling spooked by the creepy shadows and quiet of the fifth floor, and collided with George, who was resting against the wall. Louise tottered up behind, her tall body hunched over her cane.

"Whoa," Louise whispered, wheezing as she leaned against the wall. "This ain't a horse race."

"Did you spot anything?" Nancy murmured.

"Nah, did you?" Louise's gravelly voice echoed in the hall.

Nancy put a finger to her lips and herded them toward the elevators and away from the apartments. "I checked a lot of possible hiding places. Didn't see anyone in the halls or anything suspicious."

"Neither did we," growled George. "Most of the hidey holes were full of dust—and nothing else."

Louise leaned on her cane and attempted to keep her voice low. "This is probably a useless search. All the thief had to do was conceal the stolen items in his or her apartment or throw them out in the trash." She held a hand out toward the wall. "I asked the Insomniac Club, but none of them noticed anyone wandering around who shouldn't be. Of course, a member of the club could be the culprit, I guess."

As Louise caught her breath, Nancy said, "The thief can't mean to sell them." She looked from Louise to George. "None of the items stolen was valuable."

"That's why the thefts are either a petty harassment or pilfering by one of our dotty friends here." Louise peered into the dark shadows of the library.

"We might as well call it a night," said George.

Nancy pressed the down elevator button.

"Yep." Louise gestured toward the library. "The only thing you could hide in the library is a book." She lowered her voice. "Something funny is going on in the basement."

"Did you notice the smell down there?" asked George. "An odd smell—I can almost recognize it, but then my smeller isn't too good any more. Age, I guess."

Nancy hadn't checked the basement herself. "Maybe you smelled glue or paint from the classrooms and hobby areas down there."

"The smell came from the steel door at the end of the hall, the one we always wonder about. It was open a crack," said George. "The closer I got to it, the stronger the smell, but then some guy on the other side of the door poked his head out, saw me, and shut the door. I heard him lock it."

"I can't imagine why they've got a guard down there," Louise thumped her cane, "for a storage area."

Nancy watched the floor numbers over the elevator. "Is that what they say? That the door leads to a storage area?"

Louise shrugged. "That's what everyone says."

"That door was always locked when I've tried it." Nancy folded her arms. "What was that guard doing? Nothing goes on down there this late at night."

Louise nodded. "Yeah, but during the day that hall is busy with residents involved in their own arts and crafts projects."

"Something to ask the Residents Council about," Nancy said. "Or Harry Doyle." She turned toward the elevator as she heard it reach their floor and stop. The doors opened.

"Yep. Now I'm ready to turn in." George entered the elevator.

"I'll take the stairs, in case someone's hiding there," said Louise, opening the stairwell door and leaning against it. "I only have one floor to go down."

George laughed. "What are you going to do if they are there? They'll make short work of you."

"You think so?" Louise pulled apart her cane, revealing a rapier-like steel weapon on the end of the handle.

"Wow," said Nancy. George looked stunned.

Louise winked and replaced the handle so her cane again became the innocent aid it appeared to be. "I know how to use it too," she said and laughed. She waved at them as the stairwell door closed, and they heard her cane thump its way down the steps as they waited for the elevator doors to close.

Nancy returned to her apartment, endured Malone's complaints, and went to bed. She was too keyed up to sleep. She kept wondering about the missing shelf items and the steel door with its superfluous guard. Finally, she drifted off, her mind still occupied with the thefts and the search but not with the amorphous dread that usually accompanied a sleepless night.

***

Life at Whisperwood: Can't Sleep?

Yoga instructor Lara Jones can help you stretch those tense muscles and learn techniques to relax for a good night's sleep. Join her drop-in class every morning at 10 in the gym. Still can't sleep? Join the gang for games and puzzles every night in the lounge.

-From *The Whisperwood Breeze,* newsletter of Whisperwood Retirement Village

Chapter 10

After being up until after three the night before, Nancy was ready to sleep until noon. Instead, the phone dragged her to consciousness at seven. Who would call so early?

"You need to come here immediately," the bell-like voice said. "My apartment. Now. Immediately." She hung up.

Oh no, Glinda Spencer. Of course. Who else? Nancy sat on the edge of her bed, torn between annoyance and curiosity. Entering that grotesque apartment again with its staring cats repelled her. She should ignore the call, but as usual, her curiosity took control. She stepped over to her closet and stared into it, half asleep. She managed to slip into blue slacks but had to change her blouse twice before she woke up enough to find a flowered one that matched. She refused to hurry.

She washed her face, brushed her teeth, fed and petted Malone, and emerged to walk leisurely down the hall. After pouring herself a cup of coffee in the lounge, she took the elevator to the fifth floor. As the elevator doors opened, Nancy saw Glinda, oozing out on all sides of her scooter. Her pink and aqua feathered robe made her seem even more massive. She was stationed half out the door into the hall. "What took you so long?" Glinda demanded as she backed into her apartment, leaving the door open.

Nancy did not respond. *I am not your servant. You're lucky I'm here at all.* She walked in, sat down on the couch, avoiding the glassy stares of the dead cats, sipped her coffee, and waited.

"My plaque was stolen last night." Glinda leaned forward in her scooter, twisting her hands together in agitation. "You helped me put it out there." She sat up and pointed at the hall door. "It's not there now."

"You called me at seven because your plaque is missing?" Nancy's voice rose in anger. The nerve of the woman. "I told you not to put it in the hall." But she, Louise, and George had roamed the halls last night and hadn't seen anyone suspicious. Nancy wondered when the theft took place. The thief must have been a resident.

"Why shouldn't I display it so everyone can see it?" Glinda's fist pounded on the arm of her wheelchair. "I had every right to put it on my hall shelf."

Nancy sat back against the couch and stared at Glinda without speaking.

"You used to be a detective." Glinda stabbed her finger at Nancy. "You're the only one I know who can find out what happened to it." The robe's feathers quivered with her indignation.

"My friends and I are looking into the thefts." Nancy frowned at Glinda.

"I need something done now." Glinda's eyes darted around the room as if the walls could help. With her alert little head on top of her massive feathered body, she resembled an ostrich more than ever. "How dare someone take my plaque."

"A musical doll that was precious to me was stolen three nights ago," said Nancy.

Glinda stared at her. "The fan doll? Worthless. My plaque was significant. A piece of history."

Nancy watched the dramatics, keeping her expression blank. "Did anyone else here know the history of that plaque?"

Glinda sat in her chair, deflated. "A couple of people. My sister for one, but she wouldn't dare steal from me."

Nancy thought a moment. "I haven't met her, but I did read her listing in the Bio Books. She's from Alaska too, isn't she?"

Glinda waved that aside as of no importance. "Of course. Only I made it and she didn't. No talent. She even worked for me for awhile," Glinda muttered as if she spoke to herself, "till she married that no-good husband of hers." Her blue eyes turned cold. "Surprised the hell out of me when they showed up here a couple of years ago."

"So your sister Barbara knows about the plaque?"

Glinda tossed her head. "Of course she knows. You've got to get it back." Glinda leaned forward in her wheelchair. Her pudgy fingers tapped on the arm of the wheelchair.

Nancy considered with amusement the subtle undercurrents at play in Whisperwood. "Could Barbara have taken it?"

"Of course not." Glinda sat up and gripped the arms of her wheelchair. "Anyway, Barbara wouldn't sneak it away like that."

Nancy leaned forward. "Do you know Bernice Nelson? I read in the Bio Book that she's from Alaska too."

"Oh. Bernice." A secret smile crossed Glinda's face. "Sure. We go way back." She looked down at her hands. "Way back."

"Then who else might have taken it?"

"That's why I called you." Glinda glared at Nancy. "Wait a minute. Just sit there. Be quiet. I've got to think."

Nancy sipped her coffee, her eyes wandering around the room from one item to the next. Were there any other bizarre exhibits like the staring dead cats? She supposed that the knickknacks on the tables and shelves might be collectible items. They could be valuable, but they didn't look like much—more like common souvenirs from around the country. The Tiffany lamp was probably the most valuable item in the room—if it was genuine.

Glinda's eyes flashed. "I've got an idea. I'll talk to you tomorrow. Meanwhile, you look for it, okay?"

"If you expect me to help, you should tell me what you know."

Glinda rolled her wheelchair towards the door. "I don't know anything. You've got to find it."

Nancy studied her for a moment. "I'll look for your plaque while I look for the other missing items. No promises. But if you know who might have stolen it, you should tell me. The thief might retaliate if he feels threatened."

Glinda wrapped her housecoat tightly around her. "Don't you worry about me. If I'm right, I'll set the dogs on them, I will. They ought to know better than to try to put something over on me."

Nancy turned to leave. Did Glinda see herself as the heroine dashing off to confront the villain? Didn't she watch any old mystery movies? "That could be dangerous."

Glinda brushed Nancy's warning aside with a sweep of her hand. "Not if it's who I think it is. They wouldn't dare. If it isn't, then you'll have to keep looking. Don't bother about the other missing things. They were all worthless pieces of junk—like your pearls."

"Don't make one more statement about my pearls," said Nancy in cold, measured tones.

"They're fake. You want to keep that a secret? I can help you do that, if you make it worth my while. "

Nancy left without another word and returned to her apartment. Glinda was trouble, all right.

Now that she was up, Nancy decided to grab some breakfast. After that, she carried a book and walked down to the basement level and past the classrooms to the steel door at the end of the hall. The door was locked. She put her ear to it but could hear nothing on the other side. She moved away from it as the elevator opened, releasing a tall, middle-aged woman in a paint-covered smock struggling with two satchels. Nancy hurried to help her.

'Thanks," the woman said, handing a satchel to her. "First class-room on the left."

Nancy followed her into the classroom and dropped the satchel on top of a table.

The woman looked at Nancy. "Are you here for the nine o'clock class?"

Nancy shook her head. "Just walking around." She hesitated, wondering if the woman might have noticed anything unusual down there. She decided to ask. "Where do you suppose that steel door at the end of the hall leads?"

The woman opened a satchel and pulled out tubes of paint and brushes. "Have no idea. Storage? It's always locked. Administrative stuff. Maybe old records."

Nancy left that classroom, entered the one across the hall and took a chair out to the hall. She sat down and began reading her book. Occasionally, she would walk to the steel door and listen, but she never heard anything on the other side and after an hour, she replaced the chair and returned to her apartment.

***

Nancy waved to Louise and George, sitting in the Whisperwood pub with sandwiches and iced teas in front of them. Nancy stopped at the pub bar to order the same for herself. Then she joined them at a table close to the gas fireplace and nodded to the couple playing billiards by the back windows near the popcorn machine.

Nancy's annoyance had subsided, and as she told Louise and George about the early morning wake-up call, she could see the humor in Glinda's demands.

"The trouble is you're a nice woman," said Louise, sipping her tea. "She wouldn't dare try such stuff on me."

"She's always testing the waters," growled George. His chair was backed away from the table, and his legs straddled his cane. "I've seen her push other people around who didn't have the gumption to walk out the way you did, Nancy."

"I'm sure she's been a bully all her life," agreed Nancy, averting her eyes from his bright pink and yellow striped shirt. She smiled at the server who delivered her iced tea.

"You're being kind if you're referring to Glinda," said Louise, leaning back in her chair with her legs stretched out in front.

"The theft happened last night while we were roaming the halls," Nancy added.

"How could that be?" sputtered Louise. "I didn't notice anyone suspicious. Did you?"

"I didn't see anyone," said George. "except the bridge players."

"Here's another odd thing." Louise flicked her braid. "Before we quit scouting the halls early this morning," she said in her raucous voice, "I went out on the balcony over the portico." She noticed the billiard players staring at her and lowered her voice. "Did you know that they have deliveries coming in here at three in the morning?"

"Maybe it was someone coming home late." George pursed his lips.

Louise leaned toward George. "Nope. I saw a couple of huge trucks come in, moving slow as if they were real heavy, and they were covered trucks, not pickup trucks. What do you suppose they were delivering?" Louise sat back and twiddled her thumbs.

"They could have been picking something up. Maybe garbage," Nancy said.

Louise shrugged. "Those trucks were full of something when they came in. I suppose I could ask the staff."

George trumpeted, "Sure. Why don't you do that?"

"Probably just supplies, although three in the morning seems strange," Nancy added.

George rubbed his hands. "Say, anyone know what's on the menu for tonight?"

Louise sighed and rolled her eyes. "Coconut shrimp, roast lamb, and eggplant parmigiana. They finally wised up enough to put a vegetarian item on the menu."

"Tomorrow is roast beef and mashed potatoes again," said Nancy, "but I guess I'll go for the eggplant."

Louise peered at George. "I never eat roast beef," she said, pounding her cane on the floor. "Full of cholesterol, bad for the planet, bad for you. Bad stuff period."

"I'll worry about that tomorrow," said George.

***

Life at Whisperwood: Dining Hall Notes

In this month's meeting with the residents, our Dining Hall Manager Ned Ackerson emphasized that he makes every effort to ensure that all meals served at Whisperwood are healthy and nutritious. In keeping with this goal, no salt or sugar is added to any item on the menu, but salt, sugar, and their substitutes are always available on the tables. If you require a special menu because of allergies or other concerns, please alert the dining hall staff.

-From *The Whisperwood Breeze*, newsletter of Whisperwood Retirement Village

Chapter 11

The next night, the telephone woke Nancy at two in the morning. The dratted cat bit her arm in protest as Nancy struggled awake, pushed the cat away, and muttered, "It better not be Glinda this time."

"Nancy? Could you come up here right away?" The words were whispered and spoken quickly. Nancy could hear the panic.

"Who is this?"

"Thank God you're there. It's Anna Carothers, Nancy. Please get here as soon as you can."

Not Glinda this time but Anna who lived across the hall from Glinda. What could have happened? "I'll be right there," Nancy said, already throwing on her clothes.

She ran to the elevator, begrudging the minutes the elevator took to descend to her floor. It seemed another eternity before the doors opened to let her out on the fifth floor. Nancy walked as fast as she could down the hall, glancing at Glinda's apartment with its barren display shelf as she knocked on Anna's door. It opened a crack and an eye peered out, then the door opened wider, and Nancy was pulled in.

"It was only by luck that I was here at all," said Anna, a plump little woman wearing a black sweater and plaid slacks. She scooted a calico cat off the sofa and removed a pile of books. Her brown eyes grew large and luminous as she spoke in hushed tones. She gestured to the sofa for Nancy and pulled up a kitchen chair for herself.

"I was coming home from a late night bridge game and heard banging and crashing in Glinda's apartment. I wondered what she could be doing that time of night but I said to myself, 'Anna, stop being so nosy,' and anyway, it was too late to knock on her door." Anna gulped and took a deep breath. Her eyes blinked rapidly. "I was warming a glass of milk to help me get to sleep, you know." She looked at Nancy as if for reassurance.

Nancy nodded, settling back on the sofa. Anna's apartment was dark and stuffy, crowded with cheap, wooden bookcases—all overflowing with tattered books. Nancy stifled a sneeze at the smell of cat litter.

Anna's face was pale and her hands shook. Nancy reached over and took her hands. They felt like ice. What could have happened?

Anna sat on the edge of a straight-back chair and took another deep breath. "Then I heard Glinda's door open and close and footsteps go down the hall. I knew it wasn't Glinda. She didn't walk anywhere, poor thing, and anyway, the footsteps were heavy and solid—sounded like a man's shoes."

"Glinda had a visitor late at night?" Nancy frowned. "How odd."

"Wait till you hear the rest of it. I peeked out into the hall, didn't see anyone, so I went over to her apartment and knocked and then I tried the door knob and opened the door." Anna stared at Nancy. "It wasn't even locked."

Nancy wondered where this was leading. "What happened?"

"Nothing. She was on the floor next to the scooter and," Anna gulped and her eyes blinked even more rapidly. Her hands shook. "She's dead. In a pool of blood. Her place was ransacked."

"Dead! Are you sure? We should call Security." Now wide awake, Nancy's mind raced through courses of action. She stood and walked toward the door. "Maybe she's only unconscious."

"I checked her carotid artery first thing. She's dead, all right." Anna restrained her. "I already called Security. He's been there and gone. That was odd too."

"What was?" Nancy tugged Anna toward the door.

Anna hung back. "Bryerson's henchman—that's what I call him,

Perry, I mean—showed up too, with the security guard, and the guard pushed me out of the room."

Nancy stopped and looked at her. "I suppose that was standard procedure." She frowned. "If Glinda's dead, I mean."

"Sure. I didn't belong there, but I've never seen them bring in Perry before. Where did he come from? Why was he there?" Anna began pacing back and forth in front of Nancy.

Nancy's eyes followed her. "Maybe Security called Perry. What do you think happened to Glinda?" Obnoxious, bullying Glinda. Nancy immediately felt guilty for the thought, but Glinda had alienated so many people.

Anna stopped pacing and looked at Nancy. "She didn't fall out of the scooter. Her head was bashed in, Nancy. Blood was all over the place." She gulped again, eyes blinking as if on high speed, and took a deep breath.

Nancy turned toward the door. "We should see what happened. Maybe the scooter fell over on her."

"I don't think so." Anna pulled her back. "Nancy, they've locked her place up, you can't get in, and I told you. She didn't just hit her head. It wasn't an accident. Her head, her head was all caved in on the wrong side." Anna glanced around the apartment as if there were enemies in the walls.

"On the wrong side," said Nancy, turning towards Anna. "So she didn't hit her head as she fell."

"And the scooter was overturned away from her." Anna began pacing again in front of Nancy. "Someone hit her on the head and then they must have pushed over her scooter."

For a moment, Nancy's head buzzed, and she felt as if the wind had been knocked out of her. She stared down at the floor and took several deep breaths before she could speak.

Anna stopped pacing. "Are you all right, Nancy?"

Nancy pulled herself together to ask the obvious question. "Could she have moved after she hit her head?"

"Not likely," Anna sniffed. "Nothing looked as if it happened in an accident."

"So someone hit her." Poor Glinda. Poor obnoxious, busybody

Glinda. She didn't deserve this. Nancy glanced up at Anna. "Horrible that you had to see it."

"I'm used to that kind of thing. Army nurse, you know." Anna wrung her hands as she resumed pacing. "Someone searched her place too. It was a mess. Desk drawers were pulled out and overturned, papers scattered all over the rug along with pens, paper clips, newspapers. Even those stuffed cats had been tossed off the shelf and across the room. Gave me the creeps."

"You didn't touch anything, did you?" Nancy reached over to Anna, stopped her pacing and looked directly at her.

"No, no. I knew I shouldn't impact the crime scene."

Nancy hugged Anna. "Army nurse or not, it must have been a terrible shock for you."

Anna's eyes blinked. "I saw it before they could clean it up and restage it. Really make it look like an accident. That's what they're gonna do." She nodded her head. "You wait and see. They're going to try to pass it off as an accident, but it wasn't an accident."

Nancy kept her arms around Anna and led her to the couch.

"Who did you hear leaving her apartment?" Nancy asked as they sat down.

"I don't know." Anna shrugged. "Maybe that's who killed her. I can't imagine what they were searching for. Her apartment was a mess."

"Be careful, Anna." Nancy said. "These are murderers."

"Oh I will. I'm getting another lock, first thing tomorrow morning." Anna shivered.

Nancy left Anna's apartment not knowing what to believe. Glinda wasn't a popular person at Whisperwood, but murder was too extreme for dislike. Yet Nancy had played bridge with Anna and knew she was sharp. There was nothing wrong with her mind, ears, or eyes.

She stopped outside Glinda's door and listened. She could hear voices, but they were too low to understand. She walked to the elevator, remembering some of the cases she used to handle and the dishonesty and greed she had encountered. She had seen the worst in human behavior, and she could believe that Perry was ruthless enough to protect Whisperwood's reputation at all costs even if it meant concealing a murder, but surely Bryerson and Harry would want the culprit caught before he struck again. Surely the sheriff would want to investigate.

When she reached her apartment and opened the door, the cat sat on the windowsill, tail swishing as he watched the red and blue lights flashing outside the window. The sheriff had arrived.

Despite Nancy's cautions, Anna could not stay quiet. The next day Nancy heard versions of Anna's wide-eyed account of Glinda's murder from residents up and down the hall. Shaken from their complacency, they had begun locking their doors, and Nancy was not alone in scrutinizing every stranger she met in the halls.

***

Life at Whisperwood: In Memoriam

The Whisperwood Community regrets the passing of the following residents during the week of June 1-7.
JOHN HANSON
ELIZABETH COCHRAN
RALPH P. ALLWRIGHT
PAGE BURLINGTON
ANTHONY MORELLI
GLINDA SPENCER

-From *The Whisperwood Breeze*, newsletter of Whisperwood Retirement Village

Chapter 12

Nancy sat in the lounge sipping her morning coffee and waiting for Glinda's sister, Barbara Elmo, to leave the social worker's office. Nancy lingered in case Barbara might need company and comfort. Losing your sister had to be a terrible blow.

Nancy was an only child, but fifty years ago when her father had died and then only two years later, her first husband, she had spiraled down into deep depressions that didn't dissipate for months. Her second husband had died just four years ago, and Nancy could feel the depression creep in if she dwelled too long on her memories. She was ninety years old, and no one who'd known her as a child and young woman still existed. She was alone. This thought had lost its terror but left a deep sadness that she buried in activity—new courses, new friends, walking, swimming, bridge, anything that would push away the dark thoughts.

Nancy looked across the lobby to the place where Glinda used to sit in the mornings and raised her cup in a silent salute. She drank her coffee and waited. Creeping down the hall towards her was an elderly woman in a nightgown leaning on a walker. An aide stepped alongside and kept a guiding hand on the woman's elbow.

"Take it real slow," said the aide.

"I can go faster than this," her patient said.

"No, you go real slow now."

"But I want to go faster," the woman said.

"You're old and need to go slow. If you were younger, like me, then you could go faster."

Nancy groaned. They should train these aides better. What good does it do to insist that because someone is old, she can't do much? That aide was purposely keeping her patient down. It was all Nancy could do to sit there and not interfere right on the spot. She decided to talk to the administrator instead. *I'm ninety, and no one better tell me to go slow.*

She saw the office door opening. Barbara stepped out, nodding to the social worker who patted Barbara's back sympathetically. Barbara was wearing a faded housedress in a pink checkered pattern and her hair was unbrushed. Nancy walked over to her.

"I was so sorry to hear about your sister," Nancy said.

Barbara turned around to stare at Nancy through pale blue eyes that seemed awash. "Thank you," she mumbled.

"Is there anything you need? Anything I can do?" Nancy matched her pace to Barbara's as they headed toward the elevator.

Barbara shook her head. "I'm sorry. I don't believe I've met you, have I?" She peered over at Nancy.

"We've met in passing briefly. I'm Nancy Dickenson."

Barbara sighed. "Glinda mentioned you. You've been helping her, haven't you? The detective?"

"Used to be. I only helped her put the plaque on her display shelf." Nancy glanced at Barbara. "Not my idea, I assure you."

"I know that. What Glinda wanted, Glinda got." Barbara gave a short laugh. "She finally got more than she bargained for."

Nancy absentmindedly took a mint from the candy dish on a hall shelf as she considered what to say.

"And now the plaque is gone too," Barbara added bitterly.

"Do you know what happened to it?" Nancy asked, looking over at Barbara.

"Of course not. Someone saw what it was and took it. My guess." Barbara frowned. "My husband Donald warned her that would happen." She shook her head. "Glinda was so darned pigheaded." She glanced over at Nancy. "I'm sorry. We didn't have the best relationship." Barbara stopped speaking as an old man on a power scooter crept up behind them. They stepped aside to let him pass, then Barbara shrugged. "But I never was as good an actress as my sister. The funny thing is that we moved here because of her."

"Because of her?" Nancy stepped behind Barbara to let an elderly jogger trot by.

"Older sister syndrome. Thought we should stay together. Why, I don't know. She sure wasn't interested—and she wasn't very nice to me or my husband."

They reached the elevator, and Nancy pushed the up button. Neither spoke, but Nancy could hear the sadness behind Barbara's words and wanted to hug her. She instinctively knew that Barbara would be affronted by the touch. "Did Glinda have any other family that we should notify? Can I help you do that?"

Barbara tapped her foot as she stared at the glacial pace of the changing floor numbers above the elevator door. She glanced at Nancy. "She had two sons, Cary and Clark—you can guess why she named them that. Fortunately, they're both accountants, so they managed to build some stability in their lives. They've been notified, but I'll have to call them."

Nancy preferred the stairs but for once was glad that the elevator's slow pace down to pick them up allowed her to keep asking questions. "I've never met them. Do they live nearby?"

"In Morgantown. Not too far away, but they rarely visited their mother."

"That's too bad," Nancy said.

"Good for them, I say." She looked at Nancy. "Glinda moved here because of them, you know, and she was always begging them to visit."

Nancy smiled at this revelation. Glinda had another unexpected dimension. A loving mother. Who would have thought? "Are her sons married?" Nancy asked.

"One is. Two children. The other one is going through a messy divorce." She sighed.

"Do you have any children?" Nancy glanced at Barbara.

"No. My husband and I weren't blessed that way." She sighed, looking down at her feet. "Funny how life works, isn't it?"

"I never had children either," said Nancy. She had long ago made peace with this and often reminded herself that it had left her free for quite an exciting and adventurous life. "I do have five honorary nieces and nephews. Children of friends. Hardly do more than exchange Christmas cards now. They're all busy with their lives."

The elevator finally arrived and opened. Feeling that she ought to stand by for companionship, Nancy accompanied Barbara to the third floor and then down the hall to her apartment. Neither spoke, but as Barbara fumbled for her key, she turned to Nancy. "My husband and I have calls to make, Nancy, but thanks for your interest."

"Of course. Call me if there's anything I can do."

Barbara nodded, entered her apartment, and closed the door. Nancy walked toward the stairs but changed her mind as a woman raced down the hall on her power scooter to the elevator. As she passed, Nancy read the Whisperwood name tag that dangled from a ribbon around her neck. "Bernice Nelson." The woman reached the elevator as the doors opened, discharging an elderly man. Nancy followed her in and punched the down button. Here was an opportunity.

Nancy introduced herself, adding, "I understand you're from Alaska."

"Who told you that?" Bernice squinted up at Nancy, but Nancy noticed that Bernice's hands were gripping the handlebar and her body seemed ready to flee.

"Glinda Spencer," Nancy waved a hand, "before she died. She was telling me about people she knew."

Bernice frowned up at her. "What did that," her mouth twisted in distaste, "woman tell you?"

Nancy reared back in surprise at the venom in Bernice's voice. "Nothing," she said. "Nothing. Just that you were from Alaska too."

"That's good. You can't believe anything you heard from her." The elevator opened on the first floor, and Bernice drove herself silently forward without looking back. Nancy followed her out of the elevator and stared after Bernice as she scooted down the hall toward the lobby.

That afternoon, Nancy met Louise, George, and Tom for bridge in the card room behind the lobby. The other two tables were already filled with players bidding and passing.

Tom leaned on his walker, his bald head gleaming under the lights as he moved awkwardly toward the third table. Louise and George were already seated opposite each other. Nancy took the seat farthest away from the door, leaving the nearest and most accessible seat for Tom. He wore black jeans and a blue polo shirt. Hanging from his walker was a canvas bag with a book in it. Nancy sneaked a peek at the book cover as the canvas bag swung. A mystery. Nero Wolfe, it looked like.

"I enjoy Nero Wolfe too," she said to Tom. "Maybe we can exchange books."

He looked at her, then glanced at the bag and grinned. "I'd like that. Read all the ones in the library."

She picked up a deck of cards and asked the burning question. "You've all heard the news about Glinda?"

Louise grimaced as she shuffled the other deck. "I walk the halls everyday for exercise. Hard to go by her place now with the police tape and the sheriff's men in and out."

"Yes, I know." Nancy had hovered in the hall that morning and watched the deputies at work until one of them asked her to move on. She nodded at Louise, and the bright blue *Dogs Deserve Better* button on Louise's white cotton shirt caught her eye.

Louise noticed Nancy's glance. "For the dogs, Ham and Eggs. They shouldn't be penned up like that every day." She returned to the subject. "I don't think anyone cared much for Glinda. I dropped out of a painting class 'cause of her."

Nancy nodded. "Glinda was obnoxious in our Spanish class, too," she said. She thought of the dining room. So many tables, so many people. Some of them were amiable, pleasant companions; some were grouchy, sarcastic, or had limited social skills. Only a few were as obnoxious as Glinda.

George nodded, his Adam's apple wobbling up and down above a bright blue bow tie with white polka dots. It matched the royal blue sweater he wore. "I'm still gonna put her in my novel."

"Always the queen, our Glinda." Louise spread the cards out for the draw to be first dealer.

"Do any of you know her sister Barbara or Barbara's husband?" Nancy asked. She picked a card and turned it face up for the others to see, using the arm without the cat bites and scratches. Ten of spades.

"Barbara couldn't stand her," said Louise. She also drew a card and turned it face up. A deuce. "Glinda treated Barbara as if she were second class, substandard, deficient. Always asking Barbara to take care of the menial things."

George drew an eight and Tom, a three. Nancy picked up the deck and dealt. "Barbara doesn't seem that upset about Glinda's death." Nancy looked from George to Louise. "But some people just don't show their grief."

"I don't know," Louise said, arranging the cards in her hand. "Maybe Glinda held something over her head."

"Yeah," added George. "Barbara seemed pretty meek when she was around Glinda."

"She's not meek now," Nancy said. "One spade."

"One spade?" George eyed his cards. "Okay. Two clubs."

"I met Clark—that's one of Glinda's sons—one day when he had dinner with his Mom." Tom joined the conversation. "I was part of their foursome here for dinner. He's been going through rough times, what with the divorce. No kids, but his wife wanted everything she could get. Oh, two hearts."

"You mean someone got close enough to Glinda to get her pregnant?" Louise peered at Tom in mock disbelief, and then added, "Pass."

"She was a looker in the old days." Tom shrugged. "I saw her on stage, you know, back in Anchorage."

"Three hearts," said Nancy.

"Must have been a long, long, long, long time ago," George winked at her and said. "Pass."

Tom studied his cards. "It was. Four hearts."

Louise nodded. "I remember stuff from way back too. Can't remember shit about what happened yesterday. Pass."

The play began and proceeded quickly around the table.

"Who do you think killed her?" asked Nancy.

"That's the question, all right," answered George. "It didn't take long to learn to dislike her."

"Most of us avoid certain people," Nancy said, "but we wouldn't dream of killing them. We'd actually be nice to them, in fact."

"Speak for yourself, Nancy." Louise glanced at Nancy with a raised eyebrow.

"What about her other son? Did you know him too?" Nancy looked at Tom over her cards.

Since he was dummy for this round, he had settled back to watch the play at another table. He turned to Nancy. "Never met him, but I know that he and Clark had to fend for themselves a lot growing up. Glinda would leave them with her mother or Barbara or even her maid for months at a time."

"A show business mom," said George, picking up his third trick.

"Please, you're giving them a bad name," said Nancy.

"No, she gave them a bad name." George shot back.

Nancy took the last trick. "Made game," she said, picking up the cards. "Maybe whoever stole my fan doll also stole Glinda's boundary plate and then killed her."

"Nobody's going to kill anyone for a broken fan doll," said George as he dealt out the cards for the next game.

"Who are our suspects so far?" asked Louise, sorting the cards in her hand.

"Barbara, for one. No love lost there for her sister." Nancy said.

"Her sons," added Louise. "And don't forget me and the art teacher." She winked at them.

"Or Señora Lopez," added Nancy. She grinned.

George sat up. "Did she have any close friends here? Anyone she spent time with?" He looked at the cards in his hand. "Pass."

The play again advanced quickly around the table.

"We're going to have to ask around," Nancy said. "I met Bernice Nelson in the elevator and talked to her about Glinda. Bernice is from Alaska too. She's another one who didn't care much for Glinda."

"To know Glinda was to dislike her. The better question is who liked her. I haven't found anyone yet." George grimaced as Tom took another trick.

Nancy and Louise nodded but Louise added, "The Humane Society here liked her. And the local taxidermist. She gave them both a lot of money."

"Motive. What you need is a motive," said Tom, adding another trick to the pile in front of him.

"Money? Revenge? Hatred? I can come up with anything you want," said George. "They're all in my book."

"Can you come up with a stolen boundary plaque?" asked Nancy.

***

Life at Whisperwood: Trash Pick-Ups

Keep your apartments neat and clutter-free. Clutter increases your chances for an accident and stockpiling newspapers in your apartments increases the fire hazard for all of us. Throw out what you don't use or give it to Whisperwood's Second Time Around Treasure Shop. Call maintenance to schedule an extra pick-up of items too bulky or awkward for the trash chutes.

-From *The Whisperwood Breeze,* newsletter of Whisperwood Retirement Village

Chapter 13

Nancy picked up the memo that someone had slipped under her door early that morning. It asked all residents to come forward if they had anything to contribute to the investigation into Glinda Spencer's accident.

A reasonable way to proceed, Nancy thought. With a thousand residents and hundreds of staff and visitors in the retirement village, the local sheriff couldn't possibly question each one. The off-note was that they were calling her death an accident.

Later that morning, Nancy walked to the lobby to join a dozen other residents, most of them curious onlookers, for her turn to speak to the sheriff. The door to the interview room opened. Nancy watched as Anna exited. She nodded at Nancy.

"Are you all right?" Nancy asked.

"I guess so, Anna shrugged. "But I don't think he believed a word I said. You could corroborate me, Nancy. He thinks I'm just a fanciful old woman."

Nancy heard her name called. A deputy stood at the door to the interview room and gestured to Nancy as she stood. She picked up her purse and followed him into the room. He closed the door behind her but stayed outside in the lobby. She noted the papers piled on a bookshelf and the boxes stacked against the wall. This was probably another storage room most of the time.

A skinny man with narrow face, thin lips, and short brown hair parted at the side frowned at her from behind the desk. Nancy guessed he was in his late thirties. His pressed gray shirt with star over the chest pocket, gray tie, and gray pants were the standard for sheriffs in West Virginia. His hat lay on the desk next to a note pad with a few scribbled comments on it.

"Good morning, Mrs. Dickenson." He rose and extended his hand. "I'm Sheriff Ambrose." His eyes bore into her as if she were the culprit of a thousand crimes. Then he abruptly sat down and gestured to a chair. Nancy took it and sat watching him, curious about how he would conduct the interview. How competent was he?

"So you were friends with this Glinda Spencer?" Ambrose leaned back in his chair with an air of boredom and tapped his pencil on the desk.

"I didn't know her more than to greet her in the halls," Nancy began, keeping her manner straightforward and emotionless. "We were in the same Spanish class, and one evening she asked me up to her apartment. She wanted me to put the boundary plaque on her hall shelf."

The sheriff looked up. "She wanted you to do what?"

Nancy could see that she had surprised him into showing interest. "The boundary plaque. It was a rusted old iron plaque about a foot square someone had given her in Alaska." Nancy outlined its shape with her hands. "She wanted to display it in the hall. I told her not to do that, but she insisted. Then the day before she was murdered, she called me." Nancy told him the story.

The sheriff scrawled a note next to her name and then peered askance at her. "Why did she ask you, in particular, to help her display the plaque and then later to search for it?"

So the sheriff hadn't questioned her about the word, "murder." Nor did he deny it. It was bait, but the sheriff didn't bite. "Items have been disappearing from the display shelves in the halls. Ms. Spencer heard that we were watching the shelves and searching for the missing items. Naturally, when her plaque was stolen, she asked me to look for it."

The sheriff beat a staccato with his pencil and grinned as if she were being cute. "Uh huh. Who's this 'we' you're talking about?"

Okay. So he was going to be patronizing.

"Just a couple of other residents." Nancy said, hoping to avoid naming names. She needn't have worried. "And I was a licensed private detective, now retired." She paused for a response.

The sheriff laughed. "Private Eye, huh? Long time ago, I guess."

"Yes," Nancy said. "A long time ago." Nancy shrugged. "She probably thought I'd know what to do." She didn't expect that her past experience would carry any weight with this sheriff.

The sheriff lifted an eyebrow. "Had any success?"

"No." Nancy was ready to leave. The sheriff was playing her along.

"Did Ms. Spencer say anything that might give you a hint what was on her mind?"

Nancy remembered the pearls and Glinda's nasty insinuations. "She may have been testing me . . . to see if I was vulnerable."

The sheriff leaned back and studied her. "Vulnerable to what?"

"I didn't know Glinda very well." Nancy did not like to make insinuations herself, but this was important. "She was a bit of a bully and maybe she preyed on people's vulnerabilities."

The sheriff frowned. "In what way?"

Nancy hesitated before responding. "She liked to ridicule things that people held dear." That was as much of her own opinion she wanted to give the sheriff. "When you talk to the other residents here, you'll get a better idea of what kind of person she was," she paused, "And find the reason for her murder."

"Well now, I know murder makes for a better story." The sheriff sat back and drawled his words, "but we don't see any evidence of that here."

"You've just talked to Anna Carothers. She was an army nurse and she doesn't imagine things. She saw a murder scene."

"Oh now, I don't think so." The sheriff sat up and stared at her through narrowed eyes. "We have her description of the incident, and it could easily tally with an accident, which," he waved an arm, "is the kind of accident you'd expect in a place like this. Especially with all that trash cluttering up her place. Easy to slip, fall, turn your scooter over."

She watched the sheriff look down at his list and cross off her name before glancing up again. "So, Little Lady, do you have anything else to add?" He stood.

Nancy stiffened. Little Lady? She sniffed as if she smelled a bad odor. She straightened her back, stood, and took a full moment staring at him without expression before she replied. He was just another patronizing bully—and worthless.

Nancy remembered Anna's description of the murder scene, Barbara's dislike of her sister, and Bernice's bitter remarks. Then George's comment about the art teacher crossed her mind. Finally, she said, "No. Nothing."

"One more thing," he added. "I know how you people are." He leaned forward, his finger pointing at her. "Don't think you can do any investigating here. The victim was elderly, kept her place too cluttered, and had an accident. I'm sure we can quickly wrap this up, but you people stay out of it, you understand?"

Nancy could barely speak. Of course. They were going to call it an accident. Just what Anna feared. Nancy did not respond.

"As for those missing items, I imagine you all just misplaced them, don't you think?"

Nancy bristled. Of course he'd say that. Save him a lot of work.

The sheriff smiled. As if he had remembered that he might need her vote, he turned unctuous. "Thank you for your help. If you learn anything, please let us know. Here's my phone number." He handed Nancy a card.

Nancy took it without comment and walked out, closing the door behind her, head held high. She scanned the lobby and counted the number of people still waiting for an interview. Three. She took out a notepad and pen and noted their names. Two were wearing their Whisperwood name badge. She recognized the third. She walked over and sat with them.

"What did he want to know?" asked a petite blonde woman on her right.

"Just what I saw," Nancy said. "Did you see anything?"

"My apartment is next to hers," a second woman said. "But I

don't know anything, but I just thought I'd talk to the sheriff." She giggled. "In case I can be of any help."

The third person waiting, a white-bearded man with a mane of white hair, tapped his cane and said, "Weird things going on here and the sheriff should know about it."

"Like what?" Nancy asked.

"Like the two old guys like me who were found dead on the grounds. I don't like that. I don't like that at all."

"None of us do. How'd that happen? That's what I'd like to know," said the petite blonde. "Will one of us be next?"

The other woman nodded. "This is supposed to be a safe place."

"Yes, those were odd incidents," Nancy agreed. Then she spotted Louise leaning on her cane and peering around the corner.

"I'd sure like to know if you find out anything about those incidents," said Nancy as she left. She walked over to Louise.

"Our local sheriff, elected by the people, is an unmitigated bonehead," she said. "Are you waiting to see him?"

Louise shook her head. "Nah. I want a report. What did he ask you? Do they know anything?"

"Just the basics." Nancy shrugged. "He wasn't interested in anything I had to say. Going through the motions so he'd appear competent."

Louise nodded. "What are they going to do now?"

Nancy took a deep breath before she spoke. She still felt angry. "They're going to call it an accident."

"No way." Louise pounded her cane on the carpet. "Anna saw it and believe me, she wasn't looking at an accident scene."

"I know," Nancy said, glancing back toward the sheriff's room. "Let's brainstorm at dinner tonight."

Louise took Nancy's arm and walked with her down the hall. "I'll round up George and Tom. And next election, we'll run a voter registration drive and throw the bum out."

***

Life at Whisperwood: Loose Lips Sink Ships

Remember that phrase from World War II and how important it was? Here at Whisperwood, it has a different meaning. We're talking about gossip. Whisperwood President Nat Bryerson reminds us that well-meaning or not, uninformed talk about the people here is harmful and hurts everyone. Please don't spread rumors or gossip. Let's kill that poisonous weed, the grapevine.

-From *The Whisperwood Breeze*, newsletter of Whisperwood Retirement Village

Chapter 14

That evening, the 90s Club met again for dinner, early this time so they could request table fifty-six. It was Saturday night and already a line had formed at the host desk.

"Looks like we weren't early enough," said George, leaning on his cane as he waited for the line to advance. Nancy and Louise stood alongside him. Tom straggled behind.

"Movie night," said Louise. "Always an early crowd here on movie night. Auditorium fills up fast."

"Table fifty-six," George said to the hostess. She pored over her seating charts, then nodded at a server who walked them to the table and handed them menus. George gestured to his coffee cup. "Decaf, please."

Louise nodded. "Me too."

"I'd like a glass of Chardonnay," said Nancy.

The server smiled at Tom, pen poised.

"Just water."

George studied the menu. "Good. I like their Caribbean grouper. They got a vegetarian stir fry for Louise and Tom."

"Grouper for me, too," said Nancy. "And the salad and broccoli, please."

Louise smoothed the white tablecloth as she picked up the maroon napkin rolled around the silverware and scanned the dining room. "Did you notice they took away the twisted candle center-pieces? Too many complaints."

Tom looked up. "Good riddance, I say. Couldn't see across the table over them. Hope the stir fry is better than it was last time."

"The grouper is usually pretty good," Nancy tapped the menu, "but you can't count on everything being perfect every time."

Louise folded her arms and sat back. "I suppose they could order different grades of meat, prime one time, standard the next. That way we excuse a bad piece as just a fluke in the kitchen."

"I've wondered about that." Tom frowned at Louise. "And then they shrug away our complaints as nonsense from a bunch of cranky old people."

"Hell getting old." Louise glanced around the dining room.

Nancy sat up as if she were presiding. "As far as I know, the sheriff and his men have talked to Anna, Barbara, and me, and a few other people here at Whisperwood. They've probably also talked with Cary and Clark, but the sheriff isn't trying very hard and doesn't want to find anything suspicious."

Louise flicked her braid. "Yeah, I hung around the lobby and chatted up the others waiting to see the sheriff."

"I did too," said Nancy. "They didn't know anything useful. One had his own ax to grind. "

"The ones I talked to were just curious and wanted to put in their two cents about Glinda. Not well loved, our Glinda."

"Is the boundary plaque still missing?" asked Tom.

Nancy nodded. "It might have been the murder weapon except the timing is wrong."

Louise waved at a friend across the dining room who pointed to the large PETA button she wore and gave a thumbs up sign. Louise grinned and turned back to Nancy. "You're right. The plaque disappeared before she was killed, not after. Can't see anyone lugging that thing back to her place to kill her with it."

"What do the police think?" George straightened his silverware.

"I told them about the plaque." Nancy frowned. "But the sheriff is going to call Glinda's death an accident." She still felt angry.

"Accident." Louise snorted.

"Makes it a lot easier for him—and for Bryerson—and who would believe anyone would get murdered here?" Nancy reached for a roll. "Think how it would affect Whisperwood's marketing plans." She looked around for the butter.

Louise handed it to her. "A lot harder to sell. Anyway, we're all old folks. Practically senile, most of us." Louise sniffed. "They think they can put anything over on us."

"The sheriff warned me to stay out of their investigation, such as it is." Nancy glanced up as the manager arrived with the wine and the coffee pot. The server hovered until the manager left, then pulled out his order pad, and nodded at George. Once the server had disappeared with their meal orders, George resumed the discussion.

"What do we think?" he asked.

"Murder," Louise's penetrating voice broadcast the word. Nancy saw the curious glances that came their way. She winced.

"What's next?" Tom peered at them through his thick glasses.

Nancy pulled a pen and sheet of paper out of her purse. "First, we should each take a volume of the Bio Books and look for any ties to Glinda."

"Wait, let's brainstorm what these ties might be," said Louise.

Nancy nodded. "Any tie to Alaska." She jotted down a note and looked up. "I'm making a list."

"Good. You can add show business," said Tom.

"Russia," said Louise.

George looked up. "Maybe antiques, jewelry."

"Yes, look for antique and jewelry appraisers," added Nancy. "I may have missed somebody." She added to the list on the paper.

There was a pause. "Any other connections?" Nancy saw the server heading their way with a tray of covered dishes. "Here come our dinners. Hold the discussion."

George leaned back. "That was fast. Must be on a roll in the kitchen."

They waited as the server placed dishes around the table. "Everything okay?" he asked.

Impatient to continue their discussion, Nancy nodded.

Tom smiled at his own plate. "Looks good to me."

As soon as the server left, Louise jumped in. "Why do you suppose Barbara and her husband moved here? They didn't like Glinda any more than we did."

"Family?" George said.

"Bernice knew her too from somewhere else," said Tom. "Why would she move here?"

Nancy shook her head. "She didn't like Glinda."

"So what else is new?" Louise picked up her fork.

"Anna and I are driving to Morgantown to talk to Glinda's son Clark tomorrow. We want to hear what he has to say." Nancy sighed. "Wish my car weren't in the shop again." She folded up the note paper and put it in her purse.

Louise snorted. "Nancy, if that car were any older, they'd call it a roadster. It's always in the shop for something."

"Never mind." Nancy turned to the others. "After we go through the Bio Books, we'll interview everyone who has any possible connection to Glinda. Maybe we'll get a lead."

"We'll have to be smart about it," said George. "We don't want them to get suspicious."

"We can say we knew Glinda, that we're sorry she's gone and that we'd like to help her family." Nancy looked around the table.

Louise nodded. "Tell them we're trying to find out who borrowed her display item, that we thought a friend of hers might have taken it for safekeeping."

"We're all bright people. We can manage this just fine," said Nancy.

"Good plan," said Louise, "but her kids are the most likely suspects, sad to say."

"She made a lot of enemies here, don't forget. Nancy, for one." George grinned at her.

"Not my policy to murder anyone," said Nancy.

"Okay, then," said George, "unless Glinda did something strange in her will—and I wouldn't put that past her." He swiped a hand over his bald head. "Yep, her kids probably had the most to gain by her, uh, demise."

***

Life at Whisperwood: Safety at the Theater

Residents crowding into the theater at last Saturday night's movie blocked the exit aisles and the rear lobby areas, creating a hazardous situation. We know that you all would like to see the movie, but Whisperwood will not tolerate another such evening of rioting, lying down in the aisles, refusing to move wheelchairs and carts, name calling, and fisticuffs.

-From *The Whisperwood Breeze*, newsletter of Whisperwood Retirement Village

Chapter 15

Anna Carothers's straw hat slid down over her eyes. She shoved it back and hunched further over the steering wheel. She peered out at the drizzle, her head swinging back and forth with the wipers. "I see well enough," she assured Nancy. "It's all these cars and headlights coming toward me in the rain that confuse me."

"Maybe we could find a side road to Clark's place." Nancy clutched the armrest and checked her seat belt.

They had started right after lunch for the two-hour trip to Morgantown, but the afternoon was grey with a light drizzle that made the road slick and the lane lines hard to distinguish. Nancy gritted her teeth and watched the road. Her chauffeur drove erratically, alternately speeding up and slowing down on the interstate and braking at odd moments.

Oh well, Nancy sighed, at least she's willing to drive.

They exited the interstate and drove into Morgantown. Nancy sat back. She took a deep breath to calm herself and looked down at the address scrawled on the notepad she held in her lap. She'd found Clark's address on the Internet.

Anna slowed the car for a stoplight. "You used to live in this town. Where to now?" she asked.

Nancy directed her down several side streets until they found the one that led into an older development of two-story, colonial-style homes. Most were well-kept with trimmed shrubs, mowed lawns, and older trees with branches that stretched out over the sidewalks. Rain dripped from the trees and the air had a fresh, clean smell.

After four tries, Anna successfully parallel-parked the car in front of the house they identified as belonging to Clark Spencer. She looked at Nancy expectantly. "Here we are."

Nancy slid out of the car. "Lawn's full of weeds."

Anna joined her to walk up the sidewalk. "Needs mowing too. House looks rundown."

Nancy pushed aside untrimmed branches from shrubs to reach the porch steps. At the front door, she stepped forward to ring the bell. She knew someone was home. She could hear a television inside and see lights in several rooms.

She rang the doorbell again. The door opened. Nancy looked up into troubled eyes peering at her from an unshaven face. The man's shirt was hanging loose, and he wore shabby slippers. He held a glass filled with something that smelled like whiskey to Nancy.

"Yes?" he said.

"I'm Nancy Dickenson, and this is Anna Carothers." Nancy took a deep breath. "We knew your mom at Whisperwood. May we come in?"

He stared at them a minute, then stumbled aside. "Sure, sure." He gestured to the living room and walked over to shut off the television. "I need a cup of coffee. Can I get you one too?"

"Yes. We'd love some," Nancy said. Anna nodded.

"Just a moment." Clark left them alone.

"We'll have an excuse to stay at least until we've finished the coffee," Nancy whispered to Anna.

"Good. We should see if he needs our help." Anna whispered back. "I'll drink real slow."

Nancy surveyed the living room.

"Pretty shabby stuff," murmured Anna. "We could probably get him a few pieces from a consignment shop. Make it more homey."

A worn, gray sofa stretched along one wall behind a scuffed coffee table. A red kitchen chair was the only other place to sit. The television, resting on a small stand, was pushed against the opposite wall. Anna picked up a racetrack brochure from the coffee table. On the fireplace mantel was a parade of photos. Nancy stepped over to the mantel to take a closer look. She recognized Glinda in one as a younger woman; the others were of beaming jockeys and horseshoe wreaths.

"Very sad," Anna said. She brushed off the sofa with her hand and the two women sat down on the edge of it. "Ex-wife takes all, I guess."

Clark came back with a loaded tray, placed it on the coffee table and took the red chair. He poured coffee gracefully from a silver pot into dainty cups and passed them to Nancy and Anna. He took one himself and sat back, gesturing to the two matching china pieces on the tray. "Cream or sugar?"

"Black," Nancy said, noting with interest his delicate poise. She glanced at Anna and saw that, as usual, Anna could not be subtle. She stared at him with open mouth.

Clark noticed and conceded a wry smile. "Mom trained us well," he said, "for her . . . soirees. I took the role of butler." He crossed his legs and slung an arm over the back of the chair. "Now how can I help you?"

Nancy took the lead. "We are truly sorry about the loss of your mother."

He nodded, sipped his coffee, and stared off at the mantel.

"We'll all miss her," Anna added.

"She was a good mom to us," Clark said, looking down at his hands. "I grew up out west, you know." He gestured to the race-track brochure. "She had a lot of friends at the track. Used to get us into the stable area to help out. She loved the horses. Dogs, cats, too. All animals, in fact."

Nancy nodded, considering these new dimensions of Glinda.

"She sure liked a good time. Took us places. She knew how to make a buck and she made lots of them. She played people for fools, too. She knew just how to do that. We lived well, we did. Yes ma'am." Clark choked and stared down at the floor.

Nancy sipped the coffee to give Clark a moment to compose

himself. "She did seem to be a fun-loving person."

"She was, but she worked hard. She was an entertainer and a good one. She brought them in—even in Vegas." He saw their surprise. "Oh, not the big places, but she had a beautiful voice." He sipped his coffee. "She was always so full of life that it's hard to believe she's gone." He put his cup down on the coffee table and brushed a hand across his eyes.

Nancy took another sip and waited a moment. "Did she have an enemy who would want to harm her."

"Why? The sheriff said it was an accident."

Nancy paused, considering how she should respond.

"I was the one who found her, you know," Anna broke in, "along with the security guard." She leaned toward him.

"I'm so sorry," Nancy began, groping for the right words, but Anna couldn't wait. She rushed on. "Your mother didn't die of an accident. Someone killed her and then ransacked her apartment."

Oh no. This was terrible. Nancy reached out with a restraining hand toward Anna. Clark wasn't ready for this. She saw him freeze and stare at them as if he hadn't heard them. His eyes narrowed. "What? You're saying someone killed her? Why would you say such a thing?" He walked over to the mantelpiece and picked up his mother's picture.

"I'm sorry to break it to you like this, but I was there." Anna folded her arms and frowned at him.

"I know this is hard to hear." Nancy began again.

Clark interrupted. "Why would the sheriff call it an accident then?" He pushed his hair back with one hand.

Nancy took a deep breath. "You can see that for the sheriff and the Whisperwood administrators, an accident is much easier and less trouble." She peered over the cup at Clark and spoke slowly to give him time to absorb the shock. "Whisperwood is a big employer and important to the community. No one wants to make waves."

He did not respond but stared at the wall as if he could see through it to the truth. No one said anything. Nancy held her breath. She hoped Anna would keep quiet.

Anna bounced up and went over to Clark. "We hate to bring

this kind of news to you," she said, "but we're trying to find out what really happened."

Clark stepped away from her, heaved a sigh, and sat down. Anna went back to the couch. Clark leaned toward them, his arms resting on his knees. "Whisperwood is such a safe place. And there are laws."

Nancy looked at him. "The sheriff is an elected official, and Bryerson probably contributes to his campaign."

"But who would want to kill her?" Clark's eyes went from Anna to Nancy as if searching for an answer in their faces. "Sure she made enemies. She was a pistol and interested in everything, sometimes stuff people didn't want anyone looking into, but she was a loving and talented woman."

"Yes, she was," consoled Anna.

Nancy sat back. "You have no idea?"

"Of course not. She was harmless, and Whisperwood kept her busy." Clark reached for a bottle of bourbon in a wooden box behind him and poured a shot into his cup. He downed it in one gulp as he sat on the edge of a chair. "She loved it there."

"All right." Nancy paused before continuing. "Is there anything we can do to help out? Since we live at Whisperwood, I mean."

"Do? How can two old ladies help? He grimaced. "Sorry, but can you get my Mom back? Can you bring back my wife? Can you give me the name of a winning horse? Can you get me a better job?"

His voice was savage. "My life is a complete shambles, and you think you can help somehow?"

"I'm so sorry . . ." Nancy began. Anna reached over and poured coffee into his cup.

"Everyone's sorry, but no, I don't see any way that you can help. Thank you. Cary and I will handle everything."

He stood up. "Did you see what you came to see? Here it is." He gestured around the room. "Thank you for being so concerned about my mother. Maybe someone there did kill her," he sipped his coffee before adding, "but not me, not my brother."

"Of course not," said Nancy. "She was your mother."

He sat down again and stared at the floor, his head in his hands, covering his eyes. After a moment, he raised his head and looked at Nancy, his belligerence gone as quickly as it had appeared. "It could be you are right. She was on to something big, you know," he said. "Something really big, but I don't know what it was. Neither does Cary. We've talked about it."

"Something big at Whisperwood?" Nancy asked. She thought for a moment but couldn't come up with anything that would be a motive for murder. "Did she give you any hints?"

"Only that she called Whisperwood a time bomb. Have no idea what she meant, but I knew she was on to something. She was curious about everything. Most people said she was too nosy for her own good, but she was smart and interested in whatever was going on around her. I think she found out something she wasn't supposed to know. She's been in scrapes before, and this time maybe she went too far." He stared down at his cup. "Maybe."

Nancy nodded. "We think you're right, and we're looking into this. Whoever killed your mother is not going to get away with it."

"I don't know what you can do about it."

Nancy saw the disdain in Clark's glance.

"If it's true," he added. "Maybe it's time I put a bug in Bryerson's ear—or maybe that assistant of his."

Nancy felt a chill. What would Bryerson and Perry do?

Anna walked over to pat Clark's hand. "We and everyone at Whisperwood are horrified about what happened, and we sympathize. We do want to help."

Clark shook his head and eyed his bourbon. Nancy stood, and they all walked to the door.

Nancy paused. "By the way," she looked at Clark, "did you know anything about the boundary plaque?"

"The boundary plaque?" He grinned. "That old thing? Sure. She'd had it for years. Piece of junk, but Mom said it was an important historical artifact and probably worth a lot of money."

Anna jumped in. "It was stolen before she died."

Clark pursed his lips. "Is the sheriff working on finding it?"

"Supposedly," said Nancy.

"I'll check with him, then. Or Cary will." Clark bowed as he let them out. Nancy felt his eyes on her back all the way down the walk to the car.

"He's in a lot of trouble," said Anna in a low voice.

"Did you smell the alcohol?" asked Nancy.

"How could I miss it? He's been drinking all day, I'll bet. And he's a gambler. No telling how much money he's lost that way."

"That's why his wife left him. He seems to genuinely feel the loss of his mother."

"I guess so." Anna walked to her side of the car and unlocked the doors.

Nancy slid onto the front seat. "We'll have to back burner him as a possible suspect."

Anna started the car. "He could have used the money the plaque would fetch. Don't forget about that." She pulled out into the street.

"I wonder how generous Glinda was to her two sons." Nancy looked back at the shabby house.

"She didn't bail him out this time, did she?"

Nancy shook her head.

Anna glanced up at the rear view mirror. "Uh oh."

"What?"

"Nancy, I hope I'm wrong about this, but are we being followed?"

Nancy turned in her seat to scan the road behind them. "You mean that car back there with one yellow and one bluish headlight?"

Anna nodded. "I noticed a car like that following us on the way here. Those headlights are odd, and they were on because of the rain. The law, you know. I'm sure it's the same car. And just now, he pulled out of a parking space down the street when we did."

"You can't see the whole car. It's still too rainy out there."

"But the headlights are the same."

"Drive around the block."

Anna turned right. The car behind followed. She made the next right. The car kept on straight. "Whew. Okay. I guess not."

"Let's get back on the right road. I'll keep a look out behind us."

Anna made two more rights, and they were back on track towards Whisperwood. "I don't like thinking we'll be on that lonely road up to Whisperwood with someone following us."

Nancy kept her eyes on the cars behind them. They merged onto the interstate, but just as Nancy thought they'd lost their tail, she saw the car speed up the ramp onto the interstate behind them.

She turned around and looked at Anna. "They're behind us again."

"They followed us from Whisperwood," said Anna. "They know where we live."

"If it's the same car."

"Yes but I'm afraid it is." She frowned and glanced again in the rear view mirror. "I can't go any faster in all this traffic to try to lose them. What can we do?"

Nancy chewed her lip. They were in the early rush hour exodus from Morgantown, but the traffic would soon thin out and once they left the interstate, they would be vulnerable.

The car with the odd headlights speeded up and passed them, but its windows were tinted. Nancy could not see anyone inside. She watched the car disappear ahead. "If they're up to no good, they'll probably try to ambush us at some lonely spot once we get off the highway."

"I have my cell phone," Anna said tentatively.

"So do I." Nancy pulled out a West Virginia map. "We've got to find an alternate route." She unfolded the map and studied it. "Let's take a road that will get us there from the other direction. We'll have to chance the short stretch between the town and Whisperwood, but my guess is that they'll be waiting for us about ten miles off this highway. That's the loneliest stretch."

"Good plan. Tell me where to get off the interstate."

"Next exit."

***

Life at Whisperwood: Visitors Welcome

Whisperwood welcomes your family and friends to visit and tour our wonderful village. No reservations are needed in the dining rooms and pubs for up to ten guests. For large groups, you may reserve the private dining room for up to fifteen people or the Celebrations Room with catered meals for up to seventy-five guests. Contact the dining room captain to make arrangements.

-From *The Whisperwood Breeze*, newsletter of Whisperwood Retirement Village

Chapter 16

Anna pulled into her assigned parking space at Whisperwood. "We made it, Nancy."

She slid out of the car, walked over to Nancy and hugged her. Nancy also felt relieved, but she wondered if their imaginations had run away with them. Had they been in danger or not? Nancy walked into her apartment still pondering this question.

The red light on her answering machine blinked at her. She listened to the message as Malone rubbed himself against her ankles. She glanced down at him. Could it be that he missed her?

Simon Smythe had returned her call. More than a week had passed since Nancy had read the jeweler's description in the Bio Books. Receiving no response to her calls and visits, she had given up the idea of asking him about her pearl necklace. Now he was back, and they agreed to meet at his apartment the next morning.

Nancy expected him to be tanned and relaxed from his travels, but when he opened his door the next day, she saw a man as pale as a blanched asparagus and as skinny.

"Ms. Dickenson? Come in." He stepped aside to let Nancy enter, gesturing toward the living room and an antique Victorian sofa. Nancy sat gingerly on the red damask with its gold fringe.

He took a matching chair, his body round-shouldered and bent. His eyes blinked behind black-framed glasses. The draperies were closed, shutting out the sunshine and the air and making Nancy feel claustrophobic.

"How was your trip, Mr. Smythe?" Nancy asked, peering at Simon through the gloom. She would hate to live in this place. An antique roll-top desk stood against the wall behind Simon, and a reddish, floral Turkish carpet lay on the floor. A variety of dark landscape and still life oil paintings decorated the walls. Beneath the paintings were waist-high bookshelves displaying carved wooden elephants, a group of Moroccan perfume bottles on a silver tray, and several thick volumes held together by giraffe book-ends. The lamp base next to Nancy reared up as a bronze cobra. In the corner next to the door was an elephant's foot umbrella stand. Everything seemed old but not worn, and all appeared expensive. The room reflected the taste of a well-traveled man—or one with an exotic imagination. She looked up to find Smythe staring at her.

"The trip was fine, Ms. Dickenson," he said. He crossed his legs daintily, adjusting his trousers as he sat. "How did you know I was on a trip?"

Nancy smiled, determined to be friendly. "Your neighbor told me. She said you were always traveling someplace. And I can see by your mementos," she gestured at the wooden elephants, "that you've traveled to exotic places."

Smythe studied his shoes. "Yes, but that was many years ago. As it happens, I am not always traveling someplace now. I have, uh, children that I visit occasionally." He frowned at the wall. "I'm in and out all the time, just very busy."

"Good to keep busy." Nancy said, but the man fidgeted so much in his chair and avoided looking at her, so she questioned his story.

"You came about your pearls." Smythe got up, walked to the desk, and took out an odd-looking contraption which he fixed to his glasses.

Nancy recognized the device as the kind of magnifier her dentist used. Smythe grinned at her expression and tapped the device. "I like this better than the loupe," he said. "So let's see those pearls you're so worried about."

Nancy relaxed. His grin made him seem more human. She opened the blue velvet case as she handed it to him. "Glinda Spencer, who used to live upstairs in 512, insisted that they were fake."

"Ah yes, Glinda was always looking for trouble." He picked up the strand, murmuring to himself. "Lovely. Look at the luster." He glanced at Nancy. "Where did you get these, Ms. Dickenson?"

"My father gave them to my mother as an anniversary present and when she died—I was just a child—he gave them to me."

"I see." He adjusted the magnifier and squinted closely at each pearl.

Nancy watched with butterflies in her stomach. "You heard that Glinda died while you were gone?"

"Glinda Spencer," he said with distaste. "Yes, it's all the talk around here. She finally pushed someone too far."

"What do you mean?" asked Nancy. Apparently Smythe didn't think her death was accidental either. How well did Smythe know Glinda?

"She tried it with me, you know." Smythe peered at Nancy over the magnifier.

"Tried what?"

"The insinuations, the probing." Smythe was examining the clasp of the necklace. "She tried it with you too, didn't she?"

"Insisting that the necklace was fake."

"Sure. But she did know something about jewelry." Smythe turned the necklace over.

"So was she right?" Nancy asked, watching him.

"Here. Take a peek at this." Smythe held up the clasp. "Those are fine quality rose-cut diamonds set in a white gold clasp." He brought the clasp closer to Nancy's eyes, isolating it with his thumbs. "Nobody would put diamonds in a piece of junk. And there are knots between each pearl, another indication that the pearls are of good quality. They have a nice luster to them."

Nancy looked at him. "So they're genuine?"

Smythe picked up the strand and ran the pearls across his teeth. He repeated the gesture, then looked up at Nancy. "If they're natural, they'll feel gritty against my teeth." He studied the pearls, then walked over to a lamp and held the strand against a light. "What you have here is a fine, cultured pearl necklace."

"Oh, cultured." Nancy's face fell. "So they are fake," she said in a low voice.

"Absolutely not. Cultured pearls are every bit as genuine as other pearls from an oyster. A natural process creates both. The difference is that in a cultured pearl, the irritant is round, smooth, and planted instead of occurring naturally. You have every right to be proud of such a fine gift from your father." He returned to his chair, replaced the pearls in the blue box, and handed it to her.

Tears sprang to her eyes. Nancy wiped them away. "I am very glad to hear you say that, Mr. Smythe."

"Of course, if you'd like to be really sure about whether they are cultured or natural," he shrugged, "I could send them away to be X-rayed."

She gazed at the pearls, noticing the knots Simon had mentioned. "What would that do?"

"If they are genuine, the irritant will be irregular like a bit of grit or sand. The X-ray would show us the size of the irritant used, the thickness of the coating, and whether," he glanced at her, "the irritant was natural or man-made."

"I don't think that will be necessary, Mr. Smythe." She put the box into her purse and looked at him. "But what did Glinda mean when she said they were fish paste?"

He went over to the desk and opened a drawer. He removed a small white box and pulled out a strand of pearls. "These are the kind of pearls Glinda was talking about. They're made by coating a bead with layers of a solution made from fish scales." He watched Nancy pick them up and feel them. "They look good, don't they?"

Nancy nodded and placed the pearls back in the box.

Simon took the box and set it on the table. "But they're cheaper and wear out faster than cultured pearls."

He removed the magnifier from his glasses.

Nancy smiled at him. "Thank you, Mr. Smythe. I can see that Glinda was baiting me."

"She did that kind of thing to everyone," he said, "and for Pete's sake, please call me Simon. By the way, pearls benefit by being worn, so wear them often in good health."

Nancy nodded. "All right, Simon. And I'm Nancy." She stood and gathered her purse. "You said she tried baiting you?"

Simon rose with her and shook her hand as he walked her to the door. "Of course. I brushed her away. Wish I had a spray for insects like her."

He laughed, but Nancy heard the bitterness in his comment. How had Glinda taunted him?

"It's nice that you have children nearby and can visit them," she said, opening the door.

Simon coughed. "I didn't say they were nearby."

Nancy laughed. "Oh, I thought you did."

Simon shook his head. "Actually, they live in . . . in California."

"Beautiful state," Nancy said pleasantly. "I lived there once. Do they live near Los Angeles or San Francisco? Or maybe Sacramento?"

Simon made a show of looking at his watch. "I regret to say I have another appointment. I hope I've been able to help you."

Interesting that Simon sidestepped her questions. "Did you know about the boundary plaque?" she asked.

"Everyone knew about that damn boundary plaque." Simon clenched his teeth. "How dare she display it like that. She was asking to be robbed."

Nancy nodded. Supposedly he had been away when the plaque was stolen and Glinda was killed. Or had he? He could have stayed nearby or just lain low in his apartment. Where exactly did he go and when exactly did he return? And what was he doing while he was gone?

She wondered what he was hiding but decided not to press. She stepped out into the hall. "Thank you so much. It's a great relief—and I also appreciate the lesson about pearls."

"Of course. Now if you'll excuse me . . ."

Nancy walked down to the elevator, wondering about the relationship between Simon and Glinda. She had attacked Nancy through the pearls and taunted Simon, possibly with whatever he was hiding. Who else had she confronted? She must have gone too far with her innuendos and he—or she—took care of the problem.

***

Life at Whisperwood: One-Way Harrigans and Hallway Speed Demons

Please pay attention to the way you drive any vehicle at Whisperwood. Follow the one-way signs if you drive on the Whisperwood campus. Driving the wrong way causes accidents. Whisperwood residents have also been injured in the halls by speeding wheelchairs and scooters. Please be careful and follow the rules.

-From *The Whisperwood Breeze*, newsletter of Whisperwood Retirement Village

Chapter 17

The next day, Nancy stopped by Anna's apartment to visit, but no one came to the door. Across the hall, the yellow tape had been removed from Glinda's door, and it now stood open. A tall, slender man with short, graying hair was grappling with a large box. Nancy stepped over to him.

"May I help you?" she asked.

He peered at her over the box. "Thanks. It's not that heavy," the man said. "Just awkward. Would you mind walking with me to the elevator to push the button?"

"I'll be happy to," Nancy replied. She stepped alongside, helping to steady the box. When they reached the elevator, she pressed the down button. "I'm Nancy Dickenson," she said. "You must be one of Glinda's sons."

He rested the box on the rail and smiled at her. "I'm Cary," he said. "Clark couldn't make it today." He nodded at the box. "Thank you so much for helping."

The elevator doors opened, and they stepped in. Cary dropped the box on the floor and took out a white handkerchief to wipe his hands. His suit looked too expensive for hauling boxes. Nancy reached over and pressed the first floor button. "I took classes with your mother. I'm sorry about her passing and in such an awful way."

"Yes," Cary sighed. "We'll miss her." He shook his head and looked at Nancy. "She told me about you. You were a detective, weren't you?"

Nancy waved her hand as if to brush a fly away and laughed. "Used to be. Retired a long time ago." She glanced down at the box. "Are you moving your mom's things out?"

Cary nodded. "I know it seems heartless to be so quick about it, but I had some spare time so I thought I'd make a start at it." He shrugged. "Anyway, it's expensive to live here, so the sooner we can vacate this place and get the deposit back, the better off we'll be."

Nancy smiled at Cary. "Yes, but you shouldn't have any trouble with that. I hear there's a long waiting list for these units." She waited a moment, watching the floor numbers above the door as the elevator descended at its glacial pace. "When is the memorial service?"

"We're planning it for next Saturday morning in the chapel. At eleven. The notice will be on the bulletin boards around the building—and on the weekly chapel schedule."

"I'll be there, and I'll pass the word around to people here who knew her."

"We'd appreciate that."

The elevator door opened. Cary picked the box up from the floor and walked out of the elevator. Nancy walked alongside out to his car, helped shove the box into the trunk, and together they strolled back to the elevator.

"Is your wife with you?" Nancy asked, reaching over to push the up button.

"She's in the apartment still packing. Thanks again for your help. The kids are in school, so we were able to take a day to come out here. I'm an accountant and work out of my home."

"That's convenient for you."

They took the elevator back to the fifth floor. At Glinda's apartment, Nancy stepped in to meet Cary's wife.

She followed Cary to the bedroom door, stepping around a large box that was closed and securely taped.

"That box is full of the figurines you wanted," his wife said without looking up. She knelt by a flat carton pulled out from under the bed.

Cary walked over and touched her on the shoulder. "Teresa, I'd like you to meet Nancy Dickenson," he said.

Teresa, startled, gasped "Oh!" and hurriedly stood, smoothing her red, curly hair with one hand and brushing the other on her jeans, which were as neat, clean, and pressed as Cary's suit. She wore a simple green silk shirt. "I didn't know anyone was with you," she said, with a long look at Cary. Then she turned to Nancy, smiled, and held out her hand. "Pleased to meet you."

Nancy smiled back and shook hands, glancing over to peek into the box Teresa was packing. It contained small bundles wrapped in newspaper. The glass shelves which had held Glinda's "collectibles" were empty.

"I was so sorry to hear about Glinda," Nancy repeated.

"Yes, it was a terrible thing to happen. We don't understand it." Teresa shook her head.

"Tragic," Nancy agreed.

Teresa gestured around the room. "The place is a mess—I can't believe Glinda would leave it this way no matter what the police say."

Cary, hands on hips, also surveyed the room. "She wasn't a slob. Someone must have been looking for something, but I don't see anything missing . . . except the Russian boundary plaque, of course."

"The most valuable item she owned," said Teresa. "Looked like junk."

Cary shook his head at Teresa and then spoke to Nancy. "Someone saw it who knew its value and took it."

"You know the plaque was stolen the day before she died?" Nancy asked. Her eyes strayed to the desk. The computer was missing. Had Cary packed it? She didn't see it in his car, and the box they took out was awkward to carry but not heavy enough for the computer. She looked around the apartment.

The Tiffany lamp was missing too.

"Her Tiffany lamp was beautiful." Nancy gestured to the table where it had stood.

Teresa looked up. "I always admired it too. I guess she sold it because it's not here now."

"That's odd." Nancy looked around. "I saw it only a few days ago."

"Whatever." Cary shrugged. "It's not here. She may have given it to someone. She was a generous person."

Glinda generous? Nancy raised an eyebrow but didn't comment. Instead, she asked, "Did she ever say anything about what she thought of Whisperwood?"

"She liked it here." Cary stopped. "That is, until the last few months. She was worried about something but wouldn't say what."

Nancy watched him. "I've met Clark, and he said Glinda called this place a time bomb."

Cary shook his head. "Now that doesn't make sense." He turned back toward the desk, strewn with scraps of paper. "She told us she was working on a book. An exposé of sorts. That's probably what she meant. She had a couple of boxes of personal papers— newspaper clippings, stuff like that—that we can't find. She'd known a lot of famous—and infamous—people in her career."

"And a whole lot of not-so-famous," Teresa added, pulling a rubber glove up her hand as if she meant business.

"She probably had all the information she needed on her computer," said Nancy.

Cary looked around the room. "Yes, her computer. Where is it?" He glanced over at Teresa.

"Don't look at me," she said, a slight sneer on her face. "I don't have it."

Cary rubbed his eyes. "It was a dinosaur. Nobody would steal it, that's for sure. She was talking about getting a new one. I suppose she got rid of it and hadn't bought a new one yet. "

Teresa shook open a large plastic bag. "Here's something I'll be glad to see go," she shuddered. "They're hideous." She picked up the stuffed cats, one by one, holding them at arm's length, and dumped them into the bag, then closed it with a twist tie. She wrapped the tie tight as if to make sure the cats could not escape, and then brushed her gloved hands.

Nancy watched her, feeling the same repugnance. "That's good. They gave me the creeps to look at them—I always felt they were staring at me."

"They certainly kept me away," said Teresa, wrinkling her nose. "She was a weird duck, law unto herself. Incredible."

Cary frowned at her. "Now, Teresa, don't talk about Mom that way. She had a tough life."

Teresa shrugged. "By the way," she said, contemplating Nancy. "We were going through the old brass-bound steamer trunk and found a box with some miscellaneous items that mean nothing to us."

"We never saw them before," Cary added, "and don't know why she had them. Could you drop them by the thrift shop here?"

"Of course," said Nancy. "I'll be glad to help." She stepped over the debris and peered into the trunk. The blanket had been tossed aside, revealing a cardboard box filled with small items. Nancy took a sharp breath. On top lay her missing fan doll. She glanced at Cary and Teresa.

"You seem to recognize them," Teresa said, already turning away to inspect the bureau.

"Yes, I do." Nancy picked up the fan doll and examined it. "This fan doll was mine. It was on my display shelf, and it disappeared a few days ago."

"What?" Cary stared at Nancy, mouth open. Teresa stopped in the act of opening a drawer.

Nancy kissed the doll and smiled. "Yes, yes, it's true. I've been looking for it. Why would Glinda have it?"

"My mom was not a thief," said Cary. He took the doll and turned it over as if checking for a maker's mark.

"Of course not," added Teresa.

Nancy sat down on a chair beside the trunk, not knowing what to say.

"Why would my mother take anything from anyone else?" Cary

sputtered, returning the doll to Nancy. "You can look around here and see that she was a wealthy woman. She collected fine things, not junk." He looked at Nancy. "I'm sorry, but that doll is broken and can't be worth much."

Nancy felt offended at the tone. "You may think this is junk," she said, stroking the doll, "but it's a gift from people I helped long ago." She studied the other contents of the box. There was the framed photo from Tom's shelf and Ingrid's souvenir troll doll, and the plane model that had been missing from Ralph's shelf. She recognized items she'd seen on other residents' shelves.

"I don't understand it," she said, reaching down to pull aside the flannel cloth separating the top layer of items from those below and exposing several other familiar display items.

"Neither do we. Maybe my Mom found those things some-where." Cary glanced at his wife, who nodded. "She probably was going to return them."

"And never got the chance?" Nancy found that difficult to be-lieve, considering Glinda's frequent forays through the halls of Whisperwood.

"Maybe whoever ransacked this place put those things in the trunk," said Teresa. "That's the most logical explanation."

"I suppose so." Nancy picked up the box and set it in her lap. "I'll make sure these treasures are returned to their rightful owners. I'm relieved to see my fan doll again."

"Would you please leave my Mom's name out of it?" asked Cary. "I know she didn't steal those things. Why would she?"

"Honey, she was vengeful." Teresa reached out and patted Cary's arm. "I suppose she may have felt slighted . . ."

"That could be, I guess. Nobody took advantage of her," Cary frowned, "and got away with it."

Nancy stood, holding the box of stolen items. Glinda's getting even sounded like something she would do, as petty as it was. "I'll tell people the culprit was found, so there won't be any more thefts."

"Wait a minute. I don't think my mother was the culprit. I don't know why those things are here . . . ."

Teresa pulled Cary aside. "I'm sure no one will think your mother stole them, Cary." She turned to Nancy. "Thank you. We'd appreciate whatever you can do,"

Cary swept a hand across his forehead. "She had her problems, but I loved her."

Teresa began steering Nancy toward the door. "Mrs. Dickenson, so kind of you to drop by," she said with a nervous smile. She picked up the bag of dead cats. "You will tell people here about the memorial service, won't you?"

"Of course." Nancy heard dismissal.

"I'll walk down with you to the elevator and put this bag in the trash chute. A final good riddance to those awful cats, I say." Teresa opened the door and followed Nancy out.

Nancy rode down alone until the third floor, when the elevator stopped. The door opened to admit a black man with a white beard and curly white hair, wearing a blue polo shirt, jeans, and tool belt. As he saw her, he started, then grinned. "Hello, Nancy."

She stared at him, flabbergasted. "Fitzhugh Connelly! What are you doing here?" Of all the people she knew in the world, Fitz was the last one she expected to see at Whisperwood. But how wonderful!

"Got your note, don't you know?" He winked at her and pressed the first floor button. "With your change of address. I needed to move out of my house—too big for just me, you know? Thought if you liked this place, I ought to like it too. Didn't even visit it first. Just plunked the lolly and here I am."

"But but but," Nancy stammered, too surprised to be coherent. "But you mean you live here?"

The elevator opened, and he stepped out with her. They both turned right.

"Now I do. I'll carry that box for you, Nancy," he said, reaching over to it.

Nancy shook her head. "Thank you, but it's not heavy. When did you move in?"

He grinned at her. "Today."

They walked together down the hall. When Nancy reached her

apartment, she stopped and rested the box against the door while she fumbled for her keys.

"I live down the hall." Fitzhugh said, beaming at her. "I'm your new neighbor." He chuckled.

"And I'm delighted." She smiled. "We have a lot of catching up to do." She hesitated, not opening the door. The dratted cat usually attacked guests, but he knew Fitzhugh from when Bill was alive. Maybe Malone would behave this time. "Would you like to come in for some tea?"

"Thank you, luv, but I have errands to run. Perhaps you would join me for dinner tonight?"

"Perfect. You can meet my friends then."

"Let me know if I can do anything for you," Fitzhugh pointed to his tool belt. "I'm quite the handyman, don't you know?"

Nancy slipped into her apartment quickly and closed the door. The cat was nowhere in sight. Nancy leaned against the door for a moment. How wonderful. Fitz was a long-time friend. She would enjoy getting to know him again. But now she needed to talk to Louise and George. She called them and asked them to come to her apartment. Then she lured the cat into his carrier with a bit of sardine.

When George and Louise arrived, Nancy set the box from Glinda's apartment on the credenza next to her old clock. The square-faced mantel clock was another memento from an old case.

Nancy tore off a sheet of paper towel and wiped the dust off the clock and the credenza, then she removed the pieces from the box, one by one, lining them up on the credenza.

Louise ran her hand over the wooden troll figure. "Glinda stole them, every last one," she said in disbelief.

"She had enough money." George picked up the photo of the *Yorktown*. "Tom will be glad to get this back."

"Everyone will be relieved." Nancy removed the last item from the box, and then picked up the bottom layer of flannel. Louise and George stood to peer into the box. Removing the flannel revealed a floppy disk and a gold chain with a diamond pendant. Nancy gently picked up the piece of jewelry. George whistled. Louise fingered the delicate gold chain and peered closely at the pendant resting in Nancy's hand. Small rubies and diamonds set in gold sprays radiated out from a large central diamond.

"A sunburst," Louise noted. "Where did she get it?"

Nancy gazed at the pendant. "No one has mentioned the theft of any jewelry, and no one would put this out on her shelf."

They took turns examining the necklace. Remembering her visit with Simon, Nancy finally said, "The settings are so finely done, the stones must be genuine."

The three friends looked at each other then back at the unexpected treasure. Could the jewelry have belonged to Glinda or did she steal it too? The proper thing to do would be to give the necklace to Cary, but if they did that, then they would never find out the truth. Why would Glinda hide her own jewelry in a box of stolen items? The conclusion was inescapable.

Glinda's sons and the local humane society loved her, but apparently she was a thief. What else had Glinda been doing at Whisperwood?

The floppy was another surprise. Glinda had printed "Back-Up" on the label and then a date three days before her death. Nancy walked over to her own computer, a Mac, but realized that it was too new a model to accept an outdated 3.5-inch floppy disk. Nancy visualized Glinda's computer as it was placed in her apartment. The fact that it was an antiquated PC hadn't registered at the time. She bit her lip.

"You people always have to get the latest thing," said George. "I've had my computer for years and it still works fine, so I've put off getting a newfangled one. Anyway, all my files are backed up on floppies too."

"Great!. We can use your computer to see what's on Glinda's disk," said Nancy.

"But we'll have to wait a couple of days," George added.

Nancy waved the disk. "Why can't we go over to your place now?"

"You can, but it won't do you any good." George paused. "It's a perfectly good computer but it's got a little bug in it right now."

Nancy didn't say what she was thinking about George's perfectly good computer.

George went on. "The guy's coming in a couple of days to fix it. You're just lucky I haven't thrown the damn thing out. This guy has fixed it before, so I'm waiting for him."

"All right, then I'll go over to the computer lab." Nancy tapped her fingernails on the table. How frustrating.

"That won't work either," Louise said. "Don't you remember the brochure? It said 'state of the art' computer lab. Those computers are all way beyond floppies. That goes for the Internet café and library in town too."

George shook his head. "Besides, those places are way too public. People are always looking at what you're doing. My computer will be up in a couple of days. Just be patient."

Louise snorted. "You're a fine one to ask someone to be patient."

George stood and tapped his cane. "I'll hound that computer guy. I'm as anxious as you are to see what our Glinda's been up to."

***

Life at Whisperwood:
Computer Help Available

The computer lab is open daily from 9 a.m. to 5 p.m. Computers are equipped with the latest software, and volunteers staff the lab to help with any problems you experience. Contact Whisperwood's highly trained computer technician, Paul Hartney, to fix problems with your own home computer.

-From *The Whisperwood Breeze*, newsletter of Whisperwood Retirement Village

Chapter 18

Nancy answered the phone as she was leaving for dinner that evening. An odd time to call anyone at Whisperwood. She looked at the cat, still hunched over his dinner bowl.

"Nancy, have you heard the news?" Louise's voice quavered.

Nancy's stomach dropped. "What news?"

"Anna Carothers. She was found an hour ago at the bottom of the back stairs." Louise gulped. "They're saying she slipped."

"Anna? How badly is she hurt?" Anna usually took the elevator. What was she doing on the stairs?

"I'm sorry to tell you this," Louise stopped.

Nancy already knew the answer. "She's dead, isn't she?"

"I'm sorry. It must have been a terrible fall. Hit her head."

Another hit on the head accident. Nancy's hands trembled. She sat down. *I'm next.* She glanced at her door. The flimsy lock was no protection—not meant to be. She glanced over at Malone. For once he could be useful.

"Nancy, are you okay?"

Nancy stared at the phone. Louise was as disturbed as she was. "Yes, I'm okay. Upset but okay. I need some time to think, but I want to get out of here. May I stay with you tonight?"

"Of course. We should stick together till this is over, Nancy."

"Thank you, Louise. I'll pack a few things. . ."

"Come up as soon as you can. We can protect each other."

"You're right. I'll pass on dinner tonight, Louise. I'm too upset."

"Me too," Louise didn't hesitate. "I'll be waiting for you."

"Thank you. And be careful."

Nancy replaced the phone and studied the lock on her front door. *They killed Anna because she talked too much.*

Nancy packed a suitcase, took a moment to explain things to the cat, and rode the elevator up to Louise's floor. When she stepped out of the elevator, she saw Louise standing by her door. Nancy walked quickly down the hall. Louise pulled her in, and then turned on a music CD as she whispered, "Our apartments may be bugged."

Nancy nodded at the CD player. "Good thinking. This is getting too serious and too close." She took pen and paper out of her purse and wrote, "Will you be up for meeting in the library this evening? At nine maybe?"

Louise nodded and wrote. "Yes. Nobody goes there that late. Let's catch George before dinner. Don't trust phones either."

"Yes, but I have to call a friend of mine and cancel out of our dinner tonight." Nancy knew Fitz would understand. He'd be a good ally too, and he even got along with Malone.

At nine, Nancy and Louise warily made their way to the elevator from Louise's apartment on the fourth floor. They glanced at the stairway as they passed it and looked at each other. No need to say anything.

George waited in front of the fifth floor library. He opened the glass door, switched on the light, and swept the two women in. "Neutral territory," he said.

Nancy took a cursory look between the stacks to make sure they were alone and then joined George and Louise who were already sitting in the comfortable chairs at the back.

"Anna talked too much." George blew his nose. "This is getting serious now."

"I don't for a moment believe the accident bit." Louise added.

Nancy studied both of them, feeling like a doomed pariah. "Whoever it is will be after me next. Maybe we shouldn't stick together. Maybe we should stop seeing each other—at least until this is over—so you don't get dragged in. We don't need any more victims."

Louise sat up. "I hope," she said through gritted teeth, "that you didn't mean that, Nancy. We wouldn't desert you to save our own skins."

"Hell no," George bellowed, then instantly lowered his voice. "This is the most fun I've had since I moved here. Great stuff for my novel."

Nancy felt tears prick her eyelids. "But the murderer could strike at any moment. You shouldn't get hurt because of me."

Louise snorted. "And I don't think you should get hurt because of me. So what? We've gone through a lot together, you and me, Nancy. And we're going to find out what's going on here. Together."

"That goes for me too." George added, pursing his lips. "Don't think you're going to hog all the excitement."

Nancy stared at her hands for a moment, afraid to speak.

After a moment, Louise spoke. "So what do we do next?"

"They got Glinda late at night," Nancy said, "and Anna in the afternoon. They both lived alone, like most of us here. The locks on our doors are almost useless."

"I got locked out once and opened my door with a credit card. That's why I got the extra deadbolt on my door." Louise chuckled. "Management doesn't like it, but I say tough."

Nancy nodded. "I've been thinking about that."

Louise flexed her fingers. "Tomorrow first thing we take the shuttle into town and go to the hardware store. I can install the lock for you. Simple job."

"Get one for me too," said George. "Maybe install it?" He looked at Louise.

Louise smiled at him. "Sure, George." She turned to Nancy. "But till this is over, Nancy, you'll stay with me in my spare room."

"That'll foil 'em," said George. He tapped his cane twice. "Killing two at a time is harder than one. You could stay with me too," he added doubtfully.

Nancy laughed. "That's all right, George. Don't want to ruin your reputation."

"Come, come," Louise added, "we might all want to stay together if the killings continue."

"Meanwhile," Nancy frowned, "it would be good to run a length of thread on top of our doors, maybe in a drawer, on our phones, to see if anyone comes in while we're out."

"Good idea, but so far, they don't know about George and me." Louise rapped the table. "They think I'm an old hippie rabble rouser. And George has kept a low profile. But you, Nancy, you're a detective. I'll bet they're worried about you."

"Oh boy," added George, "spy stuff."

"Tomorrow's the memorial service for Glinda," Nancy said. "I'm interested in who will show up. We might learn something."

"Now we're starting to cook. Hot diggity." George stood up and swung his cane at the bookshelf.

Nancy tapped her lips. "But we must all act as if we accept Glinda's and Anna's deaths as accidents. No more leading questions. We have to go underground now."

Louise and George nodded.

"And remember," Nancy added, "our apartments and phones may be bugged. Whoever they are, they may be watching everything we do." She thought of Malone. He'd keep whoever they were out of her apartment. Probably.

They all shook hands quietly across the table.

***

Life at Whisperwood: In Memoriam

The Whisperwood Community regrets the passing of the following residents during the week of June 8 – 15.

GERALDINE SHIFRIN

WILLIAM ALLAN
ANNA CAROTHERS

-From *The Whisperwood Breeze*, newsletter,
Whisperwood Retirement Village

Chapter 19

Nancy enjoyed receiving flowers as much as anyone, but Fitzhugh needed to be reined in. She brought in a vase filled with orange daylilies that had been left at her door and placed it next to the daisies filling another vase on the sideboard. Pink carnations and baby's breath sprang out of yet another vase on the coffee table. She'd taken bouquets up to Louise's apartment, too, and was running out of places to put them.

She surveyed the room, but even the multitude of flowers couldn't disguise the clutter and the dust. She'd grown up with a housekeeper who'd kept the house clean and neat but left her no privacy. Now her place was cluttered and dusty, but she liked it this way. She didn't have to answer to anyone else. Her husband's smiling face came to mind. He'd been gone four years. He would have brought her flowers too. Thinking of Bill made her look at Malone who was walking delicately around the vases, sniffing each bloom.

Bill had hoped to train Malone for his magic act. Nancy shook her head. Bill performed well as an amateur magician in shows for hospital patients, but Malone in a hospital? Nancy laughed.

She stepped down the hall and knocked on Fitzhugh Connelly's door. He seemed startled to see her.

"Are they all right?" he asked. "Do you like them?"

"Of course, Fitz, they're beautiful, but . . ." Nancy considered how to say this. "You've given me way too many. If you give me any more, I'm going to take them over to the rehab unit."

"I guess I went overboard." Fitzhugh managed a grimace. "I'm always doing that. Anyway, I like flowers too. I was a florist in my other life."

"I do enjoy them," Nancy assured him. "Only not so many."

"How about coming in and having a cup of tea with me," he said. He glanced toward the kitchen doubtfully. "Or maybe coffee. We have some catching up to do."

Nancy smiled at him. "Yes, we do. It's been a long time." She walked past Fitz into the living room. "Tea would be nice." Nancy picked her way through the unpacked boxes to the sofa. "I am so pleased to see you again. Welcome to the neighborhood."

"Thanks, but I'm not sure about this place—a lot of old people live here." He shuddered dramatically but chuckled as he stepped into the kitchen.

Nancy laughed. "It's an easy life though," she said, perusing the room. The sofa was covered in what looked like a brown sheet. Two boxes had been placed side by side in front of the sofa. From the coffee rings and stains on top, Nancy guessed they'd been used as coffee tables. A small television was sitting on top of a tall wardrobe box and faced the sofa. Other chairs and lamps and tables were piled against one wall. Unpacked and set up in a corner was a steel drum with the drumsticks crossed on top.

"You still play the steel drum?" she asked.

"Sure," he called from the kitchen. "Part of my Jamaican heritage I'm not giving up." He poked his head out of the kitchen and nodded at the piles. "Please excuse the mess, my darlin'."

Then he withdrew and Nancy heard the microwave. In a few minutes, Fitzhugh brought out two mugs of tea on a tray with sugar and a carton of milk. He handed one mug to Nancy. "Right now it's difficult, luv, not knowing many people here yet."

"That will come in time."

Fitzhugh sat on the couch with Nancy. "So what's going on around here?" He took a sip and smiled at Nancy over the mug. "I keep hearing rumors of things disappearing and thieves and even murder. Quite scary, what I've been hearing."

Nancy nodded but hesitated. She studied Fitzhugh's open, congenial face for a moment and decided that truth was better than rumor. "That was Glinda Spencer. She had a valuable historical item on her display shelf and then she was hit over the head with something like it and killed. That's what I think happened. The police investigated, and they're calling it an accident."

"An accident?"

"Yes, but that doesn't quite fit with the fact that her place looked as if it had been ransacked. We're all wondering what actually happened. But usually this is a safe place to live, and we do have excellent security."

Nancy paused, remembering that Fitz had just moved in. "You can always pull the cord in each room if you need help." She nodded at the pull cord hanging near the kitchen doorway.

"Oh, I know there's good security here. I ran afoul of them in the basement just after I moved in."

"What happened?" Nancy asked. Maybe Fitz learned something about the basement they should know.

"I was looking for a place to stow my extra stuff and thought the basement might have some storage bays." He glanced around the crowded apartment. "Not that I need them, of course." He laughed. "Mostly classrooms down there, you know, but there was this steel door at the end. I ran into a guard on the other side of that door, and that was it. No way was he going to let me look around, luv. Found that out." He took another sip of tea.

Nancy frowned. "How odd."

Fitz waved his mug. "I didn't see any storage areas, but I peeked through the steel door. That staircase leads down to an underground driveway in a tunnel under the building. Then I got shoved aside by a guy behind me who went through the doorway and locked it in front of me. I guess he'd gone upstairs for a snack at the convenience store. Hurt my shoulder." Fitz rubbed his arm.

Nancy stared out the window into the distance. "What do you suppose that's all about?"

"Not a glimmer." Fitz added more sugar to his tea. "There was only one dim light in the stairwell, so I couldn't see far into the tunnel." Fitz sipped from the mug. "I would have thought a garage, maybe, for Whisperwood vehicles, but it wasn't that. I don't know what it was."

"Stairs into a tunnel." Nancy tapped her fingers on the box in front of her.

Fitz nodded. "So tell me about the woman who was killed."

"Two women now," Nancy said. She filled him in on Glinda Spencer and the Russian boundary plate. "I cautioned Glinda about displaying it, but she refused to listen. That may have been what killed her."

"I see." Fitz frowned. "And there was another woman?"

Nancy folded her arms. Anna's death chilled her. "Anna Carothers discovered Glinda's body. She thought it was murder and told everyone about it. Then she was found at the bottom of our back hall stairs. Dead."

"And the sheriff is calling them both accidents?"

Nancy nodded. "I talked to him about Glinda's death, but he patronized me as if I were a dotty old lady." She frowned at the memory.

"It's a political situation," said Fitz. "If they call it an accident, then they won't offend or frighten anybody, they think. I'm sure a lot of local people depend on Whisperwood for jobs." He smiled at Nancy. "The sheriff is elected, you know. He doesn't want to make any waves." He made a wave motion with his hand. "Of course, someone could have bribed him, I guess."

"Yes, but most of us are registered to vote, and we could vote him out. I don't understand why they think they can brush us off like that," Nancy said. "I would think they'd at least look into the motives and alibis of the two sons and their wives."

"That would be the logical thing to do if it was murder." Fitz glanced over at Nancy. "Did she have a lot of money?"

Nancy nodded. "And family members are always the first suspects, but somehow I don't see either Cary or Clark, her sons, involved in this. They genuinely loved their mother and miss her."

Fitz shrugged. "They can fool you."

"I agree, but so can any of the residents here. I feel undercurrents whenever Glinda's name comes up, and then there's still the missing boundary plate."

"Too bad I never met her."

Nancy glanced at him. "Oh, well, I'm speculating, you know. Maybe Glinda actually did fall and hit her head except that her place was vandalized. I've been in her apartment. She was neat, most of the time."

Fitz finished his tea and reached over to refill his mug. He looked up at Nancy.

"No thanks. I have to go." She stood. "Be careful on the stairs." She thought of Anna. Eager, alert, enthusiastic Anna.

"Yes. I don't want to be another accident." He scratched his head. "Terrible."

Nancy stared down at her feet and nodded. She looked up. "Fitz, we've been friends a long time, and I have a favor to ask."

"Go ahead. I'd love to help you."

Nancy smiled at him. "I don't believe you've met my friends George and Louise yet, but we are trying to find out what's going on around here. We need a safe place to meet. Since you're so new here and so far not connected with us, your apartment and phone are probably not bugged."

Fitz whistled. "You think yours are?"

She nodded.

"Of course you can meet here, luv. Give me a reason to spiffy up this place. Make it presentable." He looked at the stack of boxes against the wall.

"That is such a relief. Thank you, Fitz." She turned to leave. "Now I do have to get along and do my errands. Thank you for the tea—and for the flowers, but you can hold off on giving me any more for awhile."

Fitzhugh laughed. "Sorry I went overboard, luv. Just wanted you to know how happy I am to see you again."

"Glad to see you too. You are a wonderful surprise." Nancy stepped out into the hall. "I'll see you later."

She scurried back into her apartment, nodded to Malone on the window sill, and sat down on the couch. She called George. "How's your computer?" she asked.

"Still sick. I've been hounding the computer guy, and he keeps promising he'll get here but I haven't seen him yet. I'm as frustrated as you are about this."

***

Early the next morning, Nancy walked down to her apartment. She checked the thread she'd placed on top of her door—still there, she saw with relief, so no one had made any uninvited visits. She entered and fed the cat before he could bite her ankles, but he snarled and fussed and glared at her, then turned his back to the food, slunk out of the kitchen, and leapt up on the window sill where he pointedly ignored Nancy.

Malone was mad at her. Nancy shrugged. Staying with Louise for a few days, until they found the murderer, couldn't be helped. Being ignored was better than being bitten and scratched. She left extra treats for Malone near his bed, then rummaged in a desk drawer and found the tools she was looking for in a small, oblong box. She picked up the box and rattled it, a smile on her face.

She took the elevator to the basement and stepped down to the steel door at the end. She looked in the classrooms. Empty. No one loitered in the hall. She was alone. She took a small, thin, flathead screwdriver and a set of picks out of the box and began fiddling with the lock on the door.

She was out of practice. She worked for several minutes, frowning in concentration. She used to be quite quick at this. After a few more minutes she had maneuvered the pins into place and gingerly opened the door.

A stone staircase led down to a small landing at the bottom of the stairs, which was lit by a dim bulb hanging overhead. Leaning back in a chair on the landing, dozing, sat a man wearing jeans and a flannel shirt. He turned as the light from the hallway behind Nancy threw her shadow over him. Looking up, he yelled and drew a gun from a holster at his side.

Nancy threw the door shut and ran for the hall stairway up to the first floor, mentally thanking all the hours she'd spent on the tennis court and in the gym and pool. She hurried up the stairs to the first floor, then down the hall and into her apartment, locking the door behind her. She listened at her door for running footsteps but heard none. He must have given up the chase in the basement. She didn't think he could make out her features, especially since she looked like any other elderly woman and the hall light gave him only her silhouette.

Would he tell Bryerson? Maybe not. Bryerson might think he was sleeping on the job. Odds were that he'd keep the incident to himself, but what on earth was going on down there?

***

Life at Whisperwood:
Cooperation Makes Everyone's Life Easier

Whisperwood Administrator Harry Doyle reminds us that Whisperwood's rules and policies are designed to help all of us live together pleasantly and safely. They are listed in the Whisperwood Handbook you received when you moved here. Attending to these policies and cooperating with the authorities make Whisperwood a better place for all of us. Also, for your safety, please pay attention to signs posted around the campus.

-From *The Whisperwood Breeze*, newsletter of Whisperwood Retirement Village

Chapter 20

"I wish she'd had an open casket," a harsh voice whispered.

Nancy heard the whisper from the pew in front of her and identified the speaker. Donald Elmo sat next to his wife Barbara, Glinda's sister, both of them stony-faced, staring ahead at the stained glass window behind the altar in the Whisperwood Chapel. The window gleamed with a soothing pattern of white doves against a blue background.

Donald's arms were folded defiantly. "Yeah, if we'd had an open casket, I'd be sure the old bat was dead. How do we know that's her in the urn?"

Nancy sat back in the pew, shaking off Donald's words and taking a deep breath to feel the quiet calmness of the sanctuary. She looked at the walls, beige and barren of any religious artifacts or symbols. Even her Jewish or Muslim friends would feel welcome here.

She scanned the sprinkling of residents scattered among the pews, recognizing the jeweler Simon Smythe in the back row. Then Glinda's sons and their wives entered and walked toward the front of the sanctuary. Cary held Teresa's hand, both of them staring solemnly ahead as if to avoid the stares of those assembled there.

Clark brought up the rear, a brooding Heathcliff who stumbled as he turned into the first row pew. He followed a tightlipped woman who sat down stiffly beside Teresa, her arms folded and a frown on her face.

Clark's estranged wife, Susanne, no doubt. The woman's navy blue jacket was tightly buttoned over a white blouse. The suit looked expensive and nun-like, especially since she wore no jewelry to soften the effect. But then, Nancy mused, the woman might have thought that jewelry would be out of place at a memorial service.

Flowers had been arranged in front and at the sides of the altar, their fragrance heavy and cloying in the stuffy sanctuary. A woman in a curly red wig tortured somber music out of the organ at the left.

As Nancy waited for the service to begin, she slipped her hand into her purse and pulled out a pen and small notepad. Using a hymnal as cover, she noted the names or brief descriptions of everyone present. She tried to do this inconspicuously, but Louise was sitting next to her and never missed a thing. She grinned and nudged George.

George leaned over to her. "Always curious, eh, Nancy?"

"I guess old detectives never retire." Louise whispered.

"Hush, you two." Nancy put the pen and paper back in her purse. "We should know who's here. I'll check the guest book later."

She heard the whirr of a small motor in the hush and turned around. Bernice Nelson had entered in her power scooter, but she stopped inside the door as if to make a quick getaway. Behind her, lurking in the hall, was Bryerson's assistant, Perry, standing aloof with his hands in his pockets. Nancy considered what he might be doing there. He had not entered the sanctuary but was scanning it with those sapphire eyes and lazy smile as if counting the crowd and planning some use for them.

The minister strode up the aisle and took his place behind the lectern. He cleared his throat. The service began. Nancy found herself studying Cary and Clark, stiff and stoic in the front pew, and then others around the chapel as the minister droned on with his platitudes. As he completed his remarks, he invited friends and family to speak. At once, three women Nancy had never seen before rose and walked to the pulpit. The minister stepped aside. The first woman introduced herself as the president of the local Humane Society. She looked directly at the family in the front row and began speaking of Glinda's contributions to the society.

"Her support has been felt in all areas of our work. We are deeply grateful for all that she has contributed."

The woman stepped down and the second woman took the pulpit. She represented the local library and she, too, spoke of Glinda's contributions as did the third woman, who represented the local domestic violence shelter.

Nancy glanced at the faces around her in the sanctuary. They looked as stunned as she felt. Glinda had been unkind to her and others but generous to three good causes. What kind of person was she, really?

After the service, the family stood with dazed smiles in an informal receiving line in the lobby. Several tables had been set up there for refreshments. Nancy sampled a delicate finger sandwich and pineapple punch as she watched the visitors. She leafed through the guest book and noted the names she did not recognize. She looked around for Bernice, but she had disappeared before the minister said his last words. Then Cary came over and introduced Nancy to Susanne, who was cordial but distant. Nancy helped the servers clear the tables and lingered until only Clark, Susanne, Cary, and Teresa remained, resting in the lobby chairs. They looked pale and tired.

"Is there anything I can do to help?" Nancy asked.

"We're through here," said Clark, leaning his chair back against the wall and staring at her dispassionately.

Cary stood and offered Nancy his chair but she shook her head. "We're all going out to eat," he said. "Care to join us?"

Nancy studied the group. "I wouldn't want to intrude."

"Believe me," said Teresa, "we'd welcome an intrusion. It's been tense."

Clark stood and pushed his chair back against the wall. "I'd like to know if you've found out anything else about my mother."

"No, I haven't, but your mother made some outstanding contributions to the local community," Nancy said.

"Sure she did. She always supported the humane society wherever she lived," Cary said. "I was surprised about the domestic violence shelter. She had a heart of gold." His voice broke.

Nancy looked at him and made up her mind. "I'd love to join you for lunch. Where?"

Teresa gestured toward the door. "Foley's Country Restaurant—down on the main road. You know it?"

Nancy nodded. "I've been there. May I ride with you?"

"Sure." Cary picked up the urn with Glinda's cremains and placed it in a box. "Nothing else to do here."

"Will you be scattering them?" Nancy asked.

"I'm not sure what we'll do with them," Cary replied. "I wouldn't have considered cremation, but Mr. Bryerson's staff recommended it. I suppose it's a good idea."

Nancy nodded. It's what she had chosen for herself, but odd that the staff here would go so far as to recommend it. She filed the fact away in her mind for later consideration and walked with the others to their cars.

Foley's was a roadside cafe and bar with wide sunlit windows, light pine walls, and red checked tablecloths and curtains. It was a popular local hangout. The one server on hand sequestered Nancy and the family around a table at the back of the dining room.

"Kind of early for dinner, I guess," said Teresa, surveying the sparsely populated room.

"I don't care. I would like a drink and I mean now." Clark motioned to a server. "Double martini as quick as you can make it," he said.

Teresa spoke up. "I'd like an iced tea."

"Me too," said Nancy. She would have preferred a glass of wine, but Clark's attitude changed her mind. She didn't want to go down that road.

"Yes, iced tea seems like a good idea," said Susanne, staring at the tablecloth.

Cary shook his head at Clark. "Alcohol isn't going to get you anywhere."

"Did I ask you?" said Clark, leaning back in his chair.

Teresa reached over and patted Clark's arm. "Clark, we're worried about you, that's all." She glanced apologetically at Nancy. "I don't need your concern." Clark flung off her hand. "I am doing just fine."

"He doesn't need anyone," added Susanne, moving her chair away from him, "just a bottle."

"Please think about it, Clark," said Cary, lifting an eyebrow. "You're losing everything—even Susanne here."

Clark frowned. "That's none of your business."

The server brought the martini and iced teas, took their orders and disappeared. Nancy watched him go. Perhaps he sensed the gathering storm over this table. She, on the other hand, was willing to see what developed.

Teresa laughed. "I can't imagine what you must think of us, Nancy." She glanced around the table as if she were a teacher counting heads.

"The last week has been tough on all of you," Nancy said, unfolding her napkin as she smiled at them.

"Yes, it has." Teresa nodded and dabbed at her eyes with a napkin.

"You know that woman in the power scooter, what was her name?" Cary glanced at Nancy.

"Bernice Nelson," prompted Nancy.

Cary tilted his chair back and nodded. "I've seen her before."

"So have I," said Clark. His martini was half gone, and he was already scanning the room for the server.

"It must have been in Alaska." Cary said. "But I can't remember anyone in a wheelchair among Mother's friends there."

"She probably wasn't in a scooter then," said Teresa, her attention brought back to her table companions.

"She has arthritis," said Nancy. "She can walk somewhat. She leaves her scooter in the hall when she goes into her apartment."

Clark looked up. "Mom knew a lot of people in Alaska, and they knew her too. Always glad to see her show up. Bernice could have been a friend of hers."

"Tell me more about your Mom's career. I didn't know she was so famous." Nancy gave him her full attention.

"She always said she went from rags to riches. She was born in Skagway back in the early days when it was still a rough frontier town." Cary smiled. "She told us her mother ran a boarding house of some kind there. At least, I hope that's what it was. Mom used to sing for the guests as she grew up. That's where she got interested in show business."

"She never talked about those early days," said Clark, "and we always wondered what they were like. We went to Skagway once, Cary, Teresa, Susanne and I, on a cruise, to see the town our mother came from." Clark turned aside to gesture to the server for a refill.

"It looked like it had majored in bordellos, from what we could see." Cary frowned at Clark. "Of course now it's a tourist town."

"Be careful," said Teresa, tapping Cary's arm. "You'll have Nancy thinking your mother was some kind of streetwalker."

"Could have been, for all we know," said Clark. He cocked an eyebrow at Nancy. "That didn't come up in all your detectin', did it?"

"Of course not," interrupted Cary. "She worked hard all her life for us, and I'll thank you to remember that." He stopped and peered at his brother. "Clark, are you driving?"

"No, she is." Clark flicked his thumb toward Susanne and then turned to stare at Nancy. He was beginning to slur his words. "Have you found out anything you can tell us about our mother's death?"

Nancy had kept silent, hoping they wouldn't remember she was there, but Clark had put her in the spotlight. They were all looking at her. She shook her head. "No, I haven't learned anything that you don't already know."

Teresa turned to Nancy. "Alaska's a rugged place, you know. Skagway was a small, raucous town that lived on gold mining in those days. We don't know too much about Glinda's parents except that they had a rough life. Glinda's mother took in laundry too, we understand. Glinda never said anything about her dad." She shrugged. "They're all dead now, anyway, so I guess we'll never know. She didn't talk about Cary and Clark's dad either, and none of us ever met him."

"Just as well," said Clark, grinning at them. "Better to think that we might be bastards than to know that we are."

***

Life at Whisperwood: Memorial Gifts

As a gift in honor or memory of someone special in your life, consider a contribution to the Whisperwood Benevolency Fund. This fund helps our friends and neighbors here at Whisperwood who find themselves in financial difficulties and would, without the help of this fund, lose their place here. There is no more fitting way to remember those who have been important members of our community.

-From *The Whisperwood Breeze*, newsletter, Whisperwood Retirement Village

Chapter 21

Nancy returned to her apartment and was feeding the cat when she heard a knock on the door. She opened it to find a thin woman wearing a grim expression and a flowered smock standing outside with a clipboard and wheelchair. Behind Nancy, the cat hissed and snarled.

"I've come to pick you up," the woman said, peering around Nancy and frowning at the cat. "I'm Nurse Cynthia."

"Pick me up? For what?" Nancy looked up and down the hall. It was empty.

"We've got a pretty new room waiting for you," the woman said, pasting a bright smile on her face. "You'll like it."

"I'm sorry. You've made some mistake." Nancy felt a tremor of fear.

"No, I haven't. Now come on. Be a good girl and sit in the chair." The nurse advanced toward Nancy. She looked muscular and tough. "The papers are all signed and everything."

Nancy backed away and tried to shut the door in the nurse's face, but the woman had her foot in the door. She was rooting around in a satchel hanging off the back of the wheelchair.

"This is a mistake. I'm Nancy Dickenson. I am not moving anywhere." Nancy kicked the woman's foot out and pushed the door shut with her body, locked it, and ran to the phone. She called Louise and at Louise's querulous voice, Nancy called out, "Help!" while the nurse hammered on the door.

The nurse's voice had become placating. "Now don't make a big fuss. You'll like it much better over in the other building." She stopped. Nancy heard a key rattling in the lock. Thank God for the new lock. After a long pause, the nurse spoke again, in a softer voice.

"You'll make new friends, and . . ."

"What's this?" Nancy heard Louise's rough voice break in to the nurse's wheedling. "What do you think you're doing?"

"I have instructions to take Ms. Whaley to the other building."

"I'm not Ms. Whaley," called out Nancy as Louise said, "That's not Ms. Whaley."

"This isn't Ms. Whaley?" the nurse asked.

Nancy opened the door, her hands trembling. "I've never been so glad to see you," she said, reaching for Louise's hand. "This woman was going to take me to the Alzheimer's unit."

Louise glared at the nurse. "Over my dead body."

The nurse backed away. "I'm sorry. There's been some mistake." She turned away and hurried down the hall pushing the wheelchair ahead of her.

"I can't believe what just happened." Nancy shivered. "I'm still shaking from it."

Louise put her arm around Nancy and walked inside with her. The khaki shirt and slacks on Louise's thin body gave her a military look that made Nancy's green slacks and pink striped shirt seem frivolous and gay. Today, Louise wore a *Peace* button. "I'll make you a cup of tea, and then we can go to dinner."

Nancy sat on the couch. "Thank goodness you got here in time." She picked up a sweater that lay on the couch and pulled it on. "I feel chilled. I think she was getting ready to drug me."

"And then she would have called for support and restraints." Louise thrust out her chin. "Do you think her mistake was the accident she pretended it was?"

Nancy looked at her. "We're all sitting ducks here."

"The three of us are going to have to watch our step."

"What if you hadn't come along? Would I be over there now? Would you come and get me if that happened, Louise?" Nancy stopped. "Would you even have known what happened to me? Would they have drugged me? She did have commitment papers. Thank goodness they were for someone else. She said."

Louise brought a cup of tea to Nancy. "We'd get a lawyer and sue. Now you just drink this and relax."

"Thank you." Nancy laughed as she sipped the tea. "Of course, maybe this little incident was an accident."

"Sure." Louise raised an eyebrow. "Like Glinda fell and Anna tripped on the stairs, I don't think."

Nancy finished her tea.

Louise took the cup and set it down on the table. "Now are you up for dinner? I smelled good stuff from the dining hall."

"After a close call like that, I'm famished."

Nancy and Louise walked, arm in arm, down the hall. Nancy knocked at Fitz's door as they passed it, but no one answered so they walked on to the dining room where George waited, watching them arrive with a huge grin on his face.

Taneesha greeted them at the hostess desk. "I've been promoted," she said, pointing to the black vest she wore.

"Congratulations," said Nancy. "You deserve it."

Louise and George echoed the sentiment.

Taneesha grabbed three menus. "You like to sit by yourselves, so I'm not going to add a fourth person." She took them to table fifty-six at the back of the room and hovered. "Your favorite table." she said.

They grinned at her as they seated themselves. Fitz waved at Nancy from a far table. She smiled and waved back, relieved that Fitz was already meeting people on his own. He was so congenial, she shouldn't have worried about him at all.

Taneesha cleared her throat. "They say you're a detective, Ms. Dickenson."

"That was in my past life. I don't do that anymore." Nancy

looked up at Taneesha.

She pushed her lips in and out as if she were debating with herself. Nancy waited. Finally, Taneesha seemed to make up her mind. She smiled apologetically. "I'm a little puzzled about something and don't know who to talk to about it." She paused as she took a deep breath. "You've been so nice to me that I thought . . ."

"What's puzzling you?" broke in Louise.

"I see a lot while I'm doing my job. Some people, like Ms. Spencer, I know she's dead and all, but she was mean to us servers—ordering us around and making us take stuff back to the kitchen. She wasn't nice at all. Sorry. I know I shouldn't speak ill of the dead."

"My dear, you're not the only one she treated shabbily," said Nancy, picking up her water glass.

"Yes, I know that, but whenever she saw anyone's pet dog, she would run her scooter up to them and swoon all over the dog as if it were her baby. Go figure. Anyway, that's not what I wanted to talk to you about."

Louise and George sat up. Nancy wondered what was coming next.

"The night before she died, she had dinner with Mr. Smythe, you know, the man who always wears a white jacket? Looks like a scarecrow?" Nancy watched Taneesha glance nervously at the nearby tables, but the residents sitting at them were engaged in their own conversations.

"Sure, he was a jeweler before he retired," bellowed George, winking at Nancy.

She winced. "Quiet down, George."

Taneesha lowered her voice. "Uh huh. I don't think he's retired. Anyway, he and Ms. Spencer insisted on eating together at the back with no one else, and they were angry. Really angry."

Nancy sat up and leaned forward, her sharp eyes focused on Taneesha's face. "What was that all about, did you hear?"

"No, but Mr. Smythe handed over an envelope," Taneesha whispered, "and Ms. Spencer opened it. It was a bundle of money, and he was angry about it too. He threw down his napkin and left."

"Wow," Nancy said. George nodded and Louise's eyes narrowed.

"Thanks for telling us about that, Taneesha," Nancy whispered to her, "but keep it to yourself. It could be dangerous if the wrong person learned that you knew about this."

"I never talk about any of you to anyone else, but I've heard a lot of questions about what happened to Ms. Spencer. If anyone knew what was going on, you would. I feel better telling you about it." Taneesha glanced back at the entrance. "Now I've gotta go. I want to be worth this promotion." She smiled at the server who had arrived at the table with water, salad, and rolls.

"Yep," said Louise as Taneesha hurried away. "I like her." She leaned forward and whispered. "You see? No one's talking about Anna with any suspicion at all."

George held a fork to his eye and squinted at it. "Sure. She's another old fogey who had an accident."

"I'm thinking a lot of old fogies are having accidents." Nancy sipped her water.

"Comes with the territory," muttered George.

"But I've heard several comments about stuff being missing from the apartments of the deceased," added Nancy.

"They probably got rid of it themselves. Gave it away," said Louise.

"I suppose so." Nancy looked up at the server. His name badge said he was Christopher. "I'd like the baked chicken and mashed potatoes."

The others chimed in with their orders. Tilapia with shrimp sauce for George, vegetable lasagna for Louise. Christopher gathered their menus and walked over to the next table.

"But Glinda must have had some kind of hold on Simon." Nancy glanced at the other two. "What was it?"

"Yeah, and how do we find out?" George flicked at an imaginary crumb and his eyes twinkled. He grinned. "Anyway, it's fixed."

"What's fixed?" said Nancy, then realized what he meant.

Louise rapped her knuckles on the table. "The computer?"

"Yep. The computer guy just finished getting it working again—

in time for me to meet you for dinner." George arranged his knife and fork. "We can go to my apartment after we eat and check out that floppy disk."

"At last," Nancy breathed. "We should have some champagne." She scanned the dining room, spotted the manager, and pantomimed drinking. He nodded and headed their way. She held up her hand to stop the conversation as he arrived.

"Pinot Grigio," she said and then looked at Louise and George. "Maybe not champagne for dinner."

"Yeah. I'd like that Pinot what-she-said too," said Louise.

George pursed his lips as if he were thinking hard. "I'd like a Riesling, but" he shook his head, "I can't drink alcohol. Interferes with my meds. Decaf coffee for me." He leaned back in his chair and patted his stomach. The manager took off for the bar.

Nancy turned back to the group. "What do you suppose those trips Simon takes are all about?"

George smacked his lips. He lowered his voice. "Maybe he's still working as a jeweler. Or maybe Simon's a courier carting gems, diamonds even, from place to place."

"Could he be smuggling them in?" Louise suggested.

"To West Virginia?" said Nancy.

George cleared his throat. "You don't suppose he trades in illegal drugs or cheap pharmaceuticals." He laughed. "Maybe I ought to go talk to him."

"Don't you dare," Nancy said. "We might be dealing with a murderer here. Anyway, I wanted to talk to you about Glinda." She leaned closer. "I know she was a bully—she certainly tried to bully me—and we know she stole those display items, but after listening to Taneesha and some other people, I'd say she was also a blackmailer."

Louise nodded. "I've been getting that feeling myself."

"Blackmail can lead to murder," said George.

"And a reason to ransack her place," added Nancy, straightening her knife and fork.

Louise looked over at the bar where the manager stood chatting with the staff. "Where is our wine?" She peeked at her watch. "Too bad the servers are all underage to serve alcohol."

"Patience, Louise, patience," said Nancy. She turned to George. "I'm glad your computer is fixed. I'm anxious to look at that floppy disk, but it's odd that her computer disappeared."

"Her kids probably took it out," said Louise.

Nancy shook her head. "They seemed surprised it was gone." she paused. "What about the diamond pendant in that box? We do agree the stones are genuine?"

Louise and George nodded, but no one spoke for a moment. Louise gazed off across the room. "If I started complaining about my fabulous diamond necklace being missing, what would you think?" She brought her eyes back to Nancy and George.

"I'd think, uh oh," said George, tapping his head, "she's on her way to the other building."

Nancy shivered at the thought as she fiddled with her water glass. "I happen to know that you would never have a fabulous diamond necklace to lose," she paused, "but if you did and said it was missing, I'm afraid I'd think you misplaced it or were imagining it or," she glanced at George, "as George says."

"Sure," said Louise, tapping the table with a finger. "We'd be inclined to feel we misplaced it in our apartment. Better that than to think there's a jewel thief here or, worse, that we're 'losing it.' And we wouldn't make a fuss about it either. Same reasons."

"That's right," added George. "Once in a while someone does complain about thievery, but unless it's obvious, like the shelf items, we wave the complaint aside as a figment of the imagination." He raised an eyebrow and stared at Nancy and Louise. "Don't we?"

They nodded.

Nancy pulled a notebook and pen out of her purse. "I've made a list of possible suspects. Let's go through it and see if we can weed anyone out." She opened the notebook and bega writing. "Numbers one and two on my list are her sons, Cary and Clark. They'd be in line to inherit her property, but I don't see either one killing his mother, and I can't believe she would blackmail them."

"Let's put them on the back burner for now," said George.

"Along with their wives," added Louise.

"Then next I have Glinda's sister Barbara Elmo and her husband Donald. Both of them disliked Glinda but did either of them hate her enough to kill her? I can't see blackmail or extortion here."

George spoke up. "That Donald is a sneaky bastard and pretty loud-mouthed when he's not around that wife of his."

"There's also Bernice Nelson," said Nancy.

"Bernice Nelson." Louise echoed the words. "I don't know her too well."

"Neither do I," said Nancy, "but Cary thought he recognized her, and she did show up at the memorial service."

"She did?" Louise put down her drink.

"I noticed her," Nancy tapped her pen on the pad, "but she didn't stay long."

George looked again at his watch and surveyed the room. "They haven't brought our orders out yet, and I would really like my coffee." He spotted the manager heading their way.

They waited as the wine was set at Louise and Nancy's places. At the same time, the server appeared with a tray of covered dishes. Hovering behind him was a server with the coffee pot. For once, no one complained as Christopher stumbled around the table, mixing up the orders and apologizing as they exchanged plates to correct him. He picked up the tray and left.

"That's better," said George, sipping his coffee and settling back to savor the grouper.

"I'm sure Glinda has victimized others, but I don't know who they might be." Nancy frowned.

"What about that man who keeps sending you flowers," asked George. "Could he have an ulterior motive? Maybe he was a victim too and is trying to shake us off his trail by using flowers as a red herring."

Nancy laughed. "Fitz is a long-time friend, and he used to be a florist." Nancy shook her head. "Anyway, he moved in after Glinda was killed."

George pursed his lips. "We should find out who has alibis for the time when Glinda was murdered."

Louise nodded. "That's going to be difficult since she died

sometime during the night."

"We can sure give it a try," said George.

"I like Fitz, and he'll let us meet in his apartment. He's not connected with us yet so it should be safe," said Nancy. "He had a strange experience right after he moved in." She told them about Fitz's discovery in the basement and then about opening the door herself.

Louise banged her fork on the table. "Something odd is going on here."

"Yes," said Nancy. She looked around the pleasant dining room, seeing filled tables, hearing the hubbub of conversation, noting a child and parents here and there visiting the grandparents and great-grandparents. All innocent and ordinary. These people were her only family now. She didn't want anything to happen to them.

"How can we find out more about what's going on down in the basement?" George sat back, hooked his thumbs in his belt, and looked at Nancy.

Louise nodded. "Glinda talked about this place being a time bomb. We don't know what we're sitting on here. They could be storing explosives in those tunnels. Glinda was nosy, and she'd lived here longer than any of us. If this place is a time bomb, it's because of what's below us."

Nancy considered some possibilities before replying. "Let's take a walk around the grounds tomorrow and try to ferret out where that tunnel entrance is. Maybe we'll see a truck or something go in or out."

"Yeah. Maybe we can enter the tunnel from outside," said George.

"And see where it goes," added Louise.

George sat back and patted his stomach. " Maybe it's just Bryerson's private garage."

"Could be. But first," said Nancy, "after dinner, we need to see what's on Glinda's back-up disk.

***

Life at Whisperwood:
Safety Deposit Boxes Available

Harry Doyle, Whisperwood Administrator, reminds everyone that safety deposit boxes are available at the Whisperwood Village Bank for a nominal fee. Whisperwood is a very safe place to live, but for extra peace of mind, residents should consider placing valuables and important papers into the additional protection that safety deposit boxes provide. They will always be accessible during regular banking hours.

-From *The Whisperwood Breeze*, newsletter of Whisperwood Retirement Village

Chapter 22

George stopped at the door to his apartment, pulled out his key, and picked a thread out from the crack between door and wall. He showed the thread to Nancy and Louise. "I've got my own security system too, you see. Nobody's been in my place."

"Just a minute, George." Nancy pulled a small electronic device from her purse. "A friend sent this to me. Bug detector," she said. "Just in case." She ran it over the desk, phone, and other items in the living room and den, where George kept his computer.

"All clear." Nancy put the gadget back in her purse.

Then George ushered Nancy and Louise into his den where the computer winked green lights at them. He sat down at the keyboard while Nancy and Louise huddled behind him.

George looked up at Nancy as he inserted Glinda's back-up floppy disk into the slot. "This was a state-of-the-art machine when I bought it," he said. He pressed a few keys. "Now it's a dinosaur." He grinned at them. "Like me." Two files appeared on the monitor.

George read the file names out loud. The first was labeled "Clients" and the second, "Missing."

"They're both spreadsheets," said Nancy.

Louise whistled. "Quite a surprising lady, our Miss Glinda."

"What could she mean by 'Clients'?" Nancy asked.

George opened the file to a worksheet of thirteen columns. The first column was headed "Name/Amount" and the remaining twelve were headed, "Jan, Feb, Mar" and so on to December. Under the first column nine names were listed, but the amounts by each name were small, none more than twenty-five dollars.

Nancy studied the worksheet. "Looks like these people were making payments every month. I wonder why."

"For what?" Louise peered at the screen. "And to whom? Glinda?"

George looked up at her. "Who else?"

Nancy recognized Simon Smythe's and Bernice Nelson's names as well as several others. At the end of the list, three other names appeared with question marks. Nancy caught her breath. One of those names was hers, one was Perry's, and the third was Nat Bryerson's. No dollar amount was listed for them.

Louise glanced at Nancy. "I'll bet you didn't know Glinda had you lined up as a client."

Nancy shook her head. "I can't imagine what she'd think I'd pay her for."

George printed three copies of the "Clients" list, one for each of them. Then he closed the file and opened the second one, "Missing."

This file was set up with four headings: "Name," "Item," "Actor," and "Action." Seventy-three names were entered, and as Nancy read down the "Name" column, she recognized a few of the names as residents.

"I know, or knew, many of these people," said Louise. "A lot of them are dead now, though.

Nancy studied the list. One name in particular caught her interest. She pointed it out to Louise and George. "Look, 'GS' must stand for Glinda Spencer and the corresponding item is 'plaque' and there's a 'P' in the 'Actor' column."

Nancy continued to study the abbreviated notes under "Items." "Here's a listing for a 'Dia.N'" she added.

George squinted to read the list and Louise peered closer.

"'Dia.N.' has got to mean diamond necklace," she said.

"Of course," Nancy nodded. "The corresponding name is 'Emma Richards.'" She looked at George. "The actor is listed as 'SS.' I wonder what 'actor' means. Why do you suppose the necklace was in Glinda's box?"

Louise was studying her copy of the "Missing" file. "I'm getting a glimmer of what this is about."

"What?" asked Nancy.

Louise frowned. "A couple of years ago, before you came, Nancy, Gwen Fowler," Louise pointed to the name on the list, "reported that an antique vase was missing from her apartment. Priceless, she said. Here it is next to her name on this list. Under the 'Actor' column there's a "P" and a question mark."

Nancy studied her list. "Each name has a corresponding item in the "Item" column. No actions are noted for any of them."

"The trouble is," said Louise, "that Gwen Fowler was a bit fuzzy-brained so no one paid much attention to her. Then she was found drowned out at the duck pond and that was the end of it." Louise raised an eyebrow. "An accident."

Nancy frowned. "Why would Glinda put Gwen and the vase on this list?"

"Wait a minute. Glinda was stealing things." George looked up at Nancy. "She could have stolen the vase too."

"I doubt it. This was a valuable item kept inside the apartment," Louise shook her head. "Glinda stole mementos on the shelves in the hall."

"Obvious to me," George added, "that Glinda was workin' on the idea that someone had stolen the vase."

"Gwen's family wasn't interested in her stuff." Louise flicked her braid. "They breezed through and sent everything down to the consignment shop." She snorted. "What they didn't throw out, that is."

"I don't have anyone to leave my stuff to." Nancy stared at her finger tips. "Not that I have anything of value."

Louise's eyes sparked. "But if you did have valuable items here and no next of kin, what would happen to them? What's the policy?

We should find out. Maybe start up a community watchdog committee."

"Someone, Amanda, I guess, since she's resident coordinator here, would probably have to dispose of it." Nancy read through the list again. "Some of these items look like jewelry to me. Abbreviated, so it's hard to tell, but for those items, the actor's initials are 'SS.'"

Louise glanced at her watch and yawned. "I'm done for today. My brain's not working. I suggest we think about these lists and get together tomorrow and make a plan."

"Me too." George made three copies of the file and logged off the computer.

Nancy stepped toward the door. "You've met my friend Fitz. I'll ask him if we can meet in his apartment tomorrow morning to share notes. It's Number 116. Everyone knows we pal around together, but Fitz will be a dark horse."

"I talked to him at the mailboxes," said George. "Sounded kind of foreign."

Nancy laughed. "Jamaican. But he's lived all over the world. I've known him a long time. He's a good friend, and I trust him. My husband did too."

Louise looked at Nancy, "You're staying with me. Do we need to stop by your apartment?"

Nancy shook her head. "Malone's been fed and he's on patrol."

George shuddered.

"Good." Louise headed for the door, reading through the printouts as she walked.

***

The next morning, Nancy, George, and Louise sat at a square card table in Fitz's living room. Boxes still lined the walls, but the table and four chairs had surfaced.

Nancy whispered to them, "I checked this place for a bug just in case."

Fitz was shuffling through a stack of papers and books on a

dusty credenza. "I know I've got pens and blank paper here." He ripped open a cardboard box labeled "Desk," and grinned at them, pulling out a caddy holding pens, ruler, scissors, and paper clips. He placed it on the table, reached into the box again and pulled out a ream of paper. "Told you, ducks. Knew they had to be around here someplace."

Nancy glanced around the room. It still felt claustrophobic even with the boxes pushed against the wall. Several heavy framed paintings in dark colors leaned against the boxes and lent a dreary air to the room. But unless the murderer had bugged every apartment in the building, this one should be safe.

George sneezed. "Excuse me. Allergies."

"I got coffee and tea ready in the kitchen." Fitz grinned at them. "And I'm defrosting a coffee cake."

"Thanks, Fitz." Nancy smiled at him. "I hope you didn't go to much trouble."

Fitz sat back and beamed. "I'm pleased to be part of this, luv."

Louise cleared her throat. "Tom isn't here. He's out on a fact-finding trip. He's up in Pennsylvania now."

"So that's why he hasn't been playing bridge," said Nancy.

"I thought he was your environmental buddy. Botanist, wasn't he?" said George. "What's he looking for?"

"A better place than Whisperwood." Louise rapped her knuckles on the table. "He doesn't like what's going on around here. Neither do I."

Nancy pressed her lips together. "It's the management here."

"Bryerson's hand-picked board of directors plays dead, and Perry is a creep," said Louise. "Tom wants to find out how different places are organized and managed and how the payment schedule works."

"I didn't study any of them very much." Nancy shrugged. "I moved here because of you, Louise."

"I'd hate to see Tom move," said Louise, "but the contract says he can get his deposit back except for the cost of refurbishing his apartment."

George cleared his throat. "I liked that part. That deposit took all the money I got from selling my house, and I didn't necessarily want this to be the end of the road."

"Sure," Louise added. "Of course, if you give up your unit, Bryerson can turn it over to someone else for a higher deposit."

Nancy looked over at Fitz who'd been watching this interchange with open mouth. He shook his head. "You're makin' me feel nervous about moving here."

Nancy patted his hand. "Most of the time it's a wonderful place to live. As soon as we nab the culprit, it will be wonderful again." She looked at Louise. "Tom will let us know what he finds out, won't he?"

"He promised me a report every week." Louise threw the braid over her shoulder.

Nancy frowned. She really would like to cut off that braid.

George sat back and folded his arms. "I chose this place because I liked the setting and the layout . . . and Louise here." He winked at her.

Nancy hid a smile, but Louise ignored him and leaned forward. "I like West Virginia. It's wild and wonderful, at least that's what the tourism industry here says. I'd like to keep it that way."

"We all would," Nancy picked up the printouts. Did either of you come up with anything about the names and items on the 'Missing' list?"

Louise snorted. "Some of those people are dead. We need to talk to their neighbors or friends casually to pick up any scuttlebutt. Also," she paused dramatically, "I'm curious about how they died. Gwen Fowler's death was an odd accident."

"Sorry, folks. I haven't studied the lists at all yet," George said, an embarrassed grin on his face. "I went to bed as soon as you left my apartment last night. I was pooped after playing in the Scrabble tournament all yesterday afternoon. No one there said anything about Glinda or Anna."

Nancy tapped her pencil. "What about the list of clients?" They all studied the printouts in their hands.

"I've met Mark Bowen," Nancy said, "Don't know him well."

"I recognize some of the names," added George. "Don't know

any of them well enough to ask pointed questions."

Louise laughed. "Yeah, like 'Was Glinda blackmailing you?'"

Nancy held up her hand. "Be careful in your questions. Glinda seems to have thought someone was stealing valuable items from the residents. At the same time, she was also blackmailing and stealing from people. Obviously, she called those victims her 'clients.'"

"You were on the list too, Nancy." Louise grinned at Nancy. "Got to wonder what you've been up to."

Fitz laughed. "She's always up to something."

Nancy examined the printout once more. "I know this woman slightly." She underlined the name Emma Richards on the "Missing" list. "I'll pay her a visit and see what she says about missing jewelry." She pointed to the entry next to the name, "Dia.N."

Louise nodded. "You'll have to be careful. No leading questions. Even I might claim a lost diamond necklace if you worded the question right."

Nancy studied the list again. "I don't think you would do that, but you're right. I'll be careful and see what develops."

George sat back and twiddled his thumbs. "That's all about Glinda as perpetrator. What happened to Glinda as murder victim? And Anna, of course."

"That's the other question," said Louise. "Let's get down to business on tracking a murderer." She pointed to the printouts. "Every client on the list is a suspect. Even you, Nancy." She winked at Nancy. "And Bryerson, I guess."

George sneezed. "Sorry. The dust."

Louise found George a tissue. "Glinda's sons and their wives are off campus. They'd have to sign in at the gate and, anyway, they'd be conspicuous in the halls here late at night," she rapped her knuckles on the table, "if anyone happened to be up and around."

"What about the people at the memorial service? Bernice Nelson, for instance." George peered over the tissue, his eyes red and tearing. He pulled out a small pill container and took one. "Got any water, Fitz?"

"Just a minute." He brought George a glass of water. "Would

you like more coffee? Tea? Soda?"

Louise shook her head. "Nothing for me, thanks."

"I made a note of the names in the guest book, but there weren't too many, and some of them don't live here," said Nancy.

"Perry was there," Louise said. "He hung around in back, smiling and listening." Louise shuddered. "I don't like him."

"I did notice him," Nancy said. "He stood in back with the sheriff's deputy."

"Deputy too? Where was I? I didn't notice either of them." George blew his nose again.

"They did their best to be unobtrusive," said Louise. "We all know Perry. I don't like the man, even if he does have those beautiful blue eyes. They don't go with that mean-looking face."

"I've never seen either of them at any other memorial service," Nancy shook her head, "and we've had lots of them. Bryerson probably never even met Glinda."

"Oh, he met her," said Louise. "I saw her come out of his office one day. She looked smug, as if she'd just won a bet."

Nancy paused in her writing. "But there was only a question mark by his name. He's too sharp to be one of her victims."

"She wouldn't still be here if he was," said George. "That man is tough."

Louise glanced over at George. "He is smart and he's tough, and she's not here anymore."

They sat in silence. Nancy shook her head. "Bryerson seems too smooth, too sophisticated to actually hit her over the head." She paused. "But then I've been fooled before."

"I talked to him before I moved in," added Fitz. "He seemed to be genuinely committed to this place. Said he built it for his Mum."

"Maybe not him then," said Louise. "One of his henchmen, or Perry."

Nancy added Bryerson and Perry to the list. "What kind of hold could Glinda possibly have on Bryerson?"

George shook his head. "Don't know, but he was on her list."

"So was I," Nancy interrupted.

George squinted at her. "Got to wonder why, and I sure hope

we find out soon why Glinda thought we're living on a time bomb."
Louise laughed. "Maybe she was being philosophical," she said.
"You could also call this place a death trap. None of us is going to
leave alive."

Fitz cleared his throat. "I'll bring out the coffee cake."

Nancy shuffled the printouts. "Let's get back to business.
George, you see what you can find out about Bryerson, Perry, and,
in a friendly way, about Glinda's brother-in-law, Donald. I'll tackle
Glinda's sister Barbara since I've already talked to her somewhat."

Louise sighed. "I guess that leaves Bernice for me. I'm not good
at this kind of thing. Don't expect much."

Nancy patted her hand. "Do the best you can. We can all report
tonight at dinner."

Fitz brought out the coffee cake and four plates and set them
on the table.

George eyed the cake, picked up a slice, and waved it as he
talked. "Perry is always buzzing around this place, likely to be
anywhere, but Bryerson isn't around often. If anyone spotted him
on the upper floors of this place, they'd wonder about it . . . talk
about it too. I'll have to do some digging on the Internet to find out
more about him." He sat back and patted his stomach. "This will
make great fodder for my novel."

Louise groaned. She looked at George. "You have to put words
on paper to write a novel, George." She glanced at Nancy. "Anyway, we'll have a problem with Donald too. He doesn't talk very
much, and I never see him around if he's not at dinner."

Nancy nodded. "But he belongs to the model train club. You
can probably find him in their clubroom in the basement."

George peered at Nancy over a tissue. "Now how would you
know that?"

"Saw him at the hobby show in the auditorium downstairs," said
Nancy, reaching for the cake. Just one piece wouldn't have that
much sugar and fat. "The railroad club set up a miniature village
with trains running over and around and under, bridges, tunnels,
you name it."

"Maybe I'll do that. Might learn something." George grabbed

his cane and headed for the door. He paused and looked at Fitz. "That was great cake." He waved and stepped into the hall.

"I'll call on Bernice now," said Louise, rising stiffly from the chair. "Bye, Fitz. You're an excellent host."

"I'll make up some reason to drop by Barbara's apartment." Nancy grabbed her keys. "Thanks, Fitz. See you later." She followed Louise and George out the door to the elevator where they all waited for it to make its slow, tedious descent to the first floor.

The ride up was just as slow. The elevator took forever to reach the third floor. Nancy waved goodbye to Louise and George and walked down the hall to Number 311. As she knocked, she could hear the dog next door barking and sniffing. Barbara opened her door immediately.

"Oh, Nancy." She glanced down the hall beyond Nancy. She smoothed her hands on her dress and in a flat voice, she said, "Come in."

Nancy walked into the living room. She could smell the pine disinfectant and resisted the urge to run her finger across a side table. How clean and neat the apartment was. Perhaps she should hire a cleaning person after all. Some people had a real problem with dust—and cats.

Barbara gestured to the white, fuzzy sofa. It resembled the one in Glinda's apartment. Perhaps it was the same. Nancy sat there while Barbara took the green and red, plaid-covered armchair and glanced around the room with a self-satisfied nod. Her glance came back to Nancy. "Would you like some coffee?" Barbara asked, waving her own cup.

Nancy shook her head. "No thanks. Wanted to drop by for a minute to see how you're doing." She felt grubby in the sanitary blandness of the room and found herself shrinking to avoid touching the spotless couch any more than necessary. She sat on the edge of the cushion.

"Life rolls on. A bit calmer now, if you must know." Barbara stared down at her bright blue and yellow-flowered house dress. It clashed stridently with the plaid armchair.

Nancy resisted the urge to smooth her slacks and straighten her blouse. "Yes, I suppose Glinda was always busy."

"She was. You wouldn't believe what she poked her nose into."
Barbara gazed at her cup. "You sure couldn't keep her down."

Nancy sat back. "She was curious. I am myself."

Barbara glanced around the room as if expecting Glinda to appear. "Some people said she was prying and meddlesome." She laughed. "But she was harmless, really, even though there were those who took it the wrong way."

"Being nosy?"

"That's what they called it." Barbara picked up a tissue and wiped her eyes. "She was trying to better herself, and she became a wealthy woman. Nothing wrong in that, is there?" She shrugged. "Sometimes her nosiness became a problem for the rest of us, but she really didn't mean any harm. She didn't."

Barbara was being the protective older sister. "Did you see her that night?" Nancy asked. "I mean before she died?"

"We didn't socialize together much." Barbara stared at her hands. "Oh, I kept an eye on her, being big sis and all, but Donald and I have our own evening routine. After dinner we watch TV, and then we go to bed. Get up everyday at seven thirty." She folded her arms. "You ask Rhoda next door. She sets her clock by us. She can't sleep, so she hears Donald open the door every morning and get the paper. That sets her dog off." Barbara's smile was ironic. A dimple appeared in her cheek. "That dog is the one I'd like to murder."

Nancy laughed. "No dogs near me, thank goodness," she said. A vision of Malone ripping apart and munching on an innocent puppy crossed her mind. "Is the Russian boundary plate still missing?"

Barbara nodded. "She sure was proud of that hunk of metal. Go figure."

Nancy hesitated before plunging forward. "Did Cary tell you he found my fan doll and the other stolen shelf items in her trunk?"

"He did, but I had no answers for him, and I can't understand it." Barbara bristled. "Why would she take someone's worthless souvenirs?"

"You never heard of her doing that before? She wasn't a kleptomaniac, for instance?"

Barbara waved a hand dismissively. "Of course not." She sniffed and stared off toward the window. "You didn't want to cross her. She stuck up for herself one way or another. She might have taken stuff as some kind of revenge." Barbara shook her head. "I don't know."

Nancy sat in silence, hearing the grief in Barbara's voice.

"Anyway, she's dead now." Barbara stood and glanced toward the door. "Let sleeping dogs lie." She sighed.

Nancy rose. She walked with Barbara to the door. "Looks like you're getting through this all right, but if I can do anything to help, let me know."

Barbara nodded and smiled. "That's kind of you. Glinda was my only sister. I tried to keep an eye on her."

"Of course you did," Nancy said as she opened the door and walked out into the hall. Death had softened Barbara's feelings. Nancy understood that, but she had gotten what she came for. The dog next door would have alerted everyone in that hall if Donald or Barbara had ventured out of their apartment during the night. She could hear the dog now, yapping inside the apartment. Just the same, she would ask Rhoda if what Barbara said was true. Right now it seemed to Nancy that Barbara—and Donald too—both had alibis.

She headed for the stairs, changed her mind, and took the elevator instead.

***

Life at Whisperwood: Please Watch Your Pets

Whisperwood welcomes pets who are well-mannered and trained. Please don't let your dog annoy your neighbors with excessive barking, and please take your dogs out for frequent walks. Whisperwood Administrator Harry Doyle reminds us that Whisperwood must clean hall and elevator car-

pets much more often than usual because of pet accidents. This is expensive, and we all pay that bill in
our monthly statements. And please, don't forget to
pick up after your pet on the grounds.

-From *The Whisperwood Breeze*, newsletter
of Whisperwood Retirement Village

Chapter 23

The worst thing about getting your hair done at a salon in Whisper-wood was the wait. Nancy glanced at her watch again. She walked up to the salon reception desk where a young woman chatted on the phone.

Nancy waited.

Finally with a gesture of impatience, the receptionist put her hand over the phone and said, "Yes? May I help you?"

"My appointment was at two."

The receptionist glanced at the appointment book. "Uh huh. That's right."

"It is now after three." Nancy gestured at the wall clock.

The young woman shrugged. "You can see that everyone's busy. She'll get to you as soon as she can."

"We shouldn't have to wait this long."

"I can't do anything about that. We had to squeeze in a few extra appointments today."

The woman went back to her phone conversation. Nancy counted the people in the waiting room. Five. Two had come in within minutes of Nancy's own arrival and still waited patiently.

Nancy knew what the receptionist had left unsaid: "You can

wait. What else do you have to do?"

She picked up her purse and walked out, staring pointedly at the receptionist. The other women waiting there watched Nancy passively, but no one else stirred.

The salon was opposite the dining room, and Taneesha was already at her post. She smiled at Nancy, so Nancy stopped to chat.

"Thanks for telling us about Glinda and Simon the other night."

Taneesha picked up a stack of menus. "I hope it will help you in your detecting. Terrible thing to happen to Ms. Glinda."

Nancy's ears perked up. "Who did she usually sit with?"

Taneesha looked past Nancy at a couple who had walked up. "Just a minute." She smiled at the couple. "Please follow me."

When Taneesha returned, she glanced around before saying, "She'd sit with anyone who came in at the same time, but Mr. and Ms. Elmo refused to sit with her. I saw them hold back more than once when Ms. Glinda came up to be seated." She sniffed. "Lots of people do that, you know. Wait till someone they like shows up. I feel sorry for the people no one wants to sit with at dinner."

Nancy studied her hands, knowing that she was one of those who picked her dinner companions.

Taneesha went on. "Another person who didn't like Ms. Glinda was that Bernice Nelson, and you and your friends weren't fans of hers, were you?" Taneesha grinned mischievously. "I noticed the expressions on your faces when she wheeled herself into the dining room. All three, or sometimes four of you, would track her with your eyes as if she were some kind of magnet." She brought the menus she was holding up to her face and peeked at Nancy over them.

"Oh. I'm sure we were just looking around the room." Nancy felt chagrined at being so obvious. "Was there anyone she sat with regularly?"

Taneesha shook her head. "She mostly sat with whoever came in at the same time she did—except for Mr. Simon and Ms. Bernice, that is. Occasionally, she waited for them, but they weren't that pleased to join her."

"Thanks, Taneesha."

"Don't mention it." She glanced around. "I mean really don't mention it. I shouldn't be gabbing to you and your friends about what I see in the dining hall. I'm just upset about Ms. Spencer and how she died. You're the only ones who seem to care."

Nancy smiled. "We won't tell anyone else. Don't worry."

Taneesha smiled back as she straightened the stack of menus.

Nancy walked to Louise's apartment, head down, deep in thought. She missed Anna and the way Anna died frightened Nancy. She tapped three times. Louise opened the door and stepped aside to let Nancy enter. "Got to get you a key," Louise said.

"Have you talked with Bernice yet?" Nancy asked.

"Not yet." Louise sounded embarrassed. "I've been thinking how to strategize the conversation with her to find out what we want to know." There was a pause. Then Louise added, "I'm no good at this kind of thing. We have to be careful what we ask, and I always blurt out what I'm thinking. No tact at all"

"Would you mind if I tackled her instead?"

"Would I? Of course not." Louise grinned with relief. "Go ahead."

"Thanks." After a moment's thought, Nancy made the call. "How about lunch tomorrow, Bernice, in the pub?"

There was a long silence. "Yes," said Bernice. "I'd like to talk to you. You need to hear the whole story."

***

Nancy met Bernice in the far corner of the Whisperwood pub, away from the pool table and the TV set in the corner. The server arrived immediately, but they all knew the simple menu.

"A glass of iced tea and a hamburger for me, please," said Nancy.

"Merlot and roast beef sandwich," Bernice added, then sat back to stare at Nancy as the server departed. Bernice was not smiling. "So?" she said.

Nancy took a deep breath. "I wanted to ask you about Glinda. Didn't you know her in Alaska?"

"Who told you about that?" Bernice sat back, her arms folded in front of her.

Nancy leaned forward. "Glinda mentioned it to me. Did you move here to be close?"

Bernice snickered. "Not hardly. I was here first, you know. It was the shock of my life to glance around the dining room and see her staring at me." She frowned as the server arrived with their drinks.

"Odd that you should both move here," Nancy said, stirring sugar into her iced tea.

Bernice sipped her wine as she stared appraisingly at Nancy. "Not so odd. Sent Christmas cards and a note, the way you do sometimes to acquaintances, let each other know what we were doing. She wanted to be near her kids in Morgantown. I moved here because I love the mountains and the countryside—and it's not as cold as Alaska." She winked at Nancy. "No one here would ever have heard of me, but then she moved here too."

Nancy picked up her glass. "Did you work together in Alaska?"

"Yes we did. So?" Bernice sipped her wine and sat back.

Nancy wondered what Bernice was thinking. She seemed to be testing Nancy, analyzing her, almost humoring her. Nancy sat back and mirrored Bernice's posture to work toward a rapport.

"I'm trying to understand what kind of person Glinda was," Nancy said. "She was quite unpleasant with me, and then we found my fan doll in her apartment."

"I heard about that, yes." Bernice said, frowning. "Knowing her, I figured she'd probably taken those things."

Nancy drew in her breath. Bernice seemed to be unbending a little. Nancy looked around at the empty tables surrounding them and saw the server approaching with their food. She waited until he left. "Why did you think that?"

Bernice twirled the now empty wine glass. "She was spiteful and petty in a lot of ways. She never got over growing up poor." Bernice looked around for the server and motioned to her glass.

"So you knew her well?"

Bernice shrugged. "As well as anyone, I guess."

"Tell me more about her."

Bernice sat back and studied Nancy for a moment and then took a deep breath. "You've probably had it easy all your life. You wouldn't understand how hard it was for a girl on the wrong side of the tracks with a drunk for a dad and a mom who struggled with low-paying menial jobs. I got out of Skagway as quick as I could and went to Anchorage." She picked up her wine, watching Nancy over the rim of the glass. "It's an old story you've heard a thousand times."

"Still sad and still true." Nancy sat back. "You're right, I have had it easy, but I can understand how hard it was for you."

Bernice shrugged. "Whatever. I roomed with Glinda in Anchorage. We were both trying to break into show business there, pitiful as that sounds for a couple of girls from the sticks. We did whatever we could to stay alive."

Nancy nodded to show sympathy.

Bernice glanced around the room. "I don't want you blabbing this to anyone else."

"Of course not. I'm trying to understand what happened."

Bernice spoke softly, so Nancy leaned forward to hear. "I got pregnant, but Glinda was doing pretty well. She helped me out there for awhile. She introduced me to a guy, and we hit it off. I lived with him to have my baby. They always say Alaskan men are odd, you know, and they're right. Have to be odd to want to live up there."

"So I've heard." Nancy smiled.

For the first time, Nancy saw Bernice grin.

"It's for sure. I lived with this guy for a few years and got training as a beauty operator. When I could support myself, me and my baby left him." She sat back and relaxed, taking a long sip of wine. "On good terms—we'd grown tired of each other. So I worked for a few years and then met a really good man, and we got married and moved to Morgantown. I told him I was a widow."

"Didn't your first child wonder about his real father? Try to find him?"

"We talked about it, but I told him his father died in a fishing accident and that seemed to satisfy him." Bernice stared off into the distance with a faint smile. "I had another baby, and all of us did all right together."

"So you stayed in Morgantown?"

"Till my husband died several years ago. My children worried about me a lot, living alone in that big house, so they paid for me to come here."

"You have very kind children."

"Yes, I do." Bernice smiled down at her hands. "And I didn't want any dirt dug up about my past life, but Glinda, she was willing to tell everyone about me unless I paid her a little bit every month. If you can believe it, she saw nothing wrong with that. She believed she was performing a service for pay." She stared down at her plate.

"Oh, Bernice." Nancy's eyes shone with sympathy.

"Yes, it's true." Bernice lifted her chin. "But she'd helped me out in the past and loaned me money when I needed it, so I didn't mind paying her the piddling amount she wanted every month to keep her mouth shut. She didn't have to turn it into blackmail. It breaks my heart to think that my children might learn about my past." Bernice rapped on the table. "She really was a first class, triple A bitch."

Nancy munched on her burger. "Glinda would have stepped up her demands, wouldn't she?"

"Maybe. But I think it was the power she held rather than the money that drove her. She could destroy me and wanted to make sure I knew it. That's what it was all about." Bernice shrugged. "And by the way, I know what you're fishing for, but I didn't kill her. And I don't have an alibi. None at all. I watched television till late and then went to bed."

Nancy leaned forward. "Do you have any idea who did?"

Bernice sat back with a cynical smile. "The party line says it was an accident."

"I don't believe it."

"As it happens, neither do I." Bernice fluttered a hand. "Some people don't take to being in someone else's clutches. Look for them. I wasn't her only source of extortion income. I'd say someone on her list didn't want to pay up."

Nancy nodded, and then she smiled and placed her hand on Bernice's. "Your secret is safe with me," she said.

"I know." Bernice took another sip of wine.

***

Life at Whisperwood:
Services Available to Meet Every Need

Pet sitting? Rug or apartment cleaning? These services are available for Whisperwood residents from the Home Services Department. Betty Donaldson, director, and her staff have set up an exhibit with brochures next to the lobby reception desk and are on hand to answer your questions. Services also include the beauty salon, barbershop, and massage therapy center, all with trained staff ready to help you look and feel good.

-From *The Whisperwood Breeze*, newsletter of Whisperwood Retirement Village

Chapter 24

Later that afternoon, Nancy put on a robe over her pink, flowered bathing suit and strode through the halls to the pool. Hardly anyone used the pool just before dinner, and Nancy expected an undisturbed session of swimming laps. She took a deep breath before opening the glass door to shore up against the heavy chorine smell and then entered the pool area, nodding to the lifeguard on duty.

Instead of the solitude she expected, she surprised Louise and George, paddling companionably side by side. Louise blushed, and George ducked underwater.

Well, well. Nancy pretended not to notice their embarrassment as she took off her robe and gingerly stepped into the pool. The water was so heated that the water and the air seemed to be the same temperature. She swam over to Louise. George swam underwater toward them.

She waited till he surfaced. "You can scratch the Elmos off the list," Nancy reported, keeping her voice down. She glanced at the lifeguard, who looked up for a moment without interest.

George brushed the water out of his eyes and trumpeted. "You took care of Donald for me?"

Louise winced. "Not so loud, George."

George attempted to lower his voice. "I sure didn't find out anything from him except how much he loves model trains. Fascinating down there, I have to admit."

"I told you so." Nancy moved her arms and legs back and forth to keep afloat in the deep end.

George squinted at Nancy. "He told me that Glinda used to come down to the classrooms on her exploring trips. You know how nosy she was."

"If I didn't before, I do now," said Nancy, turning to Louise. "I had lunch with Bernice today."

"Thanks for letting me off the hook." Louise swam to the edge of the pool and added softly, "What did you find out?"

The lifeguard stood, stretched, and walked back toward the pool equipment. He wasn't paying attention to them.

"She's another one who knew Glinda in Alaska and disliked her, and she has no alibi."

"The sheriff should have asked for all of our alibis," said Louise. "He didn't ask me for my alibi. Did he ask you?" She glanced from Nancy to George.

They shook their heads.

Louise wrung water out of her braid. "Haven't seen him back here since that day he talked to the residents."

"He's moved on. Glinda is history," Nancy frowned, "to him. Have you heard anything from Tom?"

George looked up. "Where is he now?"

"Ohio, I think," Louise said casually. "He's staying with a friend in a church-run retirement village where they take a certain percentage every month out of the hefty deposit you put down to live there."

"That's scary," said Nancy. "After awhile you'd have nothing left."

Louise treaded water. "You'd really be stuck. If we wanted to move out of here. . . "

"Always an option," grumbled George.

"We could get most of our deposit back." Louise splashed George and swam away as he swam after her. Nancy ignored them and began her daily laps.

George swam to the steps and climbed out of the pool, followed by Louise. She looked back at Nancy. "I'll stay if you're going to be awhile."

"Don't bother. Been doing this for months." Nancy waved in the direction of the lifeguard. "And he's there."

Louise and George left, and Nancy swam her laps. The lifeguard was talking to someone on a cell phone. She stepped out of the pool. The lifeguard put away the phone.

"You finished?" he said.

Nancy nodded.

"I gotta run down the hall a minute." He strode out of the pool area, through the doors into the hall.

Nancy gradually became aware of the silence and of being alone in a remote part of the building. She had been careful to make sure she wasn't followed to the pool. Meeting Louise and George here had been fortunate, but they were gone now.

Somewhere she could hear water dripping. She finished toweling and slipped on the robe and slippers. She felt someone nearby. She could almost hear him breathing. Surely the lifeguard was on his way back by now.

She stepped to the door out of the pool area, feeling she was being watched. She steeled herself to walk, not run, and tensed her arms. Ahead of her was the long hall past the women's and men's dressing rooms.

As Nancy passed the men's dressing room, she heard the door open and swung round as a towel was thrown over her head, then she was grabbed from behind by an arm around her neck. A strong fist pulled her arm up behind her. He—it had to be a man—began dragging her back toward the pool. Nancy tried to bite the arm around her throat but could not reach it. She felt the panic rise as she screamed but stopped when he wrenched her arm up. He was going to drown her. She gulped. She would be another sad accident.

She clamped her jaw shut. She had one distinct advantage. She was elderly. Her attacker would think she was frail, fragile, weak, and an easy prey. He had a surprise coming.

She tried to shake off the towel to get a look at his face.

"Oh no you don't," her assailant muttered.

He sounded like Perry, but his grip was too strong to allow her to twist around to see his face. Nancy took a deep breath. It was now or never. Suddenly she stepped to the side and sagged as if she had fainted.

"What the..."

She felt him lose his balance and loosen his grip. She pummeled his stomach with her elbow. As his head dropped, she whipped her elbow down into his groin and then up into his chin, pushed him backwards and ran, pulling the towel off her face. She left him doubled up on the ground, groaning in the dim light with his face turned away,

His body was slim, like Perry's, but she couldn't be sure. She turned and ran before he could recover. It wouldn't take him long to catch her.

At the main hall, she found a group heading for dinner and joined them until they reached the elevators. She clutched the robe around her as she trembled with the aftermath of such an attack and rode up with a crowd on the elevator to the fourth floor and Louise's apartment.

When Louise opened the door, Nancy sank into her arms and described the attack. "It sounded like Perry, but I didn't get a look at his face."

"Why Perry?" Louise shook her head. "Why would he be killing us residents?"

Nancy shivered. She had no answer.

Louise hugged Nancy close. "We should never have left

you alone," Louise said. "We should know by now that we've got to stick together and be careful where we go."

***

Life at Whisperwood:
Exercise to Keep Fit

Whisperwood offers a wide range of physical activities to help you stay fit, have fun, and live a long, healthy life. Stop by the gym today and sign up for softball, tennis, swimming, bowling (at the rink in town), or for dance and self-defense classes taught by skilled residents.

-From *The Whisperwood Breeze*, newsletter of Whisperwood Retirement Village

Chapter 25

After she'd calmed down, Nancy and Louise walked down to Amanda's office to report the assault, but Amanda had left for the day. Bryerson and Perry were also out, but Bryerson's assistant was at first shocked, then disbelieving.

"That kind of thing just doesn't happen here," she said.

"Nevertheless, it did happen," said Nancy. "It should be looked into."

"Were you hurt?"

Nancy shook her head.

"Well, then… " The assistant handed Nancy a form. "Just fill that out and I'll give it to Mr. Bryerson first thing in the morning. He'll contact you."

The next day, Bryerson left a note at her door, requesting Nancy to visit his office at her convenience. Nancy found the note when she stopped by to feed Malone. She finished that task, then called Louise.

"Bryerson wants to see me," Nancy said. "I'd like you to be in the lobby in case he tries something."

Louise didn't hesitate. "Be right there. Stay put."

With Louise stationed in the lobby, Nancy strode to Bryerson's office. The assistant ushered Nancy in. Bryerson rose to shake her hand, gestured to a chair, then seated himself behind the massive desk in front of the window. It silhouetted him. Nancy guessed that was the intention. An intimidation tactic.

He picked up the report she'd submitted. "Where was the lifeguard?"

"He saw that I was out of the pool and no one else was there. He had an errand to do, I suppose." Nancy sat back, watching him.

"So someone came down the hall and perhaps scared you?"

"He attacked me," said Nancy firmly.

Bryerson stared at her a moment. "But you don't know who it was."

Nancy shook her head. "I didn't see his face."

"I see." He drummed his fingers on the desk. "I've talked to the lifeguard, who says you were out of the pool area when he left, and the security guards have been alerted to pay special attention to the pool area and to strangers on the grounds." He frowned at her. "We're making every effort to make sure that Whisperwood contnues to be a safe place for all of you."

He paused a moment and seemed to reflect. "Amanda will line up a social worker to talk with you."

Nancy rose. "Thank you." She walked out, leaving Bryerson still sitting at his desk. She passed Perry, standing next to the assistant. He stared at her, and she could feel his eyes on her back as she joined Louise. They took the elevator up to Louise's apartment. Neither spoke till they were inside the door.

"He's going to beef up security around the pool area," Nancy said. "Not interested once he found I couldn't identify the assailant. And he wants me to see a social worker."

"That's a good idea." Louise looked closely at Nancy's face. "Are you feeling okay?"

Nancy shrugged. "I'm fine. Whoever attacked me got the worst of it. Makes me feel as if I'm still in the game."

Louise laughed. "Bryerson and Perry." She poured two cups of coffee. " But why would they sabotage this place?"

"I don't know. We've got a lot more digging to do."

Later that morning, Nancy strode down the hall on the second floor, keeping to the right, and nodding to the frail gentleman in a white robe who clung to his walker as he crept along. She knocked at Number 203 and patted the toy beagle bobbing its head on the display shelf. A moment later, the door opened, and a bleary-eyed woman peered out.

"Good morning, Ms. Richards," said Nancy with a smile. She introduced herself. "I've seen you around and thought I would stop by to visit. I'm also asking for donations to the consignment shop. Is this a good time?"

The woman hesitated, glancing back at her living room, before nodding. "Sure. Come in. I don't get many visitors. Please call me Emma."

Nancy followed her into the living room and took a seat on the sofa. Framed family photos ranged along the top of a credenza, a small table, and a bookcase set along the living room wall.

"Tea? Coffee?" Emma asked as she stepped into the kitchen.

"I'd love a cup of tea," said Nancy. She got up and walked over to study the photos on the credenza. The central one depicted Emma, formally dressed, and a handsome man in a tuxedo. A diamond pendant on a gold chain hung from her neck. Nancy peered closer. It was identical to the necklace Nancy had found in the box with the floppy disk. No mistaking the sunburst design of rubies and diamonds surrounding the central diamond. Nancy looked up to see Emma watching her, tea cup shaking in her hand as she handed it to Nancy.

"That picture was taken at my son's wedding—just before my husband died," Emma said.

Nancy peered more closely at the photo. "What a lovely necklace you're wearing."

Emma nodded sadly. "An anniversary gift . . . from Todd. He was so good to me." Nancy saw the tears spring to Emma's eyes and returned to the sofa. Emma sat alongside.

"Do you ever wear it here?" Nancy watched Emma's response over the teacup.

Emma smiled. "I used to, but I must have misplaced it. I'll have to hunt it down." She sat tensely and sipped her tea. They chatted a few moments about various happenings at Whisperwood, then Emma set down her tea cup. "So you wanted to tell me about the consignment shop?"

"I'm talking to residents about donations of unneeded household items for sale in the shop. The proceeds go to help the people living here. I'll be glad to pick up your donations and take them over to the shop if you'd like." Nancy finished the tea and set the cup on the coffee table.

"Oh." Emma pondered this. "I'll look in my closets and drawers."

"Just call me." Nancy rose to leave. "By the way, if you find that necklace, I'd love to see it."

Emma followed her to the door. "I can't imagine where I must have put it. It'll turn up eventually, I suppose."

***

"When I first came here," said George at dinner that evening, "we maybe had one or two deaths a week, and there'd be a monthly report in the newsletter. Now there seem to be more and more—at least one a day—and the reports come out weekly instead of monthly. I bet they're hoping we won't notice the increase that way. Makes me nervous."

Nancy looked up from her vegetable soup. "I've noticed that too. Mostly long-time residents, the oldest of the old here, which is to be expected, I guess."

Louise snorted. "How about those 'accidental' deaths? Too many of them."

"This place is supposed to keep you young and active," added George, sipping his wine, "so you'd live longer and better. That's why I moved here."

"Speaking of being young and active," Nancy said as she reached for the bread basket, "I was down on the tennis courts this morning, and Craig Kendall showed up in his undershorts."

"Uh oh." Louise passed the butter to Nancy.

"He realized his mistake when he tried to stuff tennis balls into the non-existent pockets of his boxers. He was so embarrassed he ran back to his apartment." Nancy laughed. "Left us a man short on the courts, but we're an easy-going group, and I still got to play."

"I've found myself walking down the hall here with two different shoes on my feet," said Louise, leaning back in her chair and stretching out her legs.

"Me, too," said Nancy. "But I used to do that in my twenties when I had to get up too early. Anyway, I visited Emma Richards this morning. Her name was listed in Glinda's file next to 'Dia.N.'"

"So what did you find out?" asked George, looking at her with interest.

"She had a necklace exactly like the one I found in Glinda's box. Didn't have to prevaricate. First photo I saw had her wearing it, so I asked her about it, and," Nancy paused, "her necklace is missing."

"Wow," whispered Louise. "Do you suppose the necklace we found is really hers?"

"I'd say yes." Nancy pursed her lips.

Taneesha strolled by their table, her arms full of menus. "So how is everyone tonight? They treatin' you right?"

"Just fine." George pushed his soup bowl aside. "Any scuttlebutt on your end?"

"Not much. Sorry, Mr. Burroughs. I know you're looking for stuff for your novel." She winked at him.

Louise groaned.

Taneesha glanced at her and smiled. "By the way, has Ms. Fellows talked with any of you today?"

They looked at each other.

"What would she want from us?" asked Nancy.

"No idea. Heard her mention your names." Taneesha surveyed the dining room. "Oops, gotta run. Talk to you later."

They looked at each other.

"I propose that we all drop in on Amanda Fellows, our charming resident coordinator, tomorrow first thing," said George. "Tweak her a little. Find out what she's up to."

"Don't you think we should talk to Bryerson instead?" Louise asked. "He's the boss."

Nancy shook her head. "Bryerson's too good at stonewalling. We'd learn nothing. Amanda is the weakest link." She laughed. "So to speak."

"And I have some big questions for her," added George. "Lot of strange stuff going on around here."

***

Amanda dragged in an extra chair from the hall as she ushered Nancy, Louise, and George into her office the next morning. "Have a seat. I hope you'll be comfortable. Would you like tea or coffee?"

"We're fine," Louise said, waving aside Amanda's concern.

"Good." Amanda's hands fluttered. "I've got to tell you," she said with a grim expression, "that Glinda Spencer's passing has put a severe strain on all the staff." She looked at them. "As it has on you, I know. We all want to feel safe." She gulped and added, "And then Ms. Carothers's accident. We don't like accidents here, but with your age group…"

Nancy leaned forward with hands clasped. "We're sorry it's been such a problem for you."

Amanda fiddled with a pile of paper clips. "There'd be no concerns at all if Ms. Carothers hadn't raised questions. Some of the residents continue to agitate the sheriff and the staff."

All three stared at her without speaking. George leaned back and folded his arms. "But Anna died a few days ago, so she's no problem for you."

"Oh, she was never a problem." Amanda blushed. "Not really." She fingered the cameo pendant. "We're very sorry about the accident. That's why we encourage our residents to use the elevators." She rushed on. "But both Mr. Bryerson and I would be willing to listen to anyone else who can furnish information that might further explain the . . . accident." She looked down at her desk.

Nancy frowned. "We have no information. We're concerned that such accidents happen."

Louise raised an eyebrow. "We want them to stop."

"Of course. We do too," Amanda said, "Mr. Bryerson, the staff, and I do all we can to make this a pleasant place for you." Her fingers began joining paper clips into a chain.

"Yesterday I was attacked in the pool area." Nancy said. She hoped the blunt statement might push Amanda into a revealing comment. Amanda was such a sweet, gracious person. Did she know anything about what was really going on here?

Amanda only looked at Nancy with distaste. "I heard about that, but really, who would attack you? Why? There's a lifeguard there at all times."

"He'd gone on an errand since I was not in the pool."

"Do you know who the attacker was?" Amanda reached down into a file drawer and brought out a form. "We hire workmen from the area. We screen them carefully, but sometimes mistakes happen. I'll need you to fill out this form completely, and we'll notify the sheriff. But if you can't identify him. . . ." She shrugged. "Meanwhile, I'd appreciate it if you wouldn't repeat this story around. It would frighten the other residents unnecessarily for what was probably a freak incident." She frowned at Nancy.

Nancy took a deep breath to avoid saying the tart response that sprang to her lips. She knew the attack was aimed at her, personally, but she couldn't identify the man who attacked her, and the sheriff would do nothing. Nancy clamped her lips shut. She, George, and Louise were the only ones actually working at finding out what was going on at Whisperwood.

"I know you're busy handling all the turnover of residents." Nancy stopped when she saw that Amanda had dropped the clips and her hands were not fluttering. They were shaking.

Amanda gripped a notebook as if for stability. "It's been busier than ever here. But," she added with emphasis, "we're always busy as I'm sure you understand. Our residents are elderly and, like most facilities of this kind, we do lose a large number each year. That's to be expected, but we have a long waiting list, an excellent marketing team, and a fine reputation." She spoke through her teeth. "We can easily fill the vacancies, and we certainly don't insist that anyone stay here who doesn't want to. You are all free to leave at any time."

Nancy stirred in her chair, thinking that Amanda seemed tired and stressed. That speech sounded as if she had prepared it in advance to answer their questions. Maybe Amanda was trying to answer her own questions.

Amanda looked down at her desk and took a deep breath. "Mr. Bryerson is very concerned about the possibility of liability. He doesn't want anyone getting hurt." She turned to Louise. "I know you'd like to change the landscaping here, but he's afraid of what might happen with the tools you'd need to cut out those bushes and replant. He doesn't see the need since those bushes are very attractive on the grounds."

"They are noxious weeds that . . .," Louise sputtered.

"I'd like to help, but I can't do anything to change his mind." Amanda's voice was firm.

"All right, then," George coughed, "maybe you can tell us about this. A couple of nights a week I hear trucks come in around two or three in the morning. They move slow as if they're loaded with heavy stuff. What's that all about?" he asked, leaning forward with his hands clasped on top of his cane.

"What trucks?" asked Amanda. She was shuffling papers as if anxious for them to leave, but Nancy saw that her hands were still shaking. This kind of confrontation must be very hard for someone so amiable by nature.

"The heavy-duty trucks that are driven under our building."

Amanda looked up at him over her glasses. "I'm sure they were delivering supplies. We bring in everything from food to cleaning materials and paper supplies." She waved her hand. "You have no idea what it takes to run this place. Then, of course, the garbage trucks drive in and out."

George persisted. "In the middle of the night?"

"If you heard them, then yes, in the middle of the night too." Amanda stared down at her papers.

"What about the guard in the basement?" asked Nancy. "Why is he there?"

"In the basement? He's probably down there to protect the residents." Amanda spoke as if there were no doubt. She looked at Nancy. "After your experience," she paused, "I'm sure you appreciate our efforts to protect the residents."

"But he had a gun and looked like he'd use it on one of us," said George, sitting back with his arms folded.

"I'll pass along your concerns to Mr. Bryerson," answered Amanda with a trace of irritation. "Now unless you have something else to report to the sheriff, I'd appreciate your help in quashing the rumors around here." She stood.

"Nancy, I am sorry you had such a bad experience at the pool, and I hope we can find out who attacked you but that is a job for our security force and the sheriff. I have a busy schedule this morning. Thank you for coming in."

She led them to the door and waved them down the hall, her expression forced into a pleasant blankness.

"Let's go to the pub," whispered Nancy as they walked down the hall.

"Yeah, we need to talk about this," said Louise, her anger barely controlled. "She sure knows how to dance for Bryerson."

"She's his dupe," George growled. "I'll work both of them over in my novel."

Nancy shook her head. "She wants to please everyone, and she's a diplomat. That's why she does so well in her position."

Louise's hands were balled into fists. "Diplomat or not," she snapped, "I resent being treated like a kid in day care."

They sat down at a table in the pub and signaled to the server for coffee.

"What concerns me," said Nancy, "is that she will now alert Bryerson to our concerns and interest in the late-night trucks and the other odd stuff that's going on around here."

"What do you think he'll do?" asked George.

Nancy looked at him. "I don't know."

"Have you found out anything about Bryerson yet?" asked Louise.

"Yes, I have." George tapped his fingers on the table. "But I'm not sure what it means." He leaned back and stuck his thumbs in his belt. "Bryerson started out with a company that manufactured fertilizer from waste materials, then he picked up a chain of dry cleaning shops, and about ten years ago, he bought two hundred acres of land here—a reclaimed strip mine in the middle of West Virginia so he got it cheap—and built Whisperwood on top of it. He's gotten awards from geriatric associations for the design of this place, you know."

"That's one reason why I moved here," said Nancy "Besides, I love West Virginia."

"Me, too," said Louise. "And of course, the locals idolize Whisperwood."

"Do you suppose there are mining tunnels under this building?" Nancy peered at the floor as if she might see through it. "Wouldn't they have filled them in or blocked them as part of reclaiming the land."

"I don't know." George peered around the room. "They must have had to bulldoze this place flat to build on it. Could explain the guard, I guess. Bryerson wouldn't want any of us winding up in the bottom of some abandoned shaft."

"Should be a cheaper way of solving that problem than hiring guards for it," said Nancy.

Louise flicked her braid. "Strip mining's done on the surface, anyway."

"I'll keep digging into Bryerson's activities." George leaned back in his chair, hands in his pockets. "I know there's something funny going on here."

"One thing's for sure," added Nancy. "Whoever they are, they're watching us."

***

Life at Whisperwood:
Maintenance Work Scheduled

Some areas of the buildings may be closed temporarily for routine maintenance. This will include the basement crafts and class rooms and the pool. We ask all of you to be patient as we carry out this work. We apologize for the inconvenience.

-From *The Whisperwood Breeze*, newsletter of Whisperwood Retirement Village

Chapter 26

The next morning, Nancy, George, and Louise met again in Fitz's apartment around his card table. George brought his own box of tissues. He looked at them apologetically. "Allergies really kicking in." He glanced at the accummulated dust on the boxes stacked in a corner.

Fitz set a pitcher of water and four glasses on the table. "I can manage water," he laughed, "even if I don't cook."

"Next time I'll bring donuts," said Louise.

George sniffled.

"I'm still watching the threads on my door and desk. Nothing has moved so far." Nancy picked up the box of candy that she'd brought in. "Anybody get one of these?"

George and Louise shook their heads. "Looks good," said Fitz.

"This was left on my display shelf this morning. No card." Nancy frowned.

Louise snorted. "Reminds me of cyanide in the Tylenol."

"Me too. I checked with Amanda, and she knows nothing about it." Nancy laughed. "Thinks I have a secret admirer."

"I'm an admirer," put in Fitz, "but that's no secret. I'm more of a flowers man anyway."

George waved a hand. "You'd know if I gave you candy." He coughed. "Not that I don't admire you, you know."

Nancy saw Louise's grimace as she put the box aside and picked up her copy of the printouts.

"Wait a minute." George tapped his cane. "What about that candy? Can't we have it analyzed or something?"

"Where? The Whisperwood CSI lab?" Louise said.

"I checked the candy," said Nancy, "and maybe some of the pieces have been tampered with. But maybe not. I'm not eating them," She looked at the others. "Not taking the stairs anymore either. Or going to the pool. I hate to say it, but I'm scared."

Louise shivered. "Me too. We've all got to be careful. More than ever."

George picked up his printouts and waved them. "So what are we going to do about this?"

Nancy shuffled the papers. She put on her reading glasses. "We're all pretty sure Glinda was taking advantage of people's weaknesses here to rob or blackmail them."

Louise looked up from doodling. "Everybody thinks Whisperwood is so secure. A lot of people don't even lock their doors, and even if they do, the locks are simple."

Fitz nodded. "I knew the lock was flimsy, but I didn't worry about it. Gated community, security all over the place."

George sat back, his thumbs in his belt. "We all have our habits. We four, we go to dinner at five. And we do that every single night. Whoever wants to break into our apartments knows when the best time would be and also that they would have at least an hour to canvass the place and take whatever they wanted."

"No one knows we have any of this information." Louise held up her printouts. "I'm wondering how the thefts tie in with Glinda's murder. And Anna's." She looked at Nancy. "And the attacks on you."

"We also need to watch Bryerson and Perry." Nancy thought a moment. "We ought to look at their files."

"Whoa," said George. "That's getting scary—and illegal."

"Perhaps so, but we may find a way as we learn more." Nancy

looked at each of the other three. "Agreed?"

"Yes ma'am. I don't see what else we can do right now," George said, "except keep on snooping." He sneezed into a tissue and reached for his pill bottle.

"Watch out for the booby traps." Nancy straightened her papers and rose.

***

That afternoon, Nancy sat in the rocking chair on the front patio drowsily watching the afternoon sun cast the building's lengthening shadow down the lawn in front of her. Her thoughts were anything but restful. Glinda died two weeks ago, and so far they had gotten no closer to who killed her. Most people at Whisperwood had already forgotten Glinda and were going on with their lives unaware.

Nancy sat up and opened her eyes. She couldn't stop adding, I suppose that's the way it will be when I die. Sometimes depressing thoughts were hard to keep at bay. She scanned the patio for someone to chat with and get her mind off this topic. At the far end sitting on a bench with her back against the rail, sat Bernice, staring at Nancy. When their eyes connected, Bernice hoisted herself up on her walker and hobbled over to join Nancy. Bernice's thin legs and frail body, encased in clothes that hung loosely, seemed barely able to support her even while she leaned on the walker.

"No scooter today?" Nancy asked.

"I've given up the power scooter," Bernice said. "Trying to gain strength." She smiled. "I've been waiting for you to wake up." Bernice's head had a slight tremor, but her hands were steady.

"I wasn't asleep. You could have come over and tapped me on the shoulder—or said something." Nancy pulled over a chair. "Sit?"

"No. I'm heading back to my apartment."

"Has your son visited yet?"

"Not yet. Couple more weeks." Bernice coughed. "I would like to show you something in my apartment."

"Sure. Should I come now?"

"Yes. It's important."

Nancy stood. "Let's go then."

Nancy stepped slowly to match Bernice's pace as she crept along into the building. Amanda joined them in the elevator. Out of the corner of her eye, Nancy studied Amanda in faint surprise. She did not seem as poised and confident as she usually did. She looked tired and she fidgeted with her keys. Twice, Nancy caught Amanda darting glances in her direction and wondered what was on her mind.

As Nancy and Bernice stepped out into the hall, Amanda seemed to reach a decision. "Nancy, I need to talk with you about the newsletter. May I stop by your apartment later today?"

"Of course," Nancy said. "I'll be back soon."

She took Bernice's arm, and they continued on down the hall, but Nancy felt Amanda's eyes on her back as the elevator door closed. Nancy turned her attention to Bernice who hesitated at each step and glanced both ways down the hall before unlocking her door. Nancy followed her into the sparsely furnished apartment.

"Can I help you?" asked Nancy. Her shoes slid on the polished wooden floor.

"No, thanks. Help yourself. Soft drinks in the refrigerator."

"I'm fine, thank you."

Bernice saw Nancy glance at the floor. "I don't like rugs. Too many allergies." Bernice sat down on a couch covered in plain brown fabric.

Nancy nodded and sat next to Bernice. "So what is this all about?"

"I want you to go into my bedroom, open the middle drawer of my bureau, and bring out the package that's in there."

She did as Bernice asked and returned with a heavy, rectangular package wrapped in newspaper and tied with a string.

"Open it," said Bernice, gesturing to scissors on the kitchen countertop.

Nancy brought the scissors back to the sofa and laid the package in her lap. She cut the string, unwrapped the newspaper, and stared at the object inside. "The boundary plaque."

"Yes, the famous boundary plaque." Bernice shivered.

Nancy instinctively pulled her hands back to avoid touching it. She saw no blood stains on this side. She looked up to see Bernice watching her. "Did you touch it?"

Bernice shuddered. "I unwrapped it, saw what it was, and rewrapped it. Why?"

"Fingerprints." Nancy glanced at Bernice. "But how did you get it?"

Bernice shrugged and tears came to her eyes. "I don't know how it got here. It was hidden in my bureau, all wrapped up like you found it, when I came back from dinner last night." She brushed aside the tears. "Sorry. I've been so worried."

Nancy waited a moment before softly asking, "Do you have any idea who put it there?"

"If I knew that, I wouldn't need you, would I?" The old truculence returned. "The next thing you know the police will want to search my apartment, and they'll find the plaque and then they'll haul me off to jail." Bernice bit off each word and spit it out. "I didn't steal it, Nancy."

"Of course not." Nancy reached over to pat Bernice's arm.

Bernice tossed aside Nancy's hand. "Then they'll look into my background and that will be it. Everyone will know I used to be a hooker—even my son. No one will believe that this is a frame-up."

Nancy put her arm around Bernice. "All that stuff in your past was long ago. No one will have any record or memory of it."

Nancy studied her. Bernice was too frail and disabled to have stolen the plaque or to have killed Glinda, even though she did have a motive. Nancy's eyes dropped to the plaque. "We have to make sure the sheriff doesn't find the plaque here. Whoever planted it is probably going to tip him off."

"That's what I thought." A tear dribbled down Bernice's cheek. "Or I might be next to die." Her hands shook.

"No one would kill you over the boundary plaque."

Bernice's eyelashes fluttered. "They killed Glinda."

Nancy nodded. Maybe Glinda had found out who took the plaque and cornered them. But where did her Tiffany lamp go? And her computer. Gwen Fowler's accidental death and her missing vase flitted through Nancy's mind. She stared at the wall as odd bits of information fitted into a pattern.

"Nancy? Are you all right?" asked Bernice, tugging at her arm.

Nancy shook off these disquieting thoughts and took Bernice's hand. "I'm going to tell you something, but you have to keep this to yourself."

Bernice sat up. "If you can help me, I'll do whatever I can to help you."

Nancy nodded. "Louise, George, and I have been looking into Glinda's death, but we can't prove anything yet. We're not sure how the plaque is involved."

Bernice nodded. "A lot of us are scared about what happened to Glinda and to Anna, too. What is going on here?"

"I would like to call my friends to come over." Nancy nodded at the phone.

Bernice dabbed at her eyes and frowned. "But then they'll find out all about this—and about me. I've lived a good life and now it will all be ruined. Everyone will know."

"George and Louise don't need to know any more than you want to tell them. They can keep their mouths shut. This is a difficult situation, and they can help."

Bernice sat silently for a moment, her eyes on her hands folded in her lap. At last she looked up. "All right then," she said, doubt on her face and in her voice.

Fifteen minutes later, the four were staring at the plaque. "None of us has touched it so it may have useful fingerprints," Nancy said, "although I doubt it."

Louise flicked her braid. "Maybe latent blood stains."

Nancy nodded. "I propose to hide it in my apartment. You can all be eyewitnesses in case the sheriff decides to search my apartment for any reason."

Louise tapped her cane and nodded. "Yeah, get it out of here. That'll stop whoever had the bright idea of planting it on Bernice." She glanced over at the silent woman huddled on the sofa. "Why do you suppose the thief did that?"

"It's an odd item," Nancy said.

"You said it." Louise laughed.

"Hard to get rid of," Nancy tapped it lightly with her fingers. "Hard to figure out its value, and it could link the thief directly to Glinda's murder. He needed to unload it fast and chose Bernice because she's usually a loner." She reached over and patted Bernice on the back. "He didn't know we're her friends."

Bernice blinked.

"Pardon me," broke in George, "All this is just speculation. What if Bernice is trying to frame you?" He looked at Nancy. "I have her down as a possible suspect, but this means that we all believe Bernice's story?" He turned and bowed to Bernice. "Beg your pardon, ma'am."

"I'm telling the truth," said Bernice, leaning away from him against the sofa.

"If I take the plaque," Nancy said, "it keeps Bernice, Glinda's family, and the police from being manipulated by someone here who may be the real guilty party. Even if they say Glinda died by accident, there's still the question of theft."

Nancy turned to Bernice. "I'd like to wrap the package in a coat or jacket to be as inconspicuous as possible. George, you and Louise can run interference if necessary."

"There's an old jacket in the foyer closet." Bernice pointed toward the front door.

George hobbled over to the closet and retrieved a faded blue jacket. "This one?"

Bernice nodded. Nancy rewrapped the plaque in the newspaper and then covered it with the jacket.

"Don't you worry about this," Nancy said to Bernice, still sitting on the sofa with mournful eyes as they left. "We've got it all under control."

"Maybe," said George under his breath.

Later, at dinner, Nancy snapped her fingers. "Darn it," she said to George and Louise, "what with all the excitement about the boundary plate, I completely forgot that Amanda wanted to see me this afternoon."

***

Life at Whisperwood: Register to Vote Now

Resident Louise Owens has set up a voter registration table in the lobby with all the necessary forms and information you need to register to vote in this county and state. Make sure your elected officials respond to your needs and requests. Register to vote now!

-From *The Whisperwood Breeze*, newsletter of Whisperwood Retirement Village

Chapter 27

Nancy ran into Amanda the next morning in the lobby and apologized for not meeting her the day before.

Amanda glanced over at Bryerson's office. "That's all right. It was nothing. I'll check with you later."

She moved on quickly, and Nancy strolled out the entrance, meeting May Brooks on her way in. May held out a hand and stopped Nancy. "Did you get my surprise?" she asked.

"Surprise?"

"Yeah. The box of candy. My son sent it to me, but I can't eat sweets anymore. Dropped it on your shelf." May grinned.

"You gave me the candy." Nancy felt the relief well up from deep inside. "Yes. Thank you. I wondered who had given it to me."

"Probably disappointed it was me and not some secret admirer." May laughed and went on into the building.

Nancy smiled to herself as she walked across the broad lawns of Whisperwood to the picnic table. She looked back at the windows of Bryerson's office and saw the draperies move. She nodded at George and turned to Louise, already sitting at the table.

"He's watching us," Nancy said, jerking her head slightly toward Bryerson's office. "Don't look."

Louise kept her eyes on the table. "Do you suppose he has one of those long-distance listening devices?"

George dropped his newspaper and reached under the table to pick it up. "Don't see any bugs under here." He brushed aside an ant. "Except that one."

Nancy pretended to laugh. "Act like we're just having a good time."

Louise laughed too. "Is the plaque hidden away?" she asked.

"Yes. I'm waiting to see if the sheriff shows up." Nancy eyes strayed toward Bryerson's office.

"But why choose Bernice as the victim?" Louise laughed again, for the benefit of anyone watching them.

"She looks like a victim, doesn't she? I'd pick her to be the fall guy. She's a loner, too," said George, his face buried in the newspaper. "You two and me, we stick together. Whoever did this knows we'd protect each other."

"The way gossip flies around this place, everyone would know about it," Nancy added. "I don't like being so visible out here." Nancy looked back at Bryerson's office. "I feel like Bryerson's watching our every move."

"Next time let's meet over by the tennis courts or the duck pond," said George. "They're around back and the picnic tables are behind bushes."

"Yeah, the multiflora rose bushes, you mean." Louise laughed, but her eyes were angry. Nancy patted her on the back.

"I can't pretend to laugh like you gals," said George. "I'm supposed to be an old grouch. It'd ruin my reputation."

They walked back to the building and separated. Nancy stopped by Amanda's office, but she was out. Nancy left a note with the receptionist.

Later, she called Amanda, but the voice mail receiver was on. Again, Nancy left a message. The next day, Nancy still could not find Amanda, and her messages had not been answered. "She's in Morgantown," the receptionist said curtly.

Nancy walked over to the staff office where she pulled together the newsletter on the computer. Harry wandered in with a cup of coffee. "Working today?" he asked, a grin on his face.

"I needed to catch up." She looked at him. "By the way, where is Amanda?"

Harry waved his hand. "She went to Morgantown. She has family there, I believe. Should be back tomorrow." He walked on past Nancy and into his office.

Nancy nodded and returned to the papers on her desk. The next day, she walked by Amanda's office just before lunch. It was still closed, and the receptionist shook her head. "Not back yet."

Nancy stepped over to Harry's office and tapped on the door. She heard "Enter," so she opened the door and poked her head in. He was sitting at his desk, scowling as he tapped a pencil. His brows were drawn down in an angry "V."

"Any word from Amanda?" she asked.

"Yes," he snapped. "She's not coming back."

"She decided to stay in Morgantown?" Nancy walked into the office and gazed down at Harry.

"Doesn't care how she leaves us in the lurch." He spit out the words. "Now I've got to find a replacement and in a hurry too."

"But what happened?" Nancy asked.

"She up and called Bryerson from Morgantown and told him her family needed her there." Harry threw a wad of paper against the wall. "Never mind that we need her here. Forget the two weeks' notice. Now what am I going to do?"

"But she was so professional," Nancy said. "I can't believe that she'd leave like that."

"Neither can I," said Harry. "But you don't see her around here anywhere, do you?" He got up, retrieved the paper wad, and tossed it into the waste basket.

***

Life at Whisperwood:
Staff Appreciation Day

Every year, we ask residents to remember the hard and caring work of the staff and to take a few minutes to offer a thank you. Whisperwood has a no-tipping policy, but envelopes will be placed in every resident's mail cubby for a special once-a-year monetary gift contribution that will be shared equally among all hourly employees and given to them on Labor Day. We hope you will be generous in recognizing the excellent service you receive all year. Also be sure to thank them in person.

-From *The Whisperwood Breeze*, newsletter of Whisperwood Retirement Village

Chapter 28

Nancy spotted George as he straightened his bright red bow tie and in his rambling pace, walked toward her and Louise outside by the duck pond behind the residents' building.

"We've got to do a better job at detecting, Nancy," he said. "How long can we hold out against whoever is killing the residents here?"

They trekked down to the picnic table by the pond. "We've got to." Her voice was tense.

Louise nodded. In one hand she held binoculars to her eyes as she scanned the tree canopies. In the other, she kept her cane off the grass since it sank into the ground if she leaned on it. She stumbled along and collapsed onto the wooden bench. "Nice they put a picnic table here, too. Can't see the entrance or Bryerson's office."

Nancy looked over toward the building and the blank, curtained windows of the resident apartments.

George nodded. "More private like." He sat down opposite Louise.

Nancy slid in beside her. "Someone did come into my apartment last night." She spoke through gritted teeth.

Louise looked up in alarm. "Did he find the plaque?"

Nancy shook her head. "I wrapped it in aluminum foil, put it in a large flat cake pan and baked a cake on top of it."

Louise laughed. George whistled.

Nancy folded her arms. "Whoever it was went through my desk drawers but didn't take anything. Probably just snooping to find out what we're up to. Stirred up the cat. Look around for someone with scratches."

Poor Malone. Nancy had to stay an extra hour in her apartment to call him out from under the bed and comfort him. And then he had to be coaxed to eat his breakfast. The intruder had upset him, but Nancy knew from experience that Malone could take care of himself. Coaxing him to eat was a new behavior. The bizarre thought crossed Nancy's mind that maybe Malone missed her.

Louise put down the binoculars to stare at Nancy. "Good ol' Malone, but what if you'd been there? We'd be planning your memorial service now."

Nancy nodded. "We foiled them again, didn't we? Thank goodness I'm staying in your apartment, Louise." She pursed her lips. "The sheriff did search Bernice's apartment yesterday afternoon, you know." She looked at Louise. "I was working on the newsletter in Harry's office when he showed up. Said they'd had an anonymous tip, and he sounded annoyed."

"We expected it." George hoisted himself onto the other bench across from Nancy and Louise and hung his cane on the table. He reached down to pluck a blade of grass and chewed on it.

Louise grabbed the blade of grass. "I wouldn't do that if I were you. You don't know what they put on these lawns."

Nancy glanced around at the bright greenness around her. "Looks too good to be true, doesn't it? The lawn looks more like Astroturf than grass." She turned as she heard a voice shout her name. Fitz was running toward them.

"Hi, luvies," he said, out of breath.

George raised an eyebrow, and Nancy waved a greeting as Fitz joined the group.

He wore a white dress shirt tucked into his jeans, and the tool belt added an odd touch. He was still panting hard, but he held up a hand. "I beg your pardon, but I saw you heading here from the patio." He looked around. "I say, nice place for a picnic table." He turned back to Nancy. "Anything wrong with Malone?"

"He's fine," Nancy said. "Why do you ask?"

"Heard a lot of snarling and hissing from your apartment last night." He shrugged. "All kinds of strange stuff going on around here. The latest rumor," Fitz took a seat, "is that Glinda had so much cash hidden in her apartment that Cary—that's her son—had to take it out in a plastic sack."

Nancy laughed and shook her head in mock disbelief. "Probably somebody saw Cary's wife taking Glinda's odious stuffed cats to the trash chute. Her sons have been moving her things out of the apartment. When I visited them, they hadn't found much of value." She paused.

"Of course, they kept the door closed while they packed things, so who knows what they've found since I was there."

"Yeah," added George. "Especially since she stole our shelf items, too—everybody heard about that." He reached over and brushed an ant off the table.

Fitz shook his head. "And I worried that I would be bored living here."

Nancy laughed. "Not so far."

Louise grumbled. "If you ever weakened and did anything for Glinda, it would cost you something."

"And now we've got to consider Amanda as well," Nancy said. "Did you know she's not here any more?"

"Haven't seen her around," said Louise, studying the shrubs around them. She put the binoculars back to her eyes and trained them on the residents' windows.

"I try to avoid her," added George, "if I can. Too persnickety. Anyway, she had her eyes on me." George pretended to shudder. "So what happened to her?"

"Harry says she quit and went home to Morgantown." Nancy fiddled with a twig from the honeysuckle bush. "Said her family needed her. He was annoyed."

"I guess so. Lot to do around this place," George said.

Louise set down the binoculars. "Wait a minute, now." She

shook her head. "I don't think so. She came from Jacksonville, Florida. That's where she got her experience working with retired folks. She told me her parents or grandparents or somebody had retired down there."

"I suppose her kids could be in Morgantown. Did she have any?" Nancy looked at them.

"Don't know," said Louise.

George shook his head.

"I'm afraid something has happened to her," said Nancy.

Louise tugged at her braid. "We should get her address and phone number and contact her. Just to reassure us, I mean."

"I don't see Harry or the staff here," George frowned, "giving out that kind of information."

Nancy looked up. "I'll do an Internet search on her name. Wish I'd had the Internet fifty years ago." She brushed aside an ant. "I have contacts in Morgantown, too," she added, "I could ask them to stop by Whisperwood's marketing office there and inquire about her."

Louise folded her arms on the table. "She could be staying with relatives. In fact, if the story is true, then she probably is."

"We've got some good ideas here," Nancy said. "I'm worried because she wanted to talk to me a couple of days ago. She seemed uneasy—maybe even scared."

"She seemed nervous when we talked to her," said Louise.

"I thought so too." Nancy tapped her finger on the table and looked off at the mountains in the distance. "We need to get rid of our preconceived ideas and look at the whole picture with a fresh view." She paused. "If we do that, what do we have?"

"Glinda killed with the Russian boundary plaque," said George.

"Wait a minute." Nancy held up her hand. "Glinda was killed by being hit on the head with a flat object. Or as the sheriff would have it, she fell on a hard, flat object, but the boundary plaque was stolen before she was killed."

"So," said Fitz, "the two events are not necessarily connected."

"And the person who stole the plaque," added Louise, "may not be the person who killed Glinda, if she was killed. But the person who killed Glinda also killed Anna and may be after us."

"That's right. But who would want to steal the boundary plaque?" Nancy looked at them and waited. She saw only blank faces. "I'll tell you who. Simon Smythe. He knew what it was and he knew its value. He's an antique collector and a jeweler. He had a grudge against Glinda and was connected to her somehow. Maybe he felt entitled or even honor-bound to take the plaque." She sat back.

"But then who hid it in Bernice's room?" asked George.

"Maybe Simon felt the plaque was too hot to keep in his room." Nancy thought a moment. "He could have panicked when the rumors began about murder."

"But why Bernice, of all people?" George said.

"I've wondered about that." Nancy folded her arms on the table. "That plaque is the only item on Glinda's list actually known to be stolen. Glinda told everyone."

"Except the sheriff," Louise put in.

"Thought she could find the culprit herself," said George. "She was pigheaded."

Louise looked up. "Simon could have hidden it in a safety deposit box in Morgantown or wherever he went on his travels. That plaque is worth a fortune."

Nancy nodded. "Maybe someone else took the plaque." Her eyes gazed across the rows of blank windows facing them as if the answer might magically appear. "My vote is on Perry. I still think he was the one who attacked me at the pool."

"But why?" asked George. "And was the attack connected to Glinda's murder? Maybe he's a rapist or something."

"Thanks, George," said Louise. She also stared at the building. "We should put this question aside for now. Let's take another look at our list of suspects," she said.

"Okay," agreed Nancy, pulling a crumpled paper out of her pocket. She smoothed it out on the table and pointed to the names listed on it. "Barbara and Donald have alibis. Bernice is probably out of the running, too, since she was terrified about the plaque."

George frowned. "Uh huh. Doesn't necessarily mean she didn't do it," he put in. "She may be trying to be clever."

Nancy glanced at him. "That's true," she said, "but somehow I don't believe it. She is so disabled."

Fitz sat sideways at the end of the bench. He pulled a screwdriver out of his tool belt and threw it into the dirt like a knife. "So who else do we have?"

"You," said George, looking pointedly at the screwdriver.

"You don't need to consider me at all, luvies" said Fitz. He retrieved the screwdriver and wiped a hand across his brow. "I was in Baltimore, don't you know? Arguing with the moving van people. I've got an iron-clad alibi, as you people say. In books that would make me the most likely suspect, but really, I am super-nice guy. I like birds and flowers . . ." He grinned.

"He certainly does," said Nancy, smiling at him. "Anyway, I do think Fitz is on our side here. And I don't think we can put Simon out of the picture yet. Taneesha told us she saw him giving Glinda some money at dinner."

"He probably bought one of her antiques." George snapped his fingers. "Or maybe she even sold him the boundary plaque, and then had to invent a cover story for why it wasn't on her shelf." He frowned. "Course that doesn't make much sense either."

Nancy shrugged. "Most people we've considered as possible suspects don't seem to pan out for one reason or another, but there are two people we need to look at more closely."

"Who's that?" asked George.

Nancy sat back and looked at them. "Bryerson and Perry. If this place is a time bomb, then Bryerson is responsible and Glinda knew about it." She gestured in the direction of Bryerson's office on the other side of the building. "Anyone know if he's here today?"

"Bryerson? Haven't seen him," said Louise, "but his henchman is always under foot somewhere." She stared at the thick honeysuckle bushes lining the drive.

"Hardly anyone comes down here," said George, "except maybe the staff on their lunch breaks."

"Surely they wouldn't bother with us," Fitz added.

The others looked at him.

Finally, Louise said, "Whoever they are, they got rid of Glinda and Anna. Maybe Amanda. And they've tried to get Nancy. Our saving grace so far is that we usually stick together." She waved aside a green fly hovering off her nose. "And we're so old nobody expects us to know anything, do anything, hear anything—course they may be right there—or have any power at all. They expect to shove us around. And so far they've been right."

"They haven't seen Nancy on the tennis court," said George. He acted out a tennis swing.

"Or Fitz," Nancy added. "For weeks we've been saying that something funny is going on around here, haven't we? I mean, beyond the deaths of Glinda and Anna."

Fitz and George nodded. Louise sat up straighter. "I told you about Glinda coming out of Bryerson's office a couple of days before she was killed." Louise shrugged. "Doesn't mean much."

"No, but we should keep it in mind." Nancy held up a hand. "I'm wondering how many accidental deaths we've had here in the last several years. Who died? Did they have anything worth taking?" She thought of Gwen Fowler. "Was anything missing after they died?"

She glanced at Fitz. "And another thing. Fitz found out that a guarded steel door in the basement leads to a tunnel underneath our building. I picked the lock on it and opened that door, but the guard shooed me away. What is all that about?"

"That guard scares me," said Louise. "Don't see him often in the halls, but when I do, he acts like a thug and looks mean."

"I've seen him too," George added. "Scary."

Fitz sat back. "He's not a regular security guard. They're all in uniform, and they're nice people. Caring, you know. Helpful. Not like those brutes in the basement."

"Guards aren't needed. All they have to do is to keep that door locked." George sat back. "Anyway, they took care of that door a few days ago."

"How'd they do that?" asked Louise.

George blew aside a flying insect. "They closed up that end of the hall with a new wall and a new door. Locked, of course. Sign on the door says, 'Electrical Equipment. High Voltage. Keep Out.'"

"Yeah, I noticed that myself," said Fitz. "I thought for a minute I was going nuts."

"Electrical equipment, my foot." Louise snorted. "They must need a door from the hall into the tunnel for some reason and don't want anyone snooping around. So now they've double-doored it and put up a big, scary sign."

Fitz nodded. "That's how I figure it. They think we'll forget all about that steel door. Give 'em a few months or a year or so, and they'll be right."

"I'm not buying it," George growled. "We'll have to tackle those doors, but first tell them our idea, Nancy."

She looked up. "George and I have a plan about the trucks."

"Yeah. They're heavy-duty trucks, carrying barrels, some of them." George cleared his throat. "Barrels of what is what I'd like to know. They drive under the building."

"I hear them too," Louise pushed out her jaw. "Saw them one night."

Nancy tapped her pencil on the table. "We asked Amanda about them, remember? She brushed us off. She said they were bringing in supplies."

They stared at the table silently, then Fitz spoke, looking at George. "So what's your plan?"

"Hard to keep on track with this bunch," George said. "Now here's what I'm thinking. First, none of the trucks had any signs on them. I looked. And I couldn't see the license tags, but I would think Bryerson would buy supplies locally or from Morgantown."

"It might be cheaper in other states. Or lower taxes." Fitz grinned and swatted at a yellow jacket that had taken an interest in his white, wavy hair.

"They're still supposed to pay the West Virginia sales tax," growled George, keeping a wary eye on the yellow jacket.

"But of course, luv." Fitz winked at Nancy.

George pretended to whisper. "So we stand out by the road in shifts and get the license number, make, and any other information we can off the trucks that come in." He looked at them. " Also, we find out where they go on the campus."

Fitz grinned. "I like it. It's about time we did something. What nights do they come in?"

"Tuesday and Thursday nights, usually." George glanced at his watch. "Course what I mean is, really early Wednesday and Friday mornings."

"And they come in around two or three? We can start tonight. I'll take the first shift from one-thirty until three." Louise looked at George. "George, you could join me."

"Yeah. And I'll bring insect repellent."

"Okay," said Nancy, glancing around for possible eavesdroppers. "Fitz and I will take the three to four-thirty shift."

"That should cover it," George said. "I never hear those trucks after four a.m."

"Wait a minute." Fitz held up a hand. "What about the dogs?"

"The dogs." Nancy looked at the other three.

"The dogs. Ham and Eggs." Louise thought a moment. "They're around the curve so they won't be able to see us, and if we're real quiet, they won't hear us. They don't bark at the cars that come through, and they know me." She glanced at Nancy. "And Nancy too."

"Louise and I take them on walks and give them treats," Nancy said. "I don't think we need to worry about the dogs."

"You do?" said Fitz, admiration on his face. "They scare me."

Louise snorted. "They're just pussy cats."

"So to speak," added George.

"Okay. Then we'll meet at the pub tomorrow for lunch and compare notes," Nancy added. "This is just the beginning. We also have to find out where the trucks go and what they're bringing in."

"Or carrying out," said George.

"You say there's a loading dock?" Nancy asked George.

Louise looked up. "There's one between the buildings over by the dining room. No secret about that, and I've seen trucks there during the day. There's also a ramp down to some garage doors at the side of our building. Hard to spot unless you're looking for it."

"I'll bet that's where the trucks we're concerned about go," said

Nancy. "I'll walk by that entrance on the way back."

Louise stood. "Don't go looking around alone." She flashed her cane. "Maybe I remember some karate." She swatted a fly. "Damn bugs," she added.

Nancy nodded. "This is nothing. Wait until tonight."

***

Life at Whisperwood: Caution Required

Whisperwood Administrator Harry Doyle reminds all residents that storage and supply cupboards are for the use of staff only. Please respect all "No Trespassing" signs posted on the campus. They are for your protection.

-From *The Whisperwood Breeze*, newsletter of Whisperwood Retirement Village

Chapter 29

At night, the asphalt drive up to the Whisperwood buildings gleamed under the halogen lights glowing on alternating poles from the gates. Nancy and Fitz scurried along in the shadows of the rose and honeysuckle shrubs to meet George and Louise, hiding near the ailanthus tree and picnic bench.

"Never thought I'd be thankful for honeysuckle," said Louise, brushing herself off. She peered at Nancy in the shadows. "The trucks haven't come through yet."

"I feel all itchy and bit up." George waved his cane over his head. "Probably got ticks, too." The white shirt he was wearing reflected the lights, making him stand out among the foliage.

Louise looked at George, shook her head and scratched her arm. She was wearing jungle-colored fatigues that blended into the shrubbery. She nodded. "Yeah, Nancy, Fitz. Be sure you check for ticks when you get back in. Lyme disease ain't no fun. Hope you brought insect repellent."

Fitz nodded. "We sprayed before we came out here, luv."

"Good." Louise nodded. "We'll see you at lunch tomorrow . . . today, I guess."

Fitz stared up at the sky. "West Virginia's supposed to be a dark sky state, but I'll bet you can see these street lights on the moon."

"Shhhh," said Nancy, "we don't want to wake anyone. Or the dogs." She threw a couple of cushions on the ground. Her black slacks and long-sleeved black shirt made her look like a shadow. "Might as well get comfortable." She waved at Louise and George, already heading up the hill to a side door for residents.

Fitz swatted at something in the air. "I'm glad we sprayed with insect repellent. I can hear those mosquitoes smacking their lips all around me." He pulled the hood of his black sweatshirt over his white hair.

"Yeah." Nancy slapped her arm.

They waited in the dark, listening to the buzzing night sounds. In the distance, a barred owl hooted. Somewhere near them, another owl answered.

"Wish I'd brought some coffee," said Fitz, after a few minutes.

"Me too, but listen." In the distance they could hear the rumble of trucks and shifting of gears echoing from mountain to mountain. "So quiet before, except for the bugs," said Fitz. "Those trucks sound like a thundering herd coming up here."

Nancy nodded. "The crickets and frogs have stopped singing. I can't imagine how people can sleep through this."

"Only sounds loud to us out here," said Fitz. "Most of the residents keep their windows closed and are half deaf anyway."

They scrunched forward under the bushes to come as close as they could get to the road without being seen. Nancy pulled aside a branch and spotted headlights bouncing around a curve way down the road.

"Here they come." Fitz sat down and brought out a pen, piece of paper, and a penlight, turning it on and shielding it with his hand.

Nancy peered down toward the gate. The attendant hastened to open the gates and waved the trucks through. They rumbled up the drive. Nancy held her own pencil and notepad ready.

They watched as two trucks lumbered toward them, hesitated as the drivers shifted gears, then again crept forward. The trucks struggled to climb the hill. This time, Nancy was grateful for the lights on the drive. She could see the license plates—both from

Pennsylvania—but she couldn't make out the numbers as the behemoths crawled by.

Fitz crept closer to the road. Nancy edged along behind him, then pulled herself forward to stoop alongside Fitz. They watched the trucks continue up the road and then turn left and disappear around the side of the building.

"You got the license numbers?" Fitz asked, glancing back at her.

She shook her head. "Still too far away for me, and the street lights overhead put the tags in the trucks' shadows. Couldn't read them."

Fitz stood, brushing off his shirt. "Neither could I."

Nancy stood beside him. "Did you see any signs on the trucks?"

"No. All unmarked. Anonymous," whispered Fitz. "Like George said. If you ask me, that's a sure sign they're up to no good."

Nancy tugged at his sleeve. "Let's see where they go."

They hunched low and slunk along the shrubbery after the trucks, then turned the corner by the side of the building. Nancy stopped and backed into Fitz. She held one hand up and pointed with the other. The trucks seemed to be waiting, engines running, at the top of a ramp down to a garage door. As Nancy and Fitz watched, silently swatting the mosquitoes that swarmed around them, the garage door opened and the trucks lumbered through.

"Would you look at that?" whispered Fitz. "That's where they go. What do you suppose they have in those trucks?"

They waited. "I've got an idea," Nancy murmured.

"Shoot." He squirmed in place, the mosquitoes a black cloud around his head.

Nancy tugged at his shirt and began creeping back to the front of the building. "When we hear the trucks coming, let's go down on the road and walk along as if we're out for a stroll."

Fitz followed her, swatting at the bugs. "Kind of late for that, isn't it?"

Nancy nodded. "Yes, but we're elderly. People expect us to be eccentric."

"Okay," said Fitz. "We'll hold hands as if we're on a romantic date." He shivered. "These bugs don't make me feel romantic."

Nancy laughed. "I know, but the truck drivers will think we're cute."

They waited in silence. Finally, Nancy heard the trucks. She and Fitz walked to the entrance road in front of the building.

Fitz whispered, "How good are you at remembering numbers, Nancy?"

She shook her head. "Not very good, memory's shot, but I'll write down the tag numbers as soon as the trucks pass us."

They waited on the road. Eventually they heard the trucks emerge from the underground garage. Fitz took Nancy's hand and began acting the part of a lover as they walked down the road away from the building. "I hope they're paying attention," Fitz said. "Hate to be rubbed out by a bad driver at this stage of the game."

"They sure are barreling down the road." Nancy risked a look behind. The trucks were making the turn onto the road to the gate. "I suppose they're all unloaded and much lighter so they're picking up speed on the downhill run."

"Yeah. Whatever they were carrying is now in the basement under our apartments."

"And I don't think it was kitchen supplies."

"Get ready. They're about to pass us." Fitz steered Nancy onto the grass verge. "Okay, stop." They pressed back against the shrubs, giving the trucks extra room to pass. Nancy peered at the license plate numbers.

Nancy grabbed for her notebook and pen and scribbled the numbers before she could forget them. "Okay, I got the numbers."

"That should be enough. You're sure they're correct?"

"Best I could do," said Nancy.

***

Life at Whisperwood: In Memoriam

The Whisperwood community regrets the passing of the following Whisperwood residents during the week of June 16 – 22.

JANELLE GROSS
LILLIAN SLOAT
HARRY MACMILLAN
ABIGAIL POOLE
ROBERT WAGGENER
MATTHEW GEIGER
PAUL GARNER

-From *The Whisperwood Breeze*, newsletter of Whisperwood Retirement Village.

Chapter 30

Nancy returned a book to the library on the fifth floor and now stood at the elevator. She cast a wistful look at the stairs, so convenient and fast—she thought of Anna—and deadly. Then Nancy saw May Brooks coming her way.

"Guess what I did yesterday?" May said as she arrived at the elevator.

Nancy smiled. "What did you do?"

"I replaced the linoleum floor in my kitchen—by myself!" May grinned. "They must use really cheap stuff here 'cause the floor was all scuffed up and stained after only two years' wear. I hated to look at it."

"I know what you mean," said Nancy. "I've been thinking about replacing mine too."

"Harry told me the floor was too old to be under warranty, and Whisperwood wouldn't pay to replace it. Against their policy. That is, sure they'd do it, you understand, but they'd charge me a bundle. Twelve hundred dollars! Can you imagine?"

The elevator arrived. They stepped in and the doors closed. Nancy turned to May. "That's ridiculous."

"Yep. The flooring shop in town wanted six hundred dollars.

Six hundred!" May folded her arms. Her face became pugnacious. "So I bought a box of those self-adhesive tiles and did it myself."

Nancy grinned and patted May on the back. "Good for you!" May was a few months older than Nancy and a bear on the tennis court.

May laughed. "On my hands and knees. Just finished and it looks great!"

"I'll drop by and see it later."

"Sure. Come by this evening at four. I'm having a champagne party to celebrate my new floor."

"Will do." Nancy stepped off the elevator on the first floor and headed to the pub to join George, Louise, and Fitz for lunch.

George peered over his cup of coffee and waved at Nancy as she walked in. "Had enough sleep?" he asked.

"I'll need a nap later." Nancy took a chair, caught the server's eye, and pointed to George's cup.

"Me too," added Louise. "So tell us what you found. Fitz here says the trucks came through." She was drinking tea steeped so long it looked like swamp water.

"I hope I don't get Lyme disease," said George. "Or maybe yellow fever. Malaria even. Those mosquitoes meant business."

Nancy rubbed her eyes. "I'm all bit up too, but we did watch the trucks come in and found out where they deliver stuff here. We got their license numbers, and they were both from Pennsylvania." She glanced up as the server arrived with the coffee pot. "Thank goodness," Nancy said as she slid her cup and saucer towards the server.

"Uh huh. That's where Bryerson is from. Pennsylvania." George pointed to his cup for a refill.

After the server had left, Fitz added, "But they didn't have any signs of identification. No company name. No logo."

Louise drummed her fingers on the table. "So now we have to track down these license numbers. Any idea how to do that?"

"Piece of cake," George said.

"Probably cost five dollars," Nancy added. "I can afford that."

"Me too." George leaned back in his chair and eyed Nancy.

"How about I take it on, Nancy? Never been a private eye."

"Go ahead." Nancy grinned. "I got out of the business thirty years ago."

Fitz set down his coffee cup. "You know whatever those trucks are bringing in is not good, probably not even legal, and it concerns us. We need to figure out what Bryerson is up to for our own good."

"All right," Louise said, "So we need to know what they're bringing in."

"And where they're taking it." Fitz added. "That garage entrance probably leads to the tunnel I saw in the basement. That means we've got to explore the basement and that hidden staircase."

"What if we're sitting on some kind of Love Canal here?" George peered at them over his coffee cup.

"You mean a chemical waste dump?" Nancy asked.

"Sure. Nobody expects any of us to live very long, and we sure ain't going to have kids, birth defects or no birth defects. What I'm saying is that nobody would raise any eyebrows if most of us kicked off tomorrow. Who would expect a waste dump here, much less blame our deaths on anything but natural causes?"

Louise glanced down at the *Stop Invasive Species* and *Support Your Local Humane Society* buttons on her shirt. "We're sitting ducks."

Nancy looked at Louise. "There are laws about dumping wastes."

"Sure there are." Louise rapped her knuckles on the table. "But complying with the law can be expensive. That's why I belong to so many watchdog groups."

"West Virginia can be pretty lax," Nancy said. "Once we hired an electrician to rewire our cabin, and his dad was the electrical inspector who checked the work."

Louise laughed. "I'm not surprised."

Fitz looked at the concrete walls around them. "Sure makes me wonder."

"West Virginia's a poor state and a hungry one," Louise frowned, "surrounded by wealthier, more industrial states all looking for waste dumps and landfills. Pennsylvania is a big offender as far as toxic wastes are concerned. Costs a lot of money to dispose of them legally and big fines if you don't." She rapped her knuckles on the table.

"How come you know that?" asked Fitz, looking at her with interest.

Louise shrugged. "Been fighting those bastards all my life."

"That's right." Nancy nodded at Louise and leaned toward them. "Those trucks were all from Pennsylvania."

"And George already told us what he found on the Internet," added Louise. "Bryerson has fertilizer and dry cleaning plants there. Dry cleaning fluid, now that's a toxic waste for sure."

"This is bigger than all of us," said George, sticking his jaw out. "We've got to find out what's going on here. It's a matter of life and death."

"Yeah," added Louise. "They've already killed two people—that we know of. We're next." She pounded her cane on the carpet.

"This is serious business," Nancy added. "They have a lot to lose if we're right."

***

Nancy spent the afternoon in Harry's office, working on the newsletter. For once, Harry had left in a good mood to give his weekly report to Bryerson. He'd told Nancy about the cute story he was going to pass on.

"Bryerson will get a kick out of this little item," he'd said to Nancy.

"What little item?" Nancy asked.

Harry chuckled. "Seems we have another romance blooming here."

"That's nice," said Nancy, thinking of Louise and George. "Life goes on, doesn't it?"

"I guess so." Harry laughed. "One of the drivers for his Pennsylvania deliveries saw an old couple arm in arm as they walked down the drive."

Oops. Nancy felt like laughing but managed to keep a straight face. "How did you learn about that?"

"The driver told the gate attendant who passed it on to security, and they mentioned it to me." Harry cleared his throat and added, "Cute, don't you think?"

Nancy nodded. "Are those Pennsylvania deliveries the ones that come in late at night? What are they?"

Harry shrugged. "Stuff for his other businesses. Outta my baili-wick. Don't know anything about them." He rushed out of the office.

Nancy continued working on the newsletter. Harry returned and slammed his papers on his desk.

Nancy looked up. "What happened?"

"He didn't like the story." Harry's face showed his disbelief. "He wants me to lock all the doors to keep the residents from going outside at night." He took a deep breath. "Unbelievable!"

"He can't do that," said Nancy. "What if there's a fire?" She thought a moment. "On the other hand, two old men died of exposure out on the grounds late at night."

"That was different," Harry sputtered. "They were both gaga and ended up where they didn't belong."

"Where was that?"

Harry stopped and threw up his hands. "Outside. On the grounds. Didn't know where they were going."

Nancy sat back and tapped her pen on the table. She thought of the old men's wet shoes and blackened hands. "Where had they been?"

"I don't know. Anyway, now I have to write everyone a memo—you can put it in the newsletter too—telling them they are not to go outside between midnight to six a.m. They could hurt themselves and not be found until morning."

"We won't go for that," Nancy sputtered. "This isn't a prison."

"He's the boss." Harry picked up a pencil and broke it in half.

***

Life at Whisperwood:
Protecting Our Residents

Whisperwood provides a safe environment for all of us, but residents sometimes unwittingly engage in dangerous behaviors that may result in injury. One specific concern is late night walks on the roads around Whisperwood. Trucks bring in necessary supplies for our community at all hours of the day and night. At night, residents walking on the road may not hear a truck coming, and the truck driver may not see them on the road. Whisperwood Administrator Harry Doyle urges everyone to remain indoors at night to prevent accidents caused by dark roads and paths.

-From *The Whisperwood Breeze*, newsletter of Whisperwood Retirement Village.

Chapter 31

Nancy dropped by her apartment to feed Malone and clean his litter box before her morning tennis practice the next day. She found a thread on the carpet outside her door. She had placed it on top of her door as she left the night before. She studied the new lock and saw scratches on it. Hadn't taken them long to get around that. She listened at the door but didn't hear any movement inside. She opened the door.

A quick study of her desk showed that the thread there was displaced too and papers rearranged. Malone growled from under the bed. Nancy coaxed him out with a sardine and smelled an odd odor as he emerged. His face was damp. Nancy gingerly touched the dampness and sniffed it. Ammonia. No wonder Malone seemed so subdued and scared. Nancy glanced around the apartment as she backed out, then walked to Fitz's apartment and knocked.

"They've struck again," Nancy said as Fitz opened the door. "This time they sprayed Malone with ammonia. Come check my apartment with me—in case the intruder is still there. Then I'll call Louise."

"Sure, luv. One moment." He disappeared and returned with a heavy wrench. "Just in case."

Nancy nodded in approval. "Good. I want to see what else has been disturbed, and I have to wash the poor cat's face. Then I'll pack more clothes to take to Louise's apartment."

An hour later, Nancy arrived at Louise's apartment with a cart full of clothes, a bottle of milk, half full, and a china sugar bowl.

Louise looked over the assortment. "I have milk and sugar, Nancy," she said.

"See this?" Nancy took the milk bottle and slanted it. At the bottom lay a pile of white sludge. "What do you suppose that is?"

Louise peered closely at the sludge. "Milk doesn't leave sludge like that."

"I know."

Louise didn't reply for a moment. "I always thought that box of candy was way too amateurish for the person we're dealing with here."

"The candy was a gift from May." Nancy stared at the milk bottle. "But I could easily have poured this milk onto my cereal or into my coffee or given it to Malone and never noticed the sludge. They could have added something to the sugar bowl too. Bingo. Another accidental death."

"Good thing you checked."

"Yes." Nancy frowned. "I'll throw out everything that isn't sealed in a package."

"I've always been an activist, Nancy." Louise clenched her fists.

Nancy smiled at her. "I know."

"We have to organize. First step, find out who among the residents might be useful in the battle we've got ahead of us."

Nancy nodded. "We still don't know for sure who our enemy is. Simon seems too meek and prissy to be involved in murder. Jewelry theft maybe. It could be Bryerson. Perry and those basement guards are on his payroll. But what are they hiding down there?"

"Let's get those Bio Books out and see who's a possible resource for us." Louise was already heading for the door.

"Wait. I'll call George and Fitz." Nancy picked up the phone. "We can take the books up to the library and work there after lunch."

"Maybe George has checked on those license tags."

As expected, the library was unoccupied after lunch. They

cleared the table behind the stacks, and Nancy handed each of them a volume, keeping one for herself.

"Had problems accessing the Internet," George grumbled. "I'll find out about those license tags, don't you worry."

"So what are we looking for now?" Fitz asked, doubt written on his face, the volume in front of him unopened.

Nancy was already leafing through the pages. "Look for lawyers, jewelers, chemists . . ."

Louise broke in. "And people who worked for government agencies, especially Justice, EPA, CDC, HHS. . . ."

They spent the afternoon reading through the directories in silence broken by George's sneezing, the scratching of pens, shuffling of papers and sporadic comments. Occasionally a resident would drop by, search the shelves and leave, but most of the time they were undisturbed.

"I guess I never really went through these directories so carefully before," Louise said with a sigh. "Who wrote up these bits of fluff?"

"Amanda must have." Nancy glanced at Louise. "They're all saccharine with minimal information. Most of the women say their greatest accomplishment was their children."

"Barf," snorted Louise.

"Yeah." Nancy flipped over another page.

"What have you got to complain about?" George sneezed into a tissue. "All the men say their greatest achievement was marrying their wives."

"No imagination, none at all." Fitz added. "Most of these entries say nothing about their employment. You have to read between the lines."

"I suppose we could ask people we meet if they know anyone here who was a lawyer or whatever," said Nancy as she scanned a page.

George looked up. "I'm leery of doing that. We have to be careful. If Harry hears about this, he may mention it to Bryerson. I don't trust either of them."

"You're right," said Louise. "We're on to something that could blow this place wide open."

By the end of the afternoon, they had compiled a list of seventy-eight names. "The next step," said Nancy, "is to meet these people and check them out. Some of them could be in rehab or the Alzheimer's Unit or dead, I guess."

"But be careful about what you say." Louise slammed shut the volume. "All we're looking for right now are possible supporters for the next step."

George looked up. "Which is. . .?

"We don't know yet," said Nancy. "I'm on the killer's hit list." She laughed but she didn't feel amused. "Not the first time I've been targeted, but this time I'm scared."

***

Life at Whisperwood: Bio Book Revisions

Nancy Dickenson and May Brooks have volunteered to update and revise the Bio Books that are so helpful to us all. If you would like a new page describing yourself and your interests, please tell Harry Doyle, Whisperwood Administrator.

-From *The Whisperwood Breeze*, newsletter of Whisperwood Retirement Village.

Chapter 32

The next day at lunch, Nancy, George, Louise, and Fitz again met in the Whisperwood pub. In a corner, the popcorn machine was popping. Nancy's mouth watered as she smelled it. Popcorn would taste so good, but this popcorn was no good, full of salt and fat. The server dropped by their table. Nancy ordered a sandwich and iced tea. The others followed suit.

As the server headed back toward the kitchen, George blurted out, "I finally got to those truck license plates."

Nancy, Louise, and Fitz sat up. "And?" they said in unison.

"Those trucks belong to a company called Mountain Service Enterprises. I looked up the company and found that Bryerson is president and CEO." George raised an eyebrow. "The company's enterprises include his dry cleaning establishments in Pennsylvania and a manufacturing plant. Didn't specify what and I can't imagine." He sat back.

"Uh oh," said Louise. "I thought so."

"What do you mean?" Nancy asked.

"The disposal of dry cleaning fluid," Louise's eyes sparked, "has to meet federal standards. An expensive proposition. When I heard he had dry cleaning businesses, I had my suspicions."

"Do you suppose that's what's in those trucks?" asked Nancy, unfolding her napkin into her lap.

George looked at her. "What else?"

Nancy shrugged. "He also delves into mining, I've heard."

"And manufacturing too," added George.

"Sure. All nice, clean businesses," Louise snorted, "I don't think. He could hide anything, anything at all, tons of it, under our building."

Fitz sat up. "We've got to get through those two doors in the basement and look around."

"I can manage that," said Nancy. "I've already picked the lock of the steel door. The other one should be easier."

"Okay, great," George said, eyeing the popcorn machine, still popping like an evil genie in the corner. "But first I've got something else to talk about. I've been thinking about our other problem, the accidental death rate here. First step, I checked on Whisperwood's death rate to see how it compares with the national average." He sat back and put his thumbs in his belt. "The list of residents who've died at Whisperwood is getting longer and longer, and the rate seems to be increasing. I'm afraid to read the list any more. Might see my own name on it."

Louise nodded. "I've noticed the rate increase too."

Nancy held up a hand as the server approached with their iced teas. After he left, she said, "We need facts. Maybe it seems like a lot of deaths because our age group is the most vulnerable to dying off." She glanced at George. "How about checking the statistics, George. Let's see how Whisperwood compares with similar retirement villages."

"I've been planning to do that." George pursed his lips. "Yessiree, bob. I'll get back to you on what I find."

"Good. I'm going back through the Whisperwood newsletters for the last two years and compiling a list of everyone who's died here. The death notices usually don't mention cause of death, so we'll have to go over it ourselves and start asking other residents for the information."

"We can split up the list," said Louise.

Nancy turned to her. "And it's time, Louise, that you and I talked to Simon. I'll bring the printouts, so I can give him enough information to worry him."

"We're assuming that SS stands for Simon Smythe," George

said. "Excuse me." He shoved his chair back and walked over to the machine.

Fitz watched him, a doubtful expression on his face. "But Smythe will have to feel threatened if you're going to get the truth out of him."

"He'll probably try to bluff his way out of it," said Nancy. She considered how they might effectively begin the talk with Simon. "We need to find out what he knows about Glinda's activities and what's going on around here."

George placed a bag of popcorn on the table as the server arrived with their sandwiches. Nancy grabbed at the sandwich before she could succumb to the lure of the popcorn. It was so hard to keep away from salt and fat and sugar in this place.

"We'll have to stay strong." Louise sipped her tea and stared off into space.

"It's worth a try," Nancy said.

"All right." Fitz took a big bite of his sandwich. "George will check on death rates; Nancy and Louise will confront Simon, and I will continue looking into Bryerson and his background. I'll get George to help me on that too."

***

Nancy called Simon that afternoon, and an hour later, she and Louise were knocking at his door. Simon welcomed them in and gestured to the chairs in the living room.

"Just a minute while I bring out some refreshments," he said.

They listened as he bustled about in the kitchen.

"I don't often get many guests," he called out.

In a few moments, he had brought out a tray with a pot of tea and three delicate, gold-rimmed tea cups. He poured the tea and handed each of them a cup.

"Now what did you want to talk about," he said. "Do you have another necklace for me to look at, Nancy?"

"No, not today. I certainly appreciated your help." Nancy cleared her throat. "We're here about a different topic." She stole a quick peek at Louise and then took a deep breath. "You knew Glinda a long time ago in Alaska."

Simon froze. He sat down and studied them a moment. "So I did. What of it?"

"And you know jewelry and antiques." Nancy glanced around the room.

Louise broke in. "So two people have told us they saw you take the Russian boundary plaque from Glinda's shelf."

Simon started and set down his teacup. He frowned. "Absolutely not. I had nothing to do with it."

Louise folded her arms, sat back and stared at him. "Two witnesses are willing to testify that they saw you steal it."

"And," Nancy said, "if you stole the boundary plaque, then you probably also killed Glinda."

Simon sat up, startled. "What are you talking about? Glinda's death was an accident, and I did not steal the plaque."

"We think Glinda was killed." Nancy leaned forward to emphasize her point. "And someone saw you hide the boundary plaque in Bernice's apartment."

"That is pure hogwash. I couldn't hide it in her apartment because I never had it!" Simon stood with clenched fists and towered over them.

"Tell it to the sheriff." Nancy sat back and studied her fingernails.

"I'd like to meet these witnesses," said Simon, stepping back from his threatening position.

"You will but probably at the sheriff's office." Louise stared at him with hard eyes and a grim smile.

"Ridiculous," said Simon. "Why are you doing this to me?"

Louise leaned forward. "We want the truth out of you," she said. "Why did you take the plaque.?"

Simon sat back and covered his eyes. He didn't speak for several minutes. Finally, he sighed. "Listen. You know what a pigheaded ass Glinda was. She had a precious historical relic and took no more care of it than she would a rusty nail on the sidewalk. That Russian boundary plate was priceless," he shook his finger at Nancy and

Louise. "It was important, for God's sake. It deserved to be locked in a museum, cared for by experts." He brushed his hair back. "Instead it was displayed openly on a shelf accessible to cleaning people, security guards, and all sorts of riffraff. Anyone, anyone at all could have lifted that precious plaque. I tell you, she didn't deserve it!" His face was red and his fists clenched.

"I agree with you," Nancy said quietly. "But I didn't think I should steal it."

"Neither did I. I told you, I did not take it." He stopped to catch his breath, "and I did not kill Glinda—that is, if she was killed, which I don't accept."

"Someone hit her with something heavy. It could have been the plaque," said Nancy.

"But the plaque was missing." He sat down, folded his arms, and scowled at them. "And I don't have it."

"All right." Nancy watched him for a moment, waiting for him to calm down. "Then why was Glinda blackmailing you."

Simon froze. He stared at her for a few minutes. Nancy stared back.

"Why do you think Glinda was blackmailing me?" he asked after a long pause. His hands trembled.

"She left a record, and you were seen handing her an envelope of money." Nancy folded her arms.

"What record?"

"A back-up floppy disk of her transactions," said Nancy. "I have it."

There was a long pause. Nancy waited. She could almost feel Simon's brain click through possible responses as he stared down at his feet, looking exhausted. Then he got up and stepped to the door, opened it, and surveyed the hall in both directions before closing and locking it. He walked back to the couch, sat, and leaned forward. "I'm going to tell you what really happened," he said.

Nancy kept her gaze on Simon.

"Glinda was blackmailing me just as she was half the people in this building. On the night of her death, I decided I'd had enough. I had as much on her as she had on me and, by God, if she was going to play that game, I could too."

Nancy nodded her understanding, not daring to risk interrupting him.

"I went up to her apartment late that night. Too late, I know, but I wanted to get her off balance."

"Was she up?" asked Louise.

"Everyone knows she was an insomniac. I was just starting to walk down the hall when one of Bryerson's thugs came out of her apartment. You know who I mean. They're not the regular security guards. I don't know who they are."

"Did he see you?" Nancy asked.

"No, and I don't think he realized that I'd seen him. I ducked into the library until I heard him get into the elevator going down. Then I knocked at her door a couple of times—figured she had to be awake, you know, and tried the door. It opened. It wasn't latched. That meant the thug was coming back." Simon stopped and cleared his throat. "So I peeked in and that's when I saw her, sprawled on the floor, her scooter overturned. I walked in. Thought I'd better, in case she was still alive."

"But she wasn't," Nancy said. It wasn't a question.

"No, no. She was dead all right. This was about eleven-thirty." Simon shuddered.

"Did you touch her?" Nancy asked.

"Just to feel the carotid, but there wasn't any pulse." He stood and paced the floor in front of them. He stopped and glared at them. "I didn't do it!"

Nancy met his glare. "What about the vandalism?"

Simon shrugged. "That was me." He looked sheepish. "I took advantage of the situation, I'm afraid, to search for the money she stole from me and the papers she was using to blackmail me. I was so rattled and worried the thug would come back soon that I tore up the place."

"You must have worn gloves." Nancy glanced around the room as if to find them.

"Of course I wore gloves."

Nancy smiled to herself. A professional thief probably would carry gloves. "So your footsteps were the ones Anna heard."

"I guess so. I rushed to the stairs to get out of there before any-one saw me." He looked at them meaningfully. "And in case you're wondering, all Glinda had on me was a slight incident, almost insignificant but embarrassing if it got out." Simon sat down, his head in his hands.

Nancy studied him for a moment. "I don't think I'd call jewelry theft insignificant."

He jerked his head up. "What?"

"You're the one who's been stealing jewelry." Nancy's voice was firm. "You target residents who have expensive jewelry, then you enter their units while they're at dinner and take it."

"I most certainly do not," Simon blustered. "Why would you think that?"

Nancy leaned forward. "I know that's what you're doing. You're depending on your victims thinking they misplaced it or forgot what they did with it." She glanced at Louise, who was watching this exchange open-mouthed, and willed Louise to stay silent. This was the most colossal bluff on her part, but it made sense.

Simon seemed to shrivel into his skin. "That's preposterous," he managed to say.

Nancy pressed forward. "Did you take her computer?" She watched his face turn red.

He tried to laugh. "No. Of course not. Why would I want it?"

"Because of the incriminating files on it," said Nancy. "We have printouts." She waved them at him.

He grabbed for them, but Nancy quickly put them behind her back. "You had quite a racket going on here, didn't you?" she said. "Jewel theft from vulnerable human beings."

"You ought to be ashamed of yourself," Louise snapped.

Simon's eyes darted around the room as if he sought an escape. He seemed to be thinking hard. He swallowed once, then twice. At last he said, "I know nothing about any jewel thefts."

"Oh come on." Louise folded her arms and glared at Simon.

"No, no," said Simon, pushing his hands towards her as if to fend off her words. "I had nothing to do with any thievery. Glinda gave me her jewelry and asked me to sell it for her. That's all, I swear."

"I don't think so," said Nancy. "You stole it, and you will return it. We have a list of the items stolen and the people they were stolen from."

Simon put his head in his hands. He peered up at them. "So what are you going to do now?"

Nancy narrowed her eyes. "I want the truth. Did you steal the boundary plaque?"

"No!" Simon almost shouted. "And I didn't put it in Bernice's room."

Nancy stared at him, frowning. "All right. We'll accept that for now, but you have two weeks to return the stolen jewelry items."

"I can't do that," said Simon.

Nancy got up. "You must." She headed for the door. "I'll expect you to return the pieces to me at my apartment. Otherwise I will contact the victims and the sheriff. I have a list of the stolen items if you need one. And I want your assurance that this ends your thievery."

Simon covered his eyes and groaned. "I'll see what I can do."

Nancy looked down at him. "If we hear of any more missing items, we're going to the sheriff."

Louise followed Nancy to the door. "Thanks for the tea," she said.

***

Life at Whisperwood:
Lost and Found is Overflowing

What are you missing? Chances are, it might be in Whisperwood's Lost and Found Box held at the Reception Desk.

We have umbrellas, canes, sweaters, jackets, and miscellaneous other odds and ends found in the classrooms, lobbies, and benches around the campus. Drop by the Reception Desk and maybe you'll find what you've been looking for.

-From *The Whisperwood Breeze*, newsletter of Whisperwood Retirement Village.

Chapter 33

Nancy looked around at the faces of the group gathered around the picnic table by the tennis court. "Do you think I was right in not having Simon arrested immediately?"

Louise thumped the table. "Yes, I do. I was there. He was devastated. If he still has any jewelry that he hasn't pawned and can retrieve the pieces he has, I think he'll give them to us for return to the rightful owners. If he doesn't, then we'll have to go to the authorities, but I don't have much confidence in the sheriff."

"I really don't think there's enough evidence against him anyway," Nancy said. "Just initials and our word on what he said. He'll deny everything, and Glinda is dead, so there's no retribution in that direction."

"What hold do you suppose Glinda had on him?" Louise looked at Nancy.

Nancy shrugged. "She must have known about the jewelry thefts. She was nosy and always kept her ears and eyes open. She must have figured out what was going on—and demanded a share."

George sneezed into his sleeve. His face was already turning red and his eyes tearing. He brought out a handkerchief and shook it. Nancy and Louise reared away. "Not in our faces, George, for

Pete's sake," said Louise.

"Damn pollen." He blew his nose. "I agree with you about not turning Simon in. He's afraid of us, and he won't be stealing any more jewelry. We ought to let him be."

"We have to do something about getting the jewelry back to the owners," Louise said.

"I've thought about that." Nancy pulled tissues out of a pack in her purse and handed them to George. "We can start with an announcement about expensive jewelry someone has found and brought into the administration office. Ask everyone to provide a description of any missing pieces. We can match the names and items with Glinda's list and the pieces we have, and then return the pieces to the rightful owners. If we don't have it or Simon hasn't given it to us, then we can confirm its disappearance from the owner, get a full description, and put that item on a master list, which we'll later give to the sheriff to hunt down." She sat back, pleased at her plan. She'd like to avoid the sheriff altogether, but in this case he'd be useful. She smiled, thinking how much the sheriff would like being useful.

"Once we pass the list on to the sheriff," added Louise, "we're finished with the jewel thefts, but we still need to find out who killed Glinda."

"And who stole the plaque." Nancy tapped her finger on her lips. "My bet is on Perry. I'm sure that's what the 'P' stands for on Glinda's list."

George sneezed again, blew his nose, and clutched the handkerchief. "Yeah. Why did Perry come to Glinda's apartment at two in the morning? Something funny there." He took out a pill and swallowed it. "By the way, I checked on those mortality statistics."

Fitz put down the water bottle that usually hung on his belt. "So, what did you find out?"

"Hard to get any straight data. I finally found the National Vital Statistics website that had a table of death rates by ten-year age groups."

"And?" said Nancy.

"I've got it written down here." George waved a notebook at

them and pulled out a sheet of lined paper. "This is interesting."

"Go ahead," Nancy said in resignation. George was going to wring every bit of drama he could out of it.

"We've got about 1,000 residents here, right?"

"Okay," said Louise.

"I did some extrapolation to get what I wanted, you know," answered George, peering at them over his bifocals. "We mainly want to know the national death rate for our age group here at Whisperwood, which I figure to be over sixty-five, and when all is said and done, I figure that rate to be about seven percent of the total a year. This is my best guess, you understand."

"Okay," said Louise. "So that means for Whisperwood, which has about 1000 residents,"

"Fewer by the minute," interrupted Fitz.

Louise ignored him. "Then we could expect about seventy deaths per year."

"I think so, yes."

"So how many kick the bucket here each year?" Louise flicked her braid again.

"Whisperwood is about six years old now." George cocked his eyebrow. "In the first several years, the death rate here was pretty much in line with the national average. But then it gradually starts increasing, so last year the death rate here was a whopping twenty-one percent. "

"Omigosh. Say that again?" Nancy sat up. No wonder she was so depressed reading the memorial notices. There were too many of them.

"I'm telling you. It was twenty-one percent." George rapped his knuckles on the table and sat back, looking pleased at their response. "That's two hundred ten people, actually it was two hundred thirteen, who died here last year." He paused. "I also checked with a friend of mine who lives in a similar place in Maryland. They have about twenty deaths per month and three thousand residents. That's two hundred forty a year or about seven percent, which is in line with the national average. We keep saying this, and we're right. Something bad is going on here."

"Whew," said Louise, fanning herself with a hand. "A lot of work for the marketing people—and Amanda. Keeping those apartments filled."

Nancy pulled a notebook out of her purse. "George's numbers agree with mine, although I found them hard to believe. When the numbers started adding up, I decided to go back only a year and a half. That means I have three hundred twelve people who've died in that short period of time."

George whistled.

"I don't like this," said Louise. "Not at all."

"So now we have to find cause of death," added Nancy. "I've noted that next to the names when I remembered them. Maybe you can fill in others." She passed the list over to Louise, who pored over it with George.

Louise took a pen out of her pocket and started making notes next to names on the list.

"These are all recent, so I remember the ones where an accident was involved," she said. "That kind of news spreads fast."

Nancy watched them work on the list. After ten minutes, Louise looked up. "I'm finding a whole bunch of accidents here. Mostly falls. Easy to explain and easy to blame on the victim."

"That's what I thought," said Nancy.

Fitz pushed his chair back, stretched out his legs and examined his shoes. "Don't you think it rather odd that a man who has been involved in mining and manufacturing and dry cleaning, for Pete's sake, should switch fields and develop a retirement community?"

"He's done a good job," said Nancy. "We all came here because we liked what we saw." She remembered Louise's cheery endorsement and the sleepless nights of depression she'd suffered before she moved to Whisperwood.

"On the surface," added Louise, frowning at Nancy. "I know I loved it here at first. I was sick of the upkeep on my own house."

"Me too," said Fitz. "As far as we know, Bryerson doesn't have any relatives living here." He looked at the others for confirmation.

"I'll tell you what I think," George blurted. "He looked at the demographics. It's no secret that a huge pool of baby boomers is at or near retirement age. Where are they going to go?"

"Follow the money," said Fitz.

"My husband and I had a cabin in West Virginia for many, many years," said Nancy, gazing at the wall behind Fitz. "We loved the area, but we soon found out we had to know people in the community to get any work done, and then it seemed to drag on forever." She looked over at Fitz and Louise. "Not much oversight or monitoring where we lived, and just mention the "z" word— that's zoning—to the locals and they frothed at the mouth."

"Made to order for crooks," said Fitz, "and any kind of two-bit get-rich scheme."

"I'm afraid so," added Nancy.

***

Life at Whisperwood:
End of Life Plans Available

No one wants to think about their own end of life, but not planning ahead adds an extra burden to your loved ones. Make sure your will is up to date and that your family knows where it is. A copy may be filed with Harry Doyle, Whisperwood administrator, if you wish. A medical directive for your physician should also be filed with the Medical Center, your doctor, and your family. You may also like to leave plans for your memorial service with your family. Also be sure they know where important documents such as social security card, medical cards, long-term-care policy, and insurance policies may be found.

-From *The Whisperwood Breeze,* newsletter of Whisperwood Retirement Village.

Chapter 34

Nancy walked down the hall to Fitz's apartment and knocked on the door. He opened it immediately and ushered her in.

"I've been putting threads around too, luv," Fitz said, "but so far none of them has moved. So what did you find out?" he asked in a soft voice.

"Harry told me he's been trying to call Amanda on her cell phone, but she hasn't responded. He's still trying to reach her." Maybe, Nancy amended to herself. "That's what he says, anyway."

Fitz led Nancy into the living room. "Glad he's trying."

"And I did an Internet search on Amanda Fellows and found a reference to a paper she presented at a conference on aging five years ago."

Fitz pursed his lips. "I guess she was talking about people like us."

Nancy gestured toward the kitchen, away from the hall door, and Fitz followed her in. "Did it say where she was from? Any address or city?" he asked. He opened a bottle of water and filled two cups, then added tea bags and set the cups in the microwave.

Nancy nodded. "It listed her as being with the Morgantown Coalition on Aging, so I looked up the coalition and called them. They

remembered her, all right, and asked how she was doing here."
Nancy smiled as she remembered their questions. "They seemed to
like her."

Fitz leaned against the kitchen counter. "Sure. She was a nice
person."

"I told them she'd left here, and none of us knew how we could
get in touch with her. They said she had family in Morgantown, but
they couldn't divulge any information over the phone without
permission."

"Same drill here," said Fitz. "I don't blame them."

"So I did a white pages search for people named Fellows in
Morgantown and called them."

Fitz grinned. "Nancy, you are a regular detective." He turned as
the microwave buzzed, took out the two cups and handed one to
Nancy, gesturing at a small, round table. "Good idea to sit in the
kitchen."

"I was a detective for many years, you know," she said.

"And a mighty good one too," said Fitz. "I remember. . ."

"Yes well, this kind of thing is fun for me, that is, it would be if
I weren't so worried about Amanda and what's been going on here.
Then again, I'm way out of date."

Fitz stirred three packets of sugar into the tea. He laid the spoon
aside, sipped the tea and nodded, then looked over at Nancy. "So
now what?"

"Ten Fellows were listed. About the fourth one I called knew
Amanda and immediately started thinking something was wrong. I
had to calm her down—sounded elderly, you know, like someone
here."

"I guess we know what that sounds like." Fitz grinned. "Present
company excepted."

"Anyway, it was Amanda's aunt, but she believed Amanda was
still here. Of course, she might not be up on what's going on in the
family, so I asked if Amanda's mother was around. Turns out this
aunt pretty much raised Amanda so if Amanda told anyone what
she was doing, it would be her." She sipped her tea.

"Someone said she had parents in Florida."

"Yes. Apparently they traveled a lot so Amanda stayed with her aunt. I talked to this aunt awhile longer to see if she was non compos mentis, you know . . ."

"Good idea. I guess we're all at risk."

Nancy shrugged. "She sounded okay to me. Pretty sharp, actually."

Fitz laughed. "Like us. Did you get her address?"

"Yes, I did." She raised her eyebrows at him in question.

"Let's drive up to Morgantown and visit her." He stood up, eagerness radiating across his face.

Nancy grinned. "Great! I'd hoped you'd say that. We need to know what happened to her. At least I do. I still wonder if I had met with her that afternoon, she might still be here." Nancy stared out the kitchen window in an effort to ward off a vague feeling of guilt.

"You can't blame yourself, Nancy, but I agree that we need to know. We can head out right now." Fitz set down his tea.

"Let me grab my purse." She started toward the living room mirror to check her hair, thought better of it, and followed Fitz out the door.

The two-hour ride to Morgantown sped by in Fitz's sky-blue Cadillac. They used the time to catch up on old friends, but Nancy's mind was spinning with questions. If Amanda was missing, what happened to her? Why had she wanted to talk to Nancy? Why had she seemed so nervous when Nancy had spoken to her that last day? Why were Harry and Bryerson insisting that Amanda had simply quit and moved back to her home?

On the other hand, maybe she and Fitz were turning a simple quit-and-leave into a suspicious disappearance. Amanda had probably quit for reasons of her own and gone off to the beach or taken on another job. She was an adult, after all. She didn't have to answer to anyone—especially not to Nancy or Fitz or anyone at Whisperwood.

Nancy roused herself from her thoughts to watch the trees pass by. She took a deep breath. How good it felt to be away from the cloistered atmosphere of Whisperwood. The scenery sparkled on this clear, pleasant afternoon. Fitz turned off the highway at the Morgantown exit and then navigated the streets, finally stopping the car in a residential area. He backed up to park in front of a row house with a stone porch in front. "This is it," he said.

"That was fast." Nancy gathered her purse and surveyed the street in both directions as they walked up to the door. It seemed like a quiet, middle-class neighborhood. Two toddlers playing on the porch next door stopped to stare at them. Fitz knocked on the door once, then again louder a minute later. A frail, elderly woman—Nancy realized that she herself probably looked as frail and elderly—drew aside the lace curtains in the window next to the door and peered out at them.

"What do you want?" she asked in a thin, querulous voice.

"I called you this morning about Amanda," Nancy said.

Fitz spoke loudly. "We wanted to ask you some questions."

"We both knew her at Whisperwood," added Nancy, "and since she left, no one has heard from her. We'd like to know that she's all right."

"Why wouldn't she be all right?" They heard the arthritic hands fumble with the latch, and then the old woman opened the door to them. "You might as well come in then."

She walked ahead of them, hunched over, into the living room and gestured at a lumpy sofa. The whole place smelled of lavender. Nancy wondered if sachets were hidden under the sofa and chair cushions.

She nodded at them, not smiling. "Sit. I'll get you some coffee."

She disappeared into the back room and soon returned with two mugs of coffee. She held them out to Fitz and Nancy with blue-veined hands that trembled. She sat in the opposite chair, leaning forward and staring at them with bright, interested eyes. "Now, why are you concerned about my Amanda?"

"No one at Whisperwood," Nancy began, "has heard from her. We hoped you would know where she is."

"Whisperwood, yes. That's where she worked."

The old woman stared off at the wall behind them. "She was going to get me in there, you see, but she changed her mind a couple of weeks ago. Don't know why."

"She didn't mention that to us, but I would wonder why too," said Nancy. "Whisperwood is a nice place."

"Yes, she told me all about it." The bright blue eyes examined Nancy.

"Do you have any idea where she might have gone?" put in Fitz.

"I told you that I don't. This is most odd and not at all like Amanda." She frowned. "She doesn't answer her cell phone either."

Nancy leaned forward. "Can you tell us the names and phone numbers of any close friends or other family that we could contact?" She held her breath. This was the crucial part of the interview. Ms. Fellows' answer was critical. Not something she'd answer on the phone.

"Well, now, let me see." The fragile little woman stared off into space, one hand stroking her chin with shaking fingers. Nancy waited, not daring to interrupt. At last the woman seemed to make up her mind. "Cecilia is her best friend. Amanda might tell her things she wouldn't tell me." She looked at Nancy. "Cecilia's the one you want. I'll get her number and address."

"Thank you," said Nancy.

"You let me know what you find out," said Ms. Fellows. "And tell Amanda to call me."

Fifteen minutes later, Nancy and Fitz were on the road again, driving to the other side of Morgantown and Cecilia's apartment. She answered their knock as if she were waiting for them.

"Ms. Fellows called me," she said as she invited them in. "I am so worried about Amanda." Her crisp yellow sundress and curly blonde hair brightened up the drab apartment. "Come on in." She stepped aside and gestured to the sofa.

Nancy frowned at the cat hairs covering the sofa but sat on it anyway. A trim tuxedo cat stared at them from the kitchen. At least he seemed well-mannered, unlike Malone. "Thanks for agreeing to see us," she said.

Cecilia nodded. "We were thinking about getting together last Friday, but she never called back to confirm and hasn't answered her phone. I didn't want to worry her aunt, but I didn't know what to do. I've been waiting to hear from her. I thought that maybe she'd gotten very busy."

"Did you call Whisperwood?" Fitz asked. He fidgeted on the edge of the sofa and pulled in his arms and legs as if to avoid contamination. Nancy glanced at him. She felt the same way. It wasn't just the cat hairs. The ammonia smell of the litter pan in the corner permeated the apartment, and white bits of litter had sprayed out onto the rug. Nancy knew how easy it was to let the litter pan go, but the consequences, especially with Malone, were too dreadful to chance.

Cecilia's hands fluttered. "Yes, finally, but they weren't helpful. They said she was no longer there, and they didn't know how I could reach her."

"We got the same runaround from the Whisperwood staff," Nancy said.

"What can we do?" Cecilia looked from Nancy to Fitz. "I didn't want to worry her aunt unnecessarily and kept hoping Amanda would call. I was going to wait one more day. . ."

"At least now we know that she is missing," said Nancy. "Perhaps you and her aunt could file a missing persons report with the police. Meanwhile, we'll ask the other residents at Whisperwood. She may have told someone where she was going."

"Not likely," said Fitz.

"I'll call Amanda's aunt right away."

"It's time to do that." Nancy glanced at Fitz. He nodded, and they rose to go. "Please let us know immediately if you hear from her." Nancy handed Cecilia a card. "My phone number."

As they drove back to Morgantown, Fitz turned to Nancy. "So what do we do now?"

Nancy started at his voice. She had been engrossed in memories of Amanda's many kindnesses, not only to her but to all the residents. Nancy hoped Amanda was all right.

Fitz broke in on her thoughts. "We should tell Harry that Amanda is missing and see what he does about it."

"That will tip our hand," said Nancy. "Risky. They'll know we've been snooping."

Fitz stared at the road ahead. "The police will be involved now."

Nancy nodded. "About time, too."

Fitz shrugged. "Bryerson won't do anything."

"And that will speak volumes about him. I think finding Amanda will be up to us. I only hope she will be alive and well." Nancy clamped her lips shut.

***

Life at Whisperwood: In Memoriam

The Whisperwood community regrets the passing of the following residents during the week of June 23-31.

CUTHBERT P. WIGGLEY
JOHNATHAN WRIGHT
WILLIAM PELT
ALICE KAUFMAN
FULTON A. MICHAEL
LOUIS BELACQUA
LULA WEILAND

-From *The Whisperwood Breeze,* newsletter of Whisperwood Retirement Village.

Chapter 35

Fitz settled into the seat next to Nancy at table fifty-six and nodded at George and Louise. "Nancy and I have discovered something interesting."

The server appeared with their water, rolls, and salad. They gave him their orders and asked him to send the manager over. He nodded and disappeared toward the kitchen. Nancy leaned forward and cleared her throat. "Fitz and I made a trip to Morgantown today."

"And we found out for sure that Amanda is missing." Fitz chimed in.

"I knew it," said George. He held up a hand as the manager arrived. They gave him their orders—two chardonnays with Fitz the hold-out for beer. George shook his head and pointed to his water glass. The manager departed, and Louise jumped in.

"I'm not surprised," she said. "Did someone notify the police?" Nancy nodded, buttering a roll. "Her aunt."

"So what do we do now?" Louise raised an eyebrow at Nancy.

"When we got back," Nancy said, "I told Harry what we'd found out. He refused to take it seriously, said it was up to her relatives to do something if she was really missing."

Fitz sat back. "Harry prefers to think she took a vacation or eloped and isn't missing at all."

"The key to what's happening here is down that staircase in the basement," George rapped his cane on the floor, "and in those trucks."

"I agree," Nancy said, her eyes sparkled at the thought of the adventure coming up. She glanced at the tables in their vicinity. Two were still vacant, and the four women at the other one were busy with their own loud conversation. It was safe to talk. "We need to scope out the entrance those late-night trucks use and where it goes, find out what the tunnel under the building is used for, and then we have to find out what those trucks are bringing in."

Louise nodded. "I can hang out tonight and hide in the bushes next to that hidden garage entrance. Find out how they open that garage and who's guarding it. I'm wondering if we can sneak in through that entrance."

George peered at Louise over his glasses. "I could hide in the bushes farther out where I can watch you. If you put your cell phone on vibrator mode, I can call you if I see trouble."

"Good idea but with the insects buzzing and those noisy trucks, we shouldn't have any trouble covering any noise we make." Louise thumped her cane. "This is gonna be fun."

Nancy saw the grins pass between Louise and George. "Now hold it," she said. "This is a dangerous stunt you're contemplating." Nancy remembered the many close calls she'd survived in her career. Just luck she was still alive. "We're not playing games here."

"Not any more, luvies," Fitz added. "I've got another idea."

They all looked at him.

"Nancy and I will go down to the basement tonight—late—and conduct a surveillance operation, look around for hidden cameras, find out if anyone goes down there that late. Might even hear the trucks under the building." He winked at Nancy. "Nancy, my darlin', you can pick the locks on the two doors, and if there is some other barrier we don't expect, I might be able to take it down and put it back up. I wasn't a carpenter for nothing."

"Carpenter?" Nancy said. "I thought you were a florist."

"A varied career, madam." Fitz bowed to them all from his seat. "With the two locked doors and the scary warning sign on the hall door, I'm guessing they aren't bothering to guard that tunnel late at night from this end any more."

"Good thought. Even the first floor and lobby are deserted after nine p.m." Nancy grinned, thinking of the exciting night ahead of them. She quickly amended that idea. Much safer if the night proved boring for all of them.

"How's your hearing, Nancy?" Fitz asked.

"Not too bad. Hung onto that so far, I think."

Fitz hitched up his belt as if he already had tools hanging from it. "If you hear anyone coming down the stairs or elevator, luv, we'll duck into a classroom till they leave."

Nancy nodded. "No residents live in the basement, and none of us go down there late at night, so there's no reason for security to patrol it on their rounds. They have enough to do."

***

At midnight, Nancy slipped out of Louise's apartment and gently shut the door behind her. She took the elevator down to the first floor, peeked out as the elevator doors opened, saw no one and walked quickly to Fitz's apartment. She tapped at the door.

"Nobody around," she said when he opened it. He nodded.

They crept down the corridor to the back stairs and then down to the basement. Only emergency lights lit the basement corridor. The classrooms on each side were dark, but the display windows gleamed. To Nancy, the windows felt like eyes watching them, but she didn't spot any cameras, hidden or otherwise, on the barren walls and ceiling or attached to the exit signs at the stairs and elevator. Bryerson probably wouldn't approve the expense.

Fitz held up a hand and paused as they listened for footsteps or voices. Hearing none, they pulled a couple of chairs out of a classroom and sat next to the new wall, listening for sounds of activity on the other side. Nancy read the dire warning notice and she and Fitz exchanged glances.

She checked her watch periodically and after half an hour of hearing nothing, she pulled out her lock-picking tools, but waited while Fitz gently tapped across the end wall from side to side, his ear to the wall.

"Want to see what we're dealing with," he said to Nancy. "Sounds like a piece of wallboard on a frame. Go ahead, now, luv."

She pulled out the thin, flat-bladed screwdriver and began playing with the lock on the new door. In a few moments, she turned the door knob and opened the door. She and Fitz peered inside.

"It's like we thought," said Nancy, pleased that their deduction was correct.

"Yep," added Fitz. Nothing here. No electrical high-voltage anything." He stepped inside the little room. "Absolutely vacant," he said.

"No storage either." Nancy walked over to the steel door and put her ear to it. After a minute, she said, "I don't hear anything."

Fitz leaned against the steel door, too, with his ear against it. "Me neither."

"I know I can open this door, so let's not try it tonight," Nancy said. "We've got this situation figured out, now. Tomorrow night we'll come back with George and Louise.

She grinned. "That is, unless they find a better way tonight to get into the tunnel.

"Right. Let's go," Fitz said. "We've found out enough."

The next afternoon, Nancy and Fitz met George and Louise in the fifth floor library. They sat around the long table in the back. "So what happened?" asked Nancy, looking at Louise.

"I was in the bushes by midnight," she croaked.

"You shoulda seen her," boomed George. "Her face was all blacked up, and the rest of her was covered in old Army surplus. Scared me, but you sure couldn't see her in the bushes."

Nancy winced. George sometimes talked so loud. She put her finger to her lips and glanced at the door. "Pipe down, George. We don't want the whole world to know about this."

Louise nodded. "Yeah, pipe down." She looked at Nancy. "I got there way before the trucks would come. Plenty of time to hide someplace close to the entrance."

"So what did you find out?" asked Fitz, leaning forward.

"We can't get in that way." Louise rapped her knuckles on the table. "They've got the place sewn up. The trucks must have some kind of signal that alerts the guard to open the door. Then the trucks drive in, stop, the guard checks the drivers' papers and opens the back of the trucks, peeks in, then lets them go through. But there's only one guard at the door. Who knows how many might be farther down into the garage or whatever that place is."

"Bryerson wouldn't pay more salaries than he had to," said Nancy. She'd read enough of Bryerson's memos complaining about expenses to know that. "I vote for only one or two guards."

George nodded. "Whatever the number, I don't see how we can break through that door and get past them."

"Two guys in the truck," added Louise. "The driver and alternate driver or helper maybe."

"All right," said Nancy. "We've got another idea. Tell them, Fitz."

Fitz leaned over the table and spread his arms out to draw the group closer. He spoke softly. "The wall that they put in to block off the end of the basement and the steel door? Nothing behind it. Just a smokescreen."

Nancy pulled the box of lock-picking tools out of her purse.

George's eyes popped. "Wow. Real lock-picking tools. I've always wanted to try my hand at that. Is it hard?"

Nancy smiled at his eagerness. "Takes practice. Tonight we break into the tunnel system."

"What if that guard's still down there?" Louise asked.

"Fitz and I didn't hear any sounds of movement on the other side of the steel door, and we didn't see any surveillance cameras in the hall."

Fitz nodded. "The guard could have been asleep, of course. If we're stopped, we'll have to think of something else."

"It's a chance we'll have to take." Nancy added.

The group looked at each other and grinned.

They joined hands together across the table and shook.

***

Life at Whisperwood:
Arts and Crafts on Display

The Whisperwood Arts & Crafts Classes invite you
to visit their exhibits in the basement classrooms.
Displays include portraits and still lifes by our residents in the oil painting class and baby quilts by our
resident quilters. The railroad modelers have also
set up their trains and will run them for your enjoyment.

-From *The Whisperwood Breeze*, newsletter of
Whisperwood Retirement Village.

Chapter 36

By eleven that night, the 90s Club adventurers had gathered in Fitz's apartment. Louise and George stood leaning on their canes, and Fitz wore his tool belt. Nancy held the box of lock-picking tools.

"Looks like we're all ready." She stepped to the door and peeked out. "All clear."

George followed her.

"This takes me back to the old days," Nancy said, then caught a glimpse of herself in the living room mirror. Oh dear. How wrinkled and frail she looked, but here she was, still getting caught up in mysteries. She shook off a fleeting sense of sadness and smiled. She was still the same Nancy.

They walked down the hall to the elevator and waited in silence, listening to the elevator clanking down the shaft and watching for any signs of life from the lobby.

The elevator eventually made its way to the first floor and the doors opened. They entered and descended to the basement. Nancy held her breath. "I never realized how noisy this thing was," she whispered.

It stopped and the doors opened. She peeked out to scan the dimly lit hall. "Nobody's here. Let's go." She felt the adrenaline.

They walked to the new wall and door and hovered around Nancy as she removed the screwdriver and the picks. "Here we go."

George muscled his way in and peered so closely at what Nancy was doing that she nudged him aside with her elbow. "A little room here, please," she said.

He stepped back as Nancy inserted the screwdriver into the lock and began juggling the picks. After a few moments, she opened the door, and they stepped into the tiny room.

They looked at each other and cheered softly at the empty space.

"What a bunch of fakes they are," Louise said as she glanced around the empty space.

"Yeah," growled George. "But why?"

Fitz stepped up to the steel door, gestured to the door knob and bowed to Nancy. "Madam?"

Nancy tested the knob. Of course it was locked. "Just thought I'd give it a try."

She grinned at the others and began working on the lock. After a few minutes, she opened that door a crack, peeked in, opened it wider and peered down the staircase. "No guard." She stepped out onto the stairs. This was the kind of stuff she was made for. "With the locked double doors, they don't think they need a guard too."

Fitz stepped in front of Nancy. "Move aside, luv, I've got a flashlight," he said, pulling one out from his belt.

Nancy felt affronted. She carried a light too.

One by one, they stepped down the stairs to the landing at the base. The guard was nowhere in sight. The dim bulb at the top of the stairs cast enough light so Nancy could see that they were in a horizontal tunnel wide enough to allow trucks to travel through it on a rough road cut out of the tunnel floor. The road disappeared around curves in both directions. Dripping sounds echoed from wall to wall.

She choked on the dust and exhaust fumes. Fitz flashed the light down the tunnel to their left. George sneezed and reached for his handkerchief.

Nancy glanced at her watch. "It's not even midnight yet," she whispered. "Way too early for the trucks."

Fitz pulled out a ball of string and tied one end to the staircase rail. "Just in case." He winked at Nancy. "Better than bread crumbs."

"I put a new rubber tip on my cane," said Louise. "Trying not to thump."

They turned left and crept along, single file. "Quiet, now," said Nancy. "Seems to me the garage door would be in this direction." Their shadows on the tunnel walls along with the constant dripping everywhere gave her goose bumps. Or maybe the goosebumps came from the damp chill.

About twenty feet from the staircase, they came to a branch in the tunnel that was blocked by stacks of large plastic bins. Fitz played his flashlight across the bins. "What do you suppose. . . ?"

Nancy stepped forward and pried open the lid of a bin in front of the stack. "Look at this!" She tucked her flashlight under her arm and pulled out a Tiffany lamp. "This was Glinda's."

Louise opened another bin and peered inside. "Bunch of stuff in here." She pulled out a bundle and unwrapped it to reveal a small bronze statue of a horse. "Remember Meg Cannon? This was hers, and she was so proud of this thing. An antique from her mother."

"I'll bet Whisperwood's high death rate is partly due to the thefts." Nancy played her light across the plastic bins. "You know, arrange a fatal accident, then take what's valuable, and tell the relatives that the victim probably sold or gave it away. Who would know?"

"Oh boy," said George. "We're onto a den of thieves and murderers."

"Put the stuff back," said Nancy. "Let's finish exploring. . . "

"And get the hell out of here," added Fitz.

Farther down the tunnel, they reached a fork and paused. The tunnel to the left appeared lighter than the one at the right. "The light must be coming from the entrance at the garage door." Nancy said. "We'll have to go quietly now."

"We can duck into the side tunnel at the right if someone comes." Nancy walked cautiously toward it and sniffed. "Uh oh," she said. "Something rotten in Denmark."

Fitz followed her with the flashlight, and they both disappeared down the right fork and around a bend for a few seconds, taking the light with them. Louise and George remained behind in the main tunnel.

Nancy crept forward. She covered her nose and mouth with a tissue, fighting the smell and the fear and a growing dread. The stench grew stronger with every step forward. Then Fitz's flashlight picked out a pile of blue cloth.

"Oh God" Nancy could see the outflung hands and what remained of a face. Amanda's face.

She turned to Fitz, unable to speak. He had been staring at the body, then he looked at her face, and grabbed her hand. They walked quickly back to Louise and George. Nancy stopped, gagging. Fitz threw up.

He wiped his mouth. "We've got to get out of here," Fitz said in a low voice. "Fast."

"What's the matter?" Even in the uncertain light, Nancy could tell that Fitz was as shocked as she was. Louise took Nancy in her arms and held her.

Fitz shook his head and leaned over, his hands on his knees, retching.

"We've found Amanda," whispered Nancy. She pulled at Louse's sleeve as Louise turned to go down the tunnel. "You don't want to see that."

"She's dead. Probably since she went missing. Horrible." Fitz choked on the words.

Nancy stood numb with shock, but her brain was racing. The ones who would know about this place were Bryerson and Perry. They did this.

George peered down the lighter tunnel. "You'd think the truckers would have smelled something."

Louise snorted. "They probably had their air conditioners on and came through here too fast to pick up on the odor."

The four walked back toward the staircase and away from the smell. Nancy shook herself and took a deep breath. "We had a feeling something was wrong, and we were right. We need to go the other way, past the staircase."

Fitz nodded. "That's where they're taking whatever they're hauling in." He walked beside Nancy, head down, playing his flashlight on the puddles.

The echoing sounds of dripping water now hammered at her as she stumbled along, avoiding the puddles. Occasionally she steadied herself with a hand against the wall and once, when she wiped her hand on her slacks, it left a sooty mark. She looked at her hand. It was black with some kind of dust.

They passed the stairs, rounded a bend and stopped, astonished at the scene before them. Fitz's light reflected off the metal of a hundred steel barrels, lined up two and three deep along the side of the tunnel ahead of them and disappearing into the darkness beyond. A chemical smell now infiltrated the air along with the dust and exhaust fumes. As they approached the barrels, Nancy saw with relief that although some of them were corroded, none of them so far seemed to have leaked their contents into the ground. A few more years, though. . . .

"I'll bet it's industrial waste, toxic stuff, from his plants. Maybe even dry cleaning fluid," whispered Louise. "If they leak, they would contaminate the groundwater, which means the wells of Whisperwood would become contaminated. We'd all be drinking poison."

As they stared at the lethal-appearing barrels in front of them, a glaring spotlight caught the small group huddled together, snaring them like a net in the darkness of the tunnel. They blinked and squinted as they turned toward the intense light, but it blinded them. They could not see beyond it, but they heard the harsh chuckles. More than one man stood behind the light.

"Hold it right there," a rough voice barked at them.

Chapter 37

"You kids ever hear of hidden video cameras?" A voice called to them from behind the light glaring in their eyes. The words echoed around them.

A tall, graceful figure stepped forward. He was silhouetted against the glare behind him, but Nancy knew the man was Perry. She bit her lip and heard George gasp. She gripped Louise's hand while Fitz put his arm around Nancy. George stepped closer to them.

"I keep a video camera instead of a guard on the staircase now," Perry said. "Imagine my surprise." The man next to him snickered and waved a gun. Someone behind Perry kept the light trained on them.

Louise lifted her chin. "You could become a victim too, you know. If those barrels started leaking."

"Don't give me that environmental crap." He stepped toward them. "We're storing these barrels here. So what if there's a little seepage."

"You little creep," Louise snorted.

"Too damned nosy, all of you," said Perry. He glanced at the man holding the spotlight. "Don't trust 'em an inch. I gotta call the boss about this." Perry trudged back down the tunnel, quickly disappearing behind the light. Nancy could hear him splashing through puddles and cursing.

She pushed aside the numbness and shock. No time for that. They had to outsmart these guys. She squinted to see the two men more clearly.

"What do you think they're going to do with us?" whispered Louise. "They can't get rid of all of us at once. Too suspicious." She shaded her eyes. "I hope."

"Hey, you!" one of the guards yelled at Louise, pointing the gun at her. "Shut up. All of you back against the wall. Now!"

The group backed against the wall.

"Yeah, but they can't let us go," whispered Fitz. "We know about Amanda."

"You can't hold us down here," Fitz called out to the guards. "People will wonder what happened to us." He paused and then added, "Other people know what we're doing. They'll be looking for us." He squeezed Nancy's hand.

"Shut up!" the shorter, stout guard shouted. "Keep one hand on the wall and walk towards the stairway." He kept the gun on them and the other man, taller and thin, motioned the direction with the light. Both wore jeans and flannel shirts. She supposed the two men spent all their time down there and came dressed for the chill.

The captives formed a single line, each one with a hand on the wall, and trudged back towards the staircase. The two guards walked backwards in front of the captives, keeping the gun and the spotlight trained on them. When the group neared the landing where the dim light from the stairwell reached out into the tunnel, the spotlight was turned off, and Nancy could distinguish the guards' features. The man holding the gun was bald with big ears. He was chewing something and occasionally spat dark liquid. The other held the spotlight at his side, his unremarkable face staring at them impassively.

Nancy hoped they were stupid, but even as the thought flashed through her mind, she realized that she was hoping for a stereotype. Tough, stupid gunmen were the TV version. In reality, they might have college degrees.

"Only one has a gun," Louise whispered. "If I attack him, the rest of you go after the other one."

Before Nancy could stop her, Louise began creeping like Quasimodo toward the guard with the gun.

He leered at her. "What do you think you're doing, old gal?" He gestured toward the others with the gun. "Get back in line."

But Louise was too close. She snarled, "You disgusting jackass," and pulled apart her cane. She slashed at the guard with her rapier, hitting his gun hand. A red gash appeared on his wrist.

"You bitch!" he growled as he dropped the gun. He swung out at Louise, knocking her to the ground.

Fitz leaped forward to grab the gun, but the guard kicked it toward the other thug, who got it first.

The first guard, his hand dripping blood, shoved Louise to the side with his foot and picked up the rapier.

"Quite a nifty gadget," he sneered. "Too dangerous for an old girl like you to be carrying around." He slipped the rapier into the cane and threw it up the stairs. "I like that. Thanks for giving it to me."

Louise lay sprawled on the ground, hatred visible in her narrowed eyes.

Nancy knelt down, hoping that Louise hadn't broken an arm or hip in the fall. Her face was white, and her wrist dangled at an odd angle. Nancy held Louise's head and looked for other injuries. She glanced at George and Fitz.

"Down, girl," whispered George.

The two guards sat down on the steps. "Make yourselves comfortable," one of them said. He laughed. The other one was wrapping his wounded hand with a handkerchief. The short guard now held the gun and the spotlight. He turned it on.

Nancy gazed at the puddles up and down the road. Her feet sloshed in her wet shoes. How many puddles had she slogged through? Was the water in them toxic? She gazed at her hands. The palm on one was black where she'd run it against the wall. She forced her thoughts back to the problem at hand.

"How long will you keep us here?" she asked.

"Till the boss gets back." The thin man sat back on the steps and dangled an unlit cigarette.

George pulled the vial of pills out of his pocket and took another one.

"It's not wet next to the wall," Louise said in an attempt to laugh, but her face was still ashen as she cradled one hand in the other. Nancy helped her to sit against the wall, and then she, Fitz, and George sat down next to Louise. It became a face-off across the tunnel, but the two guards kept them pinned by the gun and the spotlight.

Nancy's mind raced through possibility after possibility for escape. These guards wouldn't allow them to leave unharmed. They knew too much. As soon as Perry talked with Bryerson and got his orders, the captives would all be dispatched—one way or another. Perry had had plenty of practice with that.

How easy to simply place any one of them at the bottom of any stairwell in the building and say he fell and killed himself. Or give them drugs to make them appear demented, senile. Throw one of them in the pool or maybe the pond after hours. Kill one of them in an automobile accident. She could come up with numerous possibilities. She'd heard of residents dying in all those ways. Were Bryerson or Perry cold-blooded enough to carry out such murders?

Of course they were.

Nancy's eyes teared from the dust and harsh chemical smells. George coughed and sneezed despite his pills. Louise began shivering, so Nancy put her arm around her and held her close. Fitz held tightly to Nancy's other hand. The two guards alternately paced and peered up the staircase. Once one of them said, "Dang, I need a smoke." The other snarled. "Forget about it. The air's bad enough down here."

The harsh spotlight glare beat at her, forcing Nancy to keep her eyes closed against it, robbing her of whatever power she might have to plan or negotiate their escape. She knew Louise was badly hurt, but nothing could be done about that right now.

At last, Perry came down the steps and motioned for all of them to climb the stairs. George helped Louise struggle to her feet. Nancy rose gingerly, rubbing her leg, which had fallen asleep. Eventually, all were able to make their way up the stairs to the basement hall. Perry motioned them into a classroom. "Sit down," he ordered. They sat as close together as they could at two tables. Nancy felt relieved to be out of the cold, dank, foul-smelling tunnel. She put her arm around Louise and squeezed in silent reassurance.

Perry sat on the instructor's table, one leg swinging, surveying them with a frown. Even in the dim light, Nancy could see scratches on Perry's face and arms. She smiled. Good ol' Malone.

"One of you would be no problem, but four of you, now there's a problem," he said. "We're going to have to hold you here for awhile, till we figure out what to do with you. Don't think anyone's coming down to rescue you. All the doors to this place are locked for the time being, and the elevators are blocked. The boss will be here in the morning. Meanwhile, we're going to tie and gag you while we wait for him. And, by the way, don't think you can escape 'cause we'll be watching you." He motioned to a guard. "Get some duct tape—and some rope."

The guard ran down the hall and disappeared, returning a few minutes later. Perry looked at the duct tape. Little was left on the roll. "This all you got?"

The guard nodded. "I got the rope from the garden shed outside."

"You don't have to bind Louise's wrist," Nancy said, her arm around Louise whose teeth chattered in her white face.

Perry shrugged. "Tie them up, but," he glanced at Louise, "don't bother about the arm with the broken wrist." Louise glared at him, her face white with pain, but Nancy felt relieved and surprised at Perry's display of humanity, meager as it was.

As the guards tied the prisoners, Perry bit off short pieces of duct tape and stretched them across their mouths. Thirty minutes later, all four captives were bound to the chairs and gagged. The windows facing the hall were covered with shades, the light was turned off, and Nancy, George, Louise, and Fitz sat in the twilight cast by the emergency lights as Perry left with one of the guards, leaving the tall, thin one with the gun to keep guard.

Nancy scanned the room for a hidden video camera, although one in the classroom didn't make sense, despite Perry's hint. In the hall, maybe, but they hadn't seen any, and Perry mentioned only the one in the staircase to the tunnel. Meanwhile, she quietly stretched and fiddled with the ropes that bound her.

Thank goodness for Bill. She had learned so much from him, which was why she still kept Malone. She thought of the many people Bill had cheered when he performed as an amateur magician in hospitals. He'd taught her a lot of tricks, including his Houdini knock-off of escaping from rope bindings.

"Ropes stretch," he'd told her, "so while they're tying you up, take a deep breath and physically expand your body as much as possible without being obvious about it, then you can work and stretch the ropes until you're out of them."

Perry and his thugs were amateurs at tying people up. Threw their victims down the stairs most of the time, Nancy thought with grim humor. These thugs didn't think they had to be careful. After all, Nancy and her friends were all over ninety.

If her mouth hadn't been covered with duct tape, she would have laughed. It took time, of course, and she had to be careful not to attract the guard's attention. She begrudged each minute that passed, but eventually, she had loosened the ropes enough so that she could wriggle out of them when the right time came.

Now if the guard would only go to the bathroom. She watched him wiggle his leg and pace in front of the room. As if he read her mind, he stretched and sauntered to the door. "Gotta take a leak." He opened the door. "Now don't you go anywhere." He snickered and walked out into the hall, closing the door behind him..

Nancy threw off the ropes, limped over to Louise and freed her next but carefully, since her wrist might be broken. It looked bad. Then she freed Fitz and George. They gingerly pulled the duct tape off their mouths. Nancy winced at the pain of it. They stood, rubbing their arms and legs and looking at each other.

"Let's get the guard as he's coming out of the bathroom," whispered Nancy and motioned for Fitz and George to follow and shook her head at Louise. "We don't need your help with this. Your wrist needs to be looked at as soon as possible."

"Hurts like hell," Louise growled as she sank into the chair.

Nancy took the lengths of rope with her and the pieces of duct tape they had pulled off their mouths. She gave a length of rope to George and Fitz. "Stretch it across the doorway—low, so he won't see it," she said.

The three took their places just as the unsuspecting guard emerged. He tripped over the rope and fell hard on the concrete floor. The gun flew out of his hand. Before he could recover, George and Fitz had wound the rope around his ankles and tied it. George further incapacitated him with a kick in the rear as Nancy slapped tape over his mouth. George and Fitz then grabbed the guard's flailing arms and held them while Nancy tied them with another length of rope. They dragged him into the classroom and tied him to the heavy classroom table.

"Let's get out of here," said George.

"Wait." Nancy ran out of the room and hurried back with the guard's gun in her hand.

George whistled. "Okay. We got some help now."

Nancy held up her hand. "The gun's loaded, and it evens the score a little bit, but we need a plan. I doubt that anyone's watching the video cameras, if there are any, right now or they'd be here. Once they find out we're gone, they're going to launch a full-scale search for us—they can't let us go."

George had his arm around Louise. "We need an ambulance," he said.

Nancy nodded. "Did anyone bring a cell phone down here?"

"I did," said Fitz.

"Me too," added George, pulling his out of his pocket. "They don't work in here though. Gotta go outside."

"Okay. We've got to split up," said Nancy. "It'll be too easy for them if we stay together like a neat, little package. There's three of us, not counting Louise. . ."

"Wait a minute," growled Louise, "you count me in on this. I'm only nicked, I ain't dead yet." Her eyes sparked in her white face.

"Anyways, there's four of us and," her eyes took on a wicked glow, "the dogs and Malone."

"The dogs?" asked Nancy and Fitz simultaneously.

"Sure." Louise tried to laugh. "What do you think I been doing out there when I've given them treats and walks. I used to train dogs long time ago. That's how I got into Humane Society work and PETA. Perry thinks they're his dogs, but you gotta spend time with them. They ain't robots."

"Okay. Louise and George, you get into one of those golf carts—the keys are at the reception desk—and get away from the building. Drive down to the gatehouse and call for an ambulance, then the sheriff, and then everyone you can think of to tell people about what's been going on here."

Nancy handed him the gun. "You might need this the most."

George took it and nodded. "Then we'll stay down there to wait for the ambulance."

"Good." Nancy turned to Fitz. "We'll go to my apartment and start making calls too. Enough calls to everyone we know will save us."

They grasped each others' hands and shook them, each seeking strength from the others.

"Good." Nancy took a deep breath and smiled grimly at the others. "Let's go."

Chapter 38

Nancy led the way down the hall to the stairs, the others following. She glanced back to see George supporting Louise with one hand and hauling himself up the stairs with the other. His cane swung on his arm, but he looked exhausted. Louise's face was white and drawn. Her mouth was clamped shut as if to stifle her pain.

They opened the door cautiously into the lobby area. No one was there, but Nancy could see a light under the door of Bryerson's office, and she heard voices within. Probably Perry and the guard. In the lobby, the lights were turned down low as usual from midnight until six a.m., and Nancy was surprised to see that it was still dark outside. It seemed to her that they'd been in the tunnel for so many hours that it should be daytime by now. She saw no one in the lobby—too early even for the receptionist who came in at seven.

Nancy ran over to the reception desk and picked up two keys to the golf carts, handing one to George, keeping one for herself. She watched George and Louise head out the door to the cart, and then she and Fitz scurried down the hall to her apartment. Nancy unlocked the door, and they rushed in, locking it behind them.

"Whew," said Fitz.

"Yeah." Nancy leaned against the wall. "Call the county hospital for an ambulance first in case George doesn't get through—I'm worried about Louise. Then call the sheriff, and then everyone you can think of. Tell them the whole story. A lot of calls to a lot of people—that's our insurance."

"Okay. Let's get started."

"Perry and the guard are in Bryerson's office, waiting for him to show up. The sheriff will be here soon, I hope." Nancy nibbled a finger. Time to bring in reinforcements.

"Here Malone," she called. He was always trying to escape, let him do something useful for once.

Malone stalked out of her bedroom, looked at Nancy, stretched, and yawned.

"Come on, boy," Nancy coaxed. She walked over to the door.

Fitz looked up. "Whoa, Nancy. Where are you going?"

She waved a hand at him. "Don't worry about me. Keep calling. I don't want Perry to get to the sheriff first. Malone and I are going to make a ruckus to divert him." She opened the door. Malone saw the open door and ran out into the hall, then skulked along behind her as she walked to the lobby.

Nancy tiptoed by the receptionist's desk. She stood debating her next move when a car screeched to a halt under the portico. Bryerson shot out and ran through the doors. He saw Nancy and stopped, gaping at her, mouth open.

"You," he growled.

At the same time, Perry came down the hall behind her. "I thought I took care of you," he shouted.

"The game's up, you know," said Nancy, backing against the wall. "We're calling everyone we know and telling them what's been happening here." Her eyes darted to the golf cart outside the door as she saw Bryerson advancing towards her. She couldn't outrun him, but perhaps . . .

"That's what you think." Perry approached her. "We'll take care of all of you."

Nancy heard a low hiss and saw Perry's expression turn from triumphant to terrified. That was all the proof she needed that Perry had been the one who snuck into her apartment and encountered

Malone. The cat leapt at his face, surprising Perry into backing up, tripping on the rug and falling flat to the floor. The cat jumped onto Perry's chest, face to face, snarling and revealing long, sharp teeth.

"Get him off! Get him off!" Perry shrieked as he tried to push the cat away.

"It's just a cat," Bryerson said as he advanced toward Nancy.

"It'll kill me, you idiot!" Perry screamed.

Nancy picked up a heavy glass vase from the lobby table and hurled it at Bryerson as he lunged at her. It struck him on the ear. He fell on his knees and the vase crashed to the floor. She gawked at him, torn between the fear that she might have injured him and terrified that she hadn't. He sat dazed, holding his ear. Blood gushed onto his jacket and shirt.

Nancy ran out to a golf cart and hopped on. With shaking hands, she inserted the key and turned it, saying a silent prayer of thanks when she felt the machine vibrate as it came to life. She circled the drive and careened down the road towards the gate-house.

She risked a glance back and saw that Bryerson had jumped into the third cart. Perry was staggering out the door as he fought Malone and attempted to pry the cat off.

As she careened down the road, she looked back again to see that Bryerson was now racing toward her. She had to keep him busy but at bay until the ambulance and sheriff arrived. Then it would all be over.

She willed her cart to move faster, faster.

She sped down the path that circled the buildings, honking the horn, hoping that someone would see this mad chase or hear the horn. But they would pull the cord, wouldn't they? That would bring security, then they'd grab her, and Bryerson, who was their boss, after all, would call her hysterical or senile, so they'd give her a shot and that would be the end. She willed the ambulance and the sheriff to come fast.

What were Louise and George doing? Were they making those calls? She looked down toward the gatehouse. They must be down there now. Nancy could hear loud, excited barking, then she heard panting and paws pounding on the drive, but she didn't want to lead Bryerson down to Louise and George. She turned back across the grass toward the building as she saw Ham and Eggs racing her way. For a moment, she felt scared, but the dogs ran past her towards the building.

She glanced up at the lobby entrance and caught her breath. She could hear the snarling and hissing and saw that a security guard had joined the fight with Perry. They were trying to shield themselves against the cat's fangs and claws. Then the dogs saw Malone and raced toward him. Appalled, Nancy sped along but kept an eye on the dogs as they joined the fray, turning it into a ferocious, bloody brawl. The barking, snarling, yelling echoed across the mountains.

Nancy tore her eyes from this spectacle and looked back. How far away was Bryerson? About twenty feet. She seemed to be whizzing along way too fast. How could she end this insane race without losing her life? Where were the ambulance and the sheriff?

Up ahead she saw the road and the ramp down to the secret garage. She slowed her vehicle. When Bryerson closed in to within a couple of feet, she accelerated. Bryerson did the same. At the ramp, Nancy swerved as if to turn down toward the garage. When Bryerson followed her, she swung back onto the road, her tires screeching. Bryerson swept past her, roaring down the slope. She heard him shriek and then a horrific crash and the cracking of wood. She stopped her vehicle and stared back at what remained of the garage door.

Bryerson's head had gone through the windshield and smashed against the door. Blood seeped out around the crumpled body and spread across the concrete. One wheel still spun over the wreckage.

Nancy covered her eyes and trembled. She hugged herself against the chill morning air and the coldness she felt within her. She couldn't move despite her fear that Perry might have escaped Malone and the dogs and lurked somewhere searching for her.

Several minutes passed. The dawn cast a pink glow over the mountains. In the woods, the birds were stirring. Nancy took a deep breath, and as she did, she saw Fitz running towards her from the building. She began to cry as she pressed the starter button and crept forward towards him. Fitz ran the last few yards and slid onto the cart seat, folding Nancy into his arms as he caught his breath. In the distance, she heard sirens. Fitz took over the driving and steered the cart back toward the entrance to Whisperwood. As he parked the cart in its space, the sheriff's car drove up, and he jumped out.

"So what's this all about?" he asked Nancy.

***

Life at Whisperwood:
Follow the Rules of the Road

Several accidents resulting in injuries have been reported in the last week, all caused by improper use of power scooters, wheelchairs and golf carts. Please follow the standard rules of the road as if you were driving a vehicle. You are. Keep to the right and slow down before rounding a corner or approaching others. Avoid excessive speed at all times.

-From *The Whisperwood Breeze*, newsletter of Whisperwood Retirement Village.

Chapter 39

The 90s Club met in Nancy's apartment that evening. The bodies of Amanda and Bryerson had been delivered to the morgue in Morgantown, Perry and one guard to the hospital, and the other to the county jail. Louise's wrist was broken, but it had been treated and she had insisted on returning home. Malone was grooming himself in the corner after a big supper of canned mackerel, his favorite food. George had begged the dining room for steaks and taken them down to Ham and Eggs.

Yellow crime scene tape crossed Bryerson's office door and blocked access to the basement. The sheriff had obtained statements from Nancy, Fitz, George, and Louise and then departed, shaking his head.

That afternoon, Nancy bumped into Harry who was muttering to himself and shuffling through papers as he walked.

"I'm so sorry about all this," he said, shaking his head. "Thank goodness you're all right. I had no idea. . . ." His eyes searched hers as if seeking forgiveness or reassurance.

Nancy couldn't help but respond. "Who would have thought

that Bryerson and Perry were such scoundrels?"

"Never occurred to me. Sometimes Mr. Bryerson made strange requests, but you get that in any job, I'm sure." He shook the papers in his hand. "I'm going crazy, Nancy. I've got to talk to Bryerson's lawyers, see the EPA people about removing those barrels and shutting down that underground garage," he shuddered, "and figure out what to do now. They never covered this in graduate school." He ran a finger under his collar and loosened his tie.

Nancy nodded. "You'd better order gallons of bottled water, too. And shut off the water pipes until the Health Department and the EPA can give the water system an all-clear. There's also the matter of all those stolen items stored down there."

He groaned. "Nancy, can you help me out in this crisis? Just a few hours a day to get through this." He took her arm and walked her toward his office. "I don't even know if we can keep this place open now. What will the residents here do?" He groaned again. "Lawsuits. I see a thousand lawsuits ahead."

Nancy followed him into his office. "I'll be glad to help you, but you should hire your own lawyer too. The EPA, the residents, the community—they might think you were in on this."

Harry stopped at his desk and turned pale. "Oh no. Never. I had no idea what was going on underneath the buildings."

Nancy studied his callow face and thought of his new MBA degree. Bryerson knew how to choose a patsy. "I believe you," she said, "although you might have a fight proving it."

Harry wiped his brow. "I didn't murder anyone either." He gulped. "I really believed Amanda had skipped out on us."

Nancy shook her head. "I think storing the barrels was Bryerson's doing. Perry handled their storage and also had his own business stealing valuable items from deceased residents. We're pretty convinced he also managed their demise."

"They kept me in the dark." He shivered and his hands trembled. "No wonder they wanted someone just out of school. I was their pigeon, their flunkie, their . . ."

"Yes, yes." Nancy patted his arm. "But how would you know? This place has won awards. We all decided it was legitimate—that's why we bought here. If you're a pigeon, so were all of us."

"I guess that's true." Harry brightened. "I've got to get moving."

"Call the lawyer first. Get his advice. Then call a meeting for all the residents. They need to know what's happening."

"The lawyers should talk to them," said Harry. "But I don't know what they can say about this," he sighed, "this mess."

***

Nancy sat back and turned to the group meeting in her living room. "And that's how we left it. Harry was going to call the lawyers and the EPA, and after they've come up with a plan, he would arrange a meeting with all of the residents."

"Bryerson and Perry were both bastards." Louise banged her good fist on the coffee table. "They didn't care," she added through gritted teeth. "Not about us or the environment or anything but money. We should have seen all this from our first sight of the grounds. Multiflora rose. Japanese honeysuckle. Ailanthus trees. That should have said it to us. Scum of the earth."

"But what's going to happen to us now?" George sneezed, his eyes tearing. He took a pill. "We've all got our savings tied up in this place. Damn it, I liked living here." He blew his nose.

"Me too," Nancy said. "But I've got an idea." She set her coffee cup on the table.

Fitz leaned forward in a straight-backed chair, elbows on his knees, and chuckled. "Nancy to the rescue again, eh?"

She frowned at him. "Bryerson's estate is going to be faced with at least a thousand lawsuits. Every resident here will have a reason to sue, not to mention the heirs of the victims no longer with us— the ones who died before their time and were robbed of their keepsakes." She paused and shrugged. "I'm not sure how any of that could ever be proved, but . . . " Nancy rapped on the dining room table. "What do we really want?"

"A safe, pleasant place to live," said George. "All the residents will want to move out once they hear what's been going on here.

Will Bryerson's estate be able to give us our money back? All of us, all at once? Especially since this place is under such a cloud they'll never find any investors."

Fitz glanced at him and nodded. "And if we all sue for our money, how long will it be before we get it back? Years? Some of us don't have many years to go."

Nancy held up a hand. "Wait a minute. We've gone through the Bio Books, and we have a list of retired lawyers who live here. They'll want to work with us on this."

"You can bet on that," said George, thumping his cane.

Nancy smiled at him. "We'll draft a plan to present to Bryerson's lawyers."

"What plan?" asked George.

"I've got one that I've been mulling around," said Nancy, looking at each of them in turn. "And I've talked to Tom who's been visiting retirement villages across the country. He thinks this is a very feasible suggestion."

"What can possibly get us out of this mess?" asked George.

Nancy glanced at George but then addressed the group, speaking with deliberation and firmness. She knew that she had to speak with authority to gain support for this idea. "We will agree not to sue if they—and Bryerson's heirs—agree to pay for the environmental clean-up of this property," she smiled, "and then turn the property into a cooperative wholly owned by the residents. The rest of his estate can be used to settle the other lawsuits bound to come out of this."

There was a silence. Then Fitz began clapping, quickly joined by the applause of the others.

"Great idea, Nancy," said Louise. "But we also need to add that all multiflora rose and honeysuckle bushes and ailanthus trees will be replaced . . ."

"I know," groaned George, "by native species."

"Can we also stipulate that George has to finish his novel?" added Louise, poking George with her elbow.

Fitz spoke up. "But first, and this needs to be done immediately, all residents should be warned to use only bottled water for drinking, cooking, and bathing, to make sure those barrels didn't leak."

"Yes, most of the residents have already heard the word since Louise has been putting signs on all the bulletin boards," Nancy said, "but we should emphasize that with everyone. And Harry is ordering bottled water for the dining hall and all the residents."

"I know people in the environmental sanitation field. I'll call them," said Louise.

"You've got a gold mine here, George," said Nancy.

"How's that?" George looked at her over the tissue as he blew his nose.

"Think what kind of novel you can write now."

"I never did like Bryerson anyway," said George.

"None of us did," Nancy added.

***

MEMORIAL SERVICE

The entire community of Whisperwood
regrets the passing of
AMANDA FELLOWS
A memorial service will be held in
the Whisperwood Chapel
on Saturday, July 31.
All are invited to attend.

In her memory, donations are being accepted
for the Amanda Fellows Special Scholarship Fund
for high school students who work so hard for us
at Whisperwood.

***

Urgent: Special Meeting for Residents

Whisperwood Administrator Harry Doyle has called a series of special meetings for residents to be held on Thursday at 9 a.m., 10 a.m., and 11 a.m. in the auditorium to accommodate all residents. This critical meeting concerns all of us and the future of Whisperwood. It is imperative that you attend.

-Special Bulletin, *The Whisperwood Breeze*

If you liked this book, please write a review
about it on Amazon.com.

Join Nancy and friends on her next adventure!
The 90s Club & the Whispering Statue will be
published soon. Watch for it!

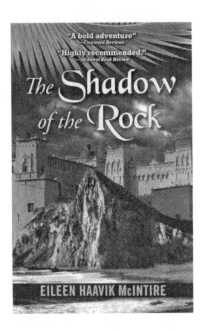

Also by Eileen Haavik McIntire

"A riveting story of time and humanity, highly
recommended." – *Midwest Book Review*

"A bold adventure…that moves "quickly in a mix-
ture of danger, excitement, and pure enjoyment…"
- *Foreword Reviews*

This compelling historical novel weaves a story of
old Florida and its Moroccan connection with a
woman's search for a relative lost in the Holocaust.

Available in print and e-book editions.